The bodies were scattered across the floor

The dark subterranean environment had contributed to the growth of mold on the bones. The clothing had largely rotted away, leaving only scattered pieces.

Sixteen skeletons lay in disarray, spread outward from the furnace as if they'd been tossed by a big hand. All of them were burned and blackened, twisted by incredible force. Rock fragments lay among them.

Annja breathed shallowly. After 150-plus years, the bacteria that triggered decomposition had done its work. All trace of the death odor was gone. But the musty thickness of the air was still filled with particulates. She took a disposable filtered mask from her backpack and fitted it over her face.

Playing the flashlight beam over the skeletons, Annja saw some of them couldn't have been much more than children. They hadn't had a chance inside the room.

Titles in this series:

Destiny
Solomon's Jar
The Spider Stone

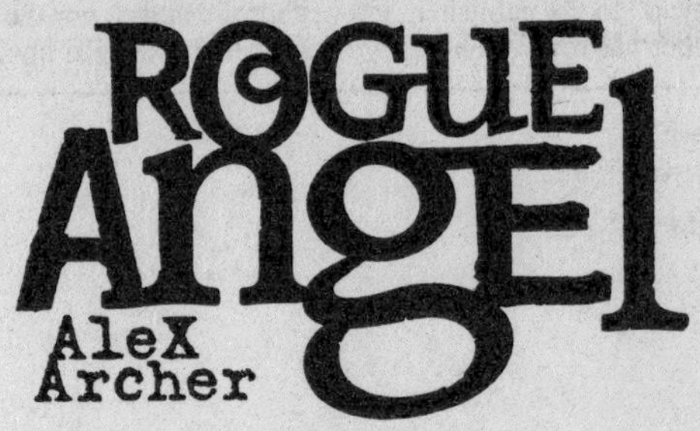

THE SPIDER STONE

A GOLD EAGLE BOOK FROM
WORLDWIDE®

TORONTO • NEW YORK • LONDON
AMSTERDAM • PARIS • SYDNEY • HAMBURG
STOCKHOLM • ATHENS • TOKYO • MILAN
MADRID • WARSAW • BUDAPEST • AUCKLAND

First edition November 2006

ISBN-13: 978-0-373-62121-7
ISBN-10: 0-373-62121-3

THE SPIDER STONE

Special thanks and acknowledgment to Mel Odom for his contribution to this work.

Printed in U.S.A.

The Legend

...THE ENGLISH COMMANDER TOOK JOAN'S SWORD AND RAISED IT HIGH.

The broadsword, plain and unadorned, gleamed in the firelight. He put the tip against the ground and his foot at the center of the blade. The broadsword shattered, fragments falling into the mud. The crowd surged forward, peasant and soldier, and snatched the shards from the trampled mud. The commander tossed the hilt deep into the crowd.

Smoke almost obscured Joan, but she continued praying till the end, until finally the flames climbed her body and she sagged against the restraints.

Joan of Arc died that fateful day in France, but her legend and sword are reborn....

Prologue

West Africa
1755

Under the blazing sun, Yohance's legs felt like stone, not flesh and blood. They seemed heavier than he could ever remember them being. He lacked the strength after so many miles to move them easily. In truth, he didn't think he could go much farther before he collapsed.

And what would happen then? The slavers who had destroyed his village and killed so many of his people were hard-eyed and merciless. If he fell, he knew they would kill him, too.

The chains pulled at his manacled wrists, jerking him once more into faster motion. Scabs on his wrists tore open. Blood stained his wrists, hands and forearms. Several times over the past few days, he'd prayed that the gods would take him. Although he'd always feared death, he was no longer so certain that death was frightening. Some of the other prisoners said he should welcome it.

"Come on, boy," the old man in front of Yohance snarled. He was abrupt and unkind. Judging from his behavior and the scars on his back, this wasn't the first time he'd been captured. A gray fringe surrounded his head and lined his seamed jaws. Several teeth were missing and the rest were yellowed wreckage in spotted gums. Like Yohance, the old man went naked. None of the prisoners were permitted clothing. "You've got to keep moving."

Yohance stared at the man. He didn't know his name. The man wasn't from Yohance's tribe. Facial scars and tattooing marked him as a warrior among his own people. But the white marks against the deep ebony of his back offered mute testimony to his servitude.

"Do you hear me, boy?" the old man demanded.

Yohance nodded. He didn't try to answer. Thirst had swollen his tongue and thickened his saliva. Until these past few days, he hadn't known he could go so long without water and food.

"If you fall behind, it's not just you that will be punished." The old man yanked on the heavy chains again. The sun had heated the iron links until they almost burned Yohance's flesh.

Yohance wanted to move more quickly, but he couldn't. He was only eleven, the smallest of the men and boys he was chained to. When the slavers had taken him, there had been some debate about whether they should try to keep him or simply put him to death. In the end, his life had been saved by the flip of a coin.

The old man quickly looked away. Hoofbeats drummed against the hard-packed earth behind Yohance.

"Move faster, you heathen!" a harsh voice thundered.

Even though he'd expected it, when the whip cracked

harshly across Yohance's narrow shoulders, he was shocked. Pain burst across his sunburned flesh, and the sudden agony dropped him to his knees on the trail. Sand and rock chafed against his legs, but it was hardly noticeable with the new injury assaulting him.

For a moment Yohance hoped that he would die. He remained on his knees and tucked his face against the ground. He didn't want to cry out. He bit his lip and his tears splashed against the dry ground.

"Get up," the old man ahead of Yohance whispered, tugging with weak desperation on the chain that bound them. "Get up or he will kill you."

Yohance knew that. The slavers relished seeing fear and weakness.

"Don't you just lay there, boy!" the slaver roared. "If you don't get up I'll run you down!"

The horse's hooves drummed against the ground again. Yohance felt the vibration echoing in his small, frail body. His hair hung loose in snarls, no longer bound by the ivory headband his mother had fashioned for him. If he'd been only a little older, if he'd participated in a hunting party, his hair would have been cut like a man's.

But he was only a boy. Too weak and afraid to defend himself against the aggressors who had destroyed his village and killed those of his people they didn't succeed in enslaving. The harsh crack of the slavers' rifles still sounded in his ears and had chased happiness from his dreams for three nights as they'd traveled toward the slave market at Ile de Goree.

For all his life, Yohance had heard about the slave market. The city was a rancid pool of despair and evil, filled with men who profited by selling other men. Some of those men were from Africa, but others were from England, Spain, France and beyond. All of those people trafficked in slaves, selling them or sending them to their colonies in the New World.

Yohance couldn't imagine the places some of the elders had described in the stories he'd been taught to memorize. He had sat around the campfires with his mentor and listened, still and silent as stone, as the warriors had recounted their adventures among the slavers. In every case, those men had lost someone, family or friends they would probably never again see. Sadness had stained every word, and Yohance had memorized that, too. He bore it in his heart like a boulder.

He had to do those things. He was a Keeper of the Ways of the People. Without Keepers to recount triumphs, as well as sorrows, his village would have lost its history. He and boys like him were chosen to devote their lives to remembering the history of his people. It was an honorable undertaking, an endeavor that Yohance had gladly promised his life to pursue.

According to the tales, rich men lived in wondrous cities where fire and water obeyed their every whim. In Yohance's village, women and small children tended the cook fires all day and carried buckets of water in from the stream. But, even with all those miracles at their disposal, the rich men desired slaves to work their fields.

For years, Yohance's village had remained safe. Then, before he had been born, his people had fought slavers again and again, and had finally gone into hiding, leaving their ancestral homes to climb higher in the mountainous terrain and escape the attacks. The move had brought new hardships to the Hausa people, and many times they had gone without good food. They had given up everything to avoid the slavers.

Still, the slavers had come. Three days earlier the raiders had found Yohance's village. His father believed the slavers had followed a hunting party back to them. The hunters had been trained to move carefully and to leave no trail, but they had been fortunate and had brought in enough antelope meat to feed the village for days. It had been a day of celebration. They had prepared for a feast.

The raiders had attacked in the night, rushing from the darkness and taking charge with their rough voices and fire-spitting rifles and pistols. Abed with their stomachs full for the first time in weeks, Yohance's people had been caught off guard. The raiders had taken the village without mercy, killing all who tried to oppose them and many of those who attempted to flee.

The next morning, after the slavers had gorged themselves on what food that the village had managed to put back and sated their evil lusts on the women, all the survivors had been placed in manacles and chained together for the long trek west to the coast.

For three days, the captives had walked from when the sun rose until it set in the evening. At that time, Yohance fell wherever he was permitted. The hated chains never came off. Mornings found his wounds thickly clustered with fat black flies. On each of those mornings, one or more prisoners had died in their sleep.

Such a death, Yohance had come to think by the second day, was a gentle thing.

Hafiz, Yohance's mentor and teacher in the ways of the Keeper, had died violently. As village elder, the raiders had executed him to take the courage from the village. The brutal tactic had worked. Everyone knew about the slavers. They knew if they didn't escape, if they weren't killed because they were too old or wouldn't stop fighting, they would be sent to live in far-off lands. Perhaps there they could hope to escape. Or perhaps the gods would provide a good life somewhere else.

"Get up!" the slaver snarled again. He jerked his horse to a stop only a few feet away from where Yohance lay. Two thick clods, torn from the earth by the horse's hooves, thudded against Yohance. "Do you hear me, boy?"

Yohance didn't look up. He couldn't. Looking into the eyes of the raiders was like looking into the eyes of demons.

Hafiz had told him that many of the Hausa's names came from the Arabian warriors. Their cultures had met before, in battle and tender embraces. The Hausa shared some of the blood of those fierce desert warriors. Yohance prayed for strength.

Another man rode up beside the first. They spoke in their language instead of that of the Hausa. Yohance didn't know what they said.

Part of him just wanted to stay there and die. He felt certain that would be easier. He didn't want to be torn from his home or his family. But it was already too late for that. His father was dead, one of the men who had fought, and his mother and two sisters were in chains as he was, all of them cruelly used by the raiders.

Without warning, Yohance vomited, giving in to the fear that was his constant companion. He retched and coughed. So little food and water were in his stomach. Yellow bile spilled on the ground. He felt the stone come up, and he was more fearful of that than anything else.

Hafiz had given him the stone to take care of. It represented Anansi's promise. Long ago, the trickster god had promised that Yohance's village would always stand, that his people wouldn't be scattered forever as so many peoples were.

As long as the stone existed, so too would his people.

Before the raiders had seized them, Hafiz had taken the stone from its altar and given it to Yohance. The slavers had taken the gold coins, ivory pieces and few jewels that had been on the altar, never realizing that the stone had been there, as well.

Yohance bent forward. He curled one hand around the stone before it could be seen. It was round and worn smooth from all the years that had passed since it had been created. The craftsman who had made the stone had carved Anansi's shape, a spider resting on its six hind legs with the front two lifted to attack or to defend—or, as Hafiz had said, merely to seek out the world.

Both spider and man, Anansi was the messenger to the gods. He was neither good nor evil. Instead, he was selfish and curious, like many people. Yohance had been taught to embrace Anansi's ways, to interact with the gods on behalf of his people, and to keep the records of their lives and triumphs.

"If you die and the stone is lost," Hafiz had told Yohance as the slavers' rifles blasted around them that night, "the home of our people will forever die with you. As long as this stone exists and our people have possession of it, Anansi's promise will exist."

And where is that promise now? Yohance thought bitterly. He had no doubt that Hafiz's body had by now been eaten by hyenas or leopards. Yohance knew that his father's body would be gone, as well. What the predators didn't take would be claimed by the ants and other insects. Spiders even made homes in large bodies to build web traps for bugs that feasted on rotting flesh.

Despite his anger, frustration and fear, Yohance struggled to get to his feet. His hand was grimed with a coating of bile and sand. He held the stone tightly.

One of the men spoke.

As Yohance stood, he lifted his head and gazed at them. One of the burnoose-clad men shoved away the rifle of another. Both men wore beards and carried curved knives and swords in their belts.

"You will walk?" the new arrival asked. He was older than the first.

"I will," Yohance whispered. It was the best his dry throat could manage.

"Only a little farther," the man said. "Then you will rest for a time. There will be water."

Yohance said nothing. Even the promise of water couldn't lift his spirits. Holding the hard stone in his fist, he willed himself to be as hard and emotionless. He had to have water. Without something to drink, he wouldn't be able to swallow the stone again.

Hafiz had told Yohance that was the best way to hide the stone. Once the raiders had taken his clothes, Yohance had seen the wisdom of his teacher's words. Hafiz had told Yohance that he had carried the stone in a similar manner on two earlier occasions.

Whips cracking in the air, the two slavers got the procession under way again. Slowly, with flagging strength, the line of human beings staggered into motion.

Yohance knew he wasn't the only one who was tired. A few of the stronger prisoners helped weaker ones. But they wouldn't be able to help them on the ship's journey to the New World. Disease and the stench of death filled the holds of those vessels. Yohance had been told that those who died were simply thrown overboard for the ever-present sharks to feed on.

The party crested a hill and peered down at the small watering hole against the side of a hill. Stones lined the hole's lip. Yohance's heart fell when he saw how little water the hole contained. The slavers would drink first, then their fine horses. Yohance doubted there would be any left for the prisoners.

Surprisingly, the slavers dismounted and brought out buckets and rope. As Yohance watched in amazement, the men brought up bucket after bucket of water.

"It is a wadi," the old man chained next to him said. "The Arabs build these along their trade routes. Water is often scarce. They dig deep holes, line them with rock, and the land guides the rain into them. When the water is deep enough, it will stay within the rocks rather than soak into the ground."

Yohance could only nod. Though he hadn't been out of his village before, he'd heard of such things. He waited his turn in line, then—when he wasn't being watched—he slaked his thirst from a hand-carved gourd and once more swallowed Anansi's Promise. Since they were given little food, he knew that the stone would stay within him for a time.

Harsh cracks suddenly rolled over the area. Several of the slavers fell from their mounts. They bled from catastrophic wounds and the dry earth sucked the liquid greedily down.

The prisoners dived to the ground even as other slavers toppled from their horses or dropped where they stood. In seconds, the surviving slavers took to the hills, their robes flowing in the wind as they rode for their lives.

A hush fell over the prisoners as they watched armed men walk down from the hills. All of them were black, wearing native garments and jewelry, but carrying rifles made by white men. A few also carried swords, spears and bows.

"We are saved," a man cried as he pushed himself to his feet. "They have come to free us."

The armed man closest to the speaker drew back his rifle and hit the man in the face with the brass-covered buttstock. Unconscious, the prisoner fell in a heap.

"You are *not* free!" a scarred warrior declared. "I have stolen you! Now you belong to me!"

"They are slavers," the old man whispered. "Just like the others."

The other prisoners drew quietly to one another and awaited their new fates.

"You will still go to Ile de Goree," the scarred warrior said in his thunderous voice. "You will still be sold to the New World of the white men. But if you listen and obey, you will live to do it." He glared contemptuously at everyone in the group. "Otherwise I will kill you and leave your bodies unmourned for the carrion feeders to take away in pieces."

A few of the women started crying.

Yohance sat back and prayed. He felt the weight of the stone in his stomach. Though he was still, he didn't feel rested, or even that he was gaining back any of his lost strength. He hoped only that even in foreign lands Anansi's Promise would find a way back to his home to protect his people.

But he had to wonder if the trickster's power could survive a trip to the white man's New World.

1

A mob surrounded the old warehouse in downtown Kirktown, Georgia. Many of the people carried signs and shouted angrily. Police cars and uniformed officers enforced the demarcation between the crowd and the warehouse. A news helicopter hovered overhead.

Seated in the back seat of the cab, Annja Creed stared through the morass of angry civilization. The car slowed, then finally came to a standstill as angry protesters slapped the vehicle and cursed. The action warred with the overall appearance of the city. Kirktown looked like the ideal tourist stop for anyone wanting a taste of genteel Southern manners.

We're not about manners today, Annja thought.

Kirktown was a small Georgia town that had limped through the Civil War, became a textile success during industrialization, but had struggled on into the twenty-first century. Old buildings stood with new as the town continued to grow around the industrial area, finally outliving the textile era and leaving the older buildings to rot at the center of the downtown area. Like many Georgia towns, and cities in the South in general, the population was almost equally divided between white and black families, with some Hispanic and Asian communities, as well.

And like a lot of small towns, Kirktown had kept its secrets close and its darkest secrets buried.

Annja Creed had come to help dig up at least one of those. Looking at the site and the crowd thronging it, she felt like an outsider—a familiar feeling. She'd been raised in an orphanage in New Orleans. No matter where she went in her life, most of the time she felt like a visitor.

The cabdriver, a barrel-chested Rastafarian with silver wraparound sunglasses and a gold tooth, turned to look back over the seat. "I'm sorry, miss, but this looks like it's as far as I can carry you."

"We can walk from here," Annja said.

"You can see what we're up against," Professor Noel Hallinger said. "Every time there's a race issue, the reactions are immediate and severe. I wasn't sure if the police would be able to hold the site clear long enough for me to bring you from the airport."

Annja nodded as she lifted her backpack from the seat and opened the door. Her head was already full of questions. She'd made notes in a notebook on the way. "How many bodies did you say you'd found?"

"Sixteen so far. But there may be more." Hallinger was a tall man in his early sixties. His hair had turned the yellow-white of old bone and hung over his ears and the back of his collar. His face held a deep tan that testified to long years spent outside in harsh weather. Bright blue eyes narrowed under the Chicago Cubs baseball cap. He wore jeans and a khaki shirt.

"Have you made any identifications so far?" Annja slipped her backpack over one shoulder, then wished she'd bought a newer, lighter-weight notebook computer.

"None."

"You're sure the bodies are all over a hundred years old?" Annja started for the warehouse.

"Who are you?" a tall black man demanded, stepping in front of her to block the way. He looked to be in his sixties, fierce and imposing. He wore a business suit with the tie at half-mast because of the heat. Even in November, Georgia insisted on being uncomfortably hot.

"Annja Creed." She stood five feet ten inches tall and wore a favorite pair of comfortable working jeans, a sleeveless olive Oxford shirt over a black T-shirt, and hiking boots. Her chestnut-colored hair was pulled back in a sleek ponytail. Blue-tinted aviator sunglasses protected her eyes from the midday brightness.

"Why are you here, Miss Creed?" the man boomed. His challenge had drawn a small crowd that was growing steadily. More and more heads turned toward them.

"I came to help," Annja responded.

"How?"

Beside her, Hallinger took out a cell phone and made a call.

"I'm here to help find out who those people are," Annja replied. "If we can, we're going to get them home."

"It's been 150 years or more," the man said in an accusing tone.

"That's what I've heard," Annja said.

"And you think you can find out who those poor unfortunates are?" The man glared at her with hostility.

"I'm going to try."

"Those people should be left alone," a broad woman shouted. "Just leave 'em alone. They been buried there for 150 years. Ain't no need in disturbin' they rest. All them folks what was gonna miss 'em back then, why, they in they graves, too. You got no call to be a-stirrin' up ghosts an' such."

I so did not need this, Annja thought. But she'd known what she was going to be getting into from the moment Professor Hallinger had outlined the situation in Kirktown. She'd come partly because of her curiosity, but also out of respect for the man. They'd had a sporadic connection over the Internet archaeology boards she liked to frequent, and they'd worked together for a short time on a dig outside London a few years ago.

But the oddities that had been found—which was why Hallinger had sent for her—drew her there. She knew she couldn't have stayed away from something like this. How often could an archaeologist expect to find a dig site inside the United States that might offer a glimpse into West African history?

Close to never, Annja had told herself back in her New York loft. She reminded herself of that again.

"We can't leave them there." Hallinger folded his cell phone and put it away. "That building is scheduled for demolition."

"That building's been abandoned for close to twenty years now," someone said. "It should just be shut up and left alone."

A police car moved forward through the crowd. The siren chirped intermittently in warning. Grudgingly, the crowd parted.

"Hey!" someone shouted. "I know that woman!"

Annja's stomach spasmed. She was betting there were more television watchers in the crowd than readers of *Archaeology Today* or any of the other magazines to which she occasionally contributed articles. Besides that, few of those articles featured any pictures of her. There was only one place that people might recognize her from.

"She's that woman from *Chasing History's Monsters!*"

And that was the place, Annja thought. It wasn't the first time that her part-time work on the syndicated television show had created problems for her.

Chasing History's Monsters was a weekly foray into the exploration of creatures, myths and whatever else the show's producers felt comfortable covering. Each week, at least two or three stories, legends or fables would be fleshed out and presented with a mix of facts and fiction.

For her part, Annja usually shot down the myths and debunked hauntings and demonic possession, blowing away legerdemain with research and study. Her concentration was on the history of the time, of the thinking and the people and how all of that related to what was going on in the world of today. Of course, even though she poked holes in fabrications, that didn't make true believers any less willing to believe.

"Kristie!" some young men shouted, mistaking Annja for her popular co-star. They jumped up and down, mired in the crowd, trying to get a closer look. They were pushed farther back as the police car rolled through. "Kristie! Over here!"

The tall black man turned to the police vehicle. He slammed both hands on the hood. The sudden loud noise quieted everyone.

"I've filed an injunction to stop this demolition," the man

roared. "The sanctity of those graves needs to be maintained."

Two policemen stepped out of the car. The older one was black and the younger one was Hispanic. Both of them had that hard-edged look that Annja recognized. She'd seen it first on the faces of the men who patrolled New Orleans, then in the faces of men serving in the same capacity around the world.

"John," the older policeman said, "I'm going to ask you to back off once, politely. And if you don't, I'm going to arrest you."

"We have the right to assemble," the man said.

"Assemble," the officer agreed, "but not to impede. The construction company and the owners of this land have graciously allowed people to come in and make the attempt to find out who those dead folks are. They didn't have to do that. They could have just cleaned them out of there."

"Like the refuse they were treated as all those years ago?"

"I'm not here to debate, John," the policeman said. "I'm asking you to step aside and let these people get on with their jobs."

"They were murdered!" John shouted.

Murmurs came from the crowd.

"We don't know that," the policeman said. "And even if they were murdered, whoever did it is dead. We're not going to find a guilty party." He took a breath. "Now step down."

Reluctantly, the big man stepped back. A corridor opened up to the police car. Annja walked forward.

"Afternoon, miss," the police officer said. The badge on his shirt identified him as A. Marcus. He opened the squad car's rear door for Annja.

"Thank you, Officer Marcus." Annja slid into the back seat.

The younger officer put Hallinger in on the other side. They were driven to the building less than a hundred yards away. The sea of protesters, driven to a new frenzy, flowed in behind them.

"You'll have to forgive them," Marcus said. "Kirktown is usually a fine city. A place where you'd want to bring your family." He glanced up at the news helicopter circling in the sky. Sunlight splintered from the frames of his glasses. "Today…well, we're just not at our best."

"Is there a chance that any of the people located under the building are ancestors of the people here?" Annja asked.

"Probably. The Civil War and the Underground Railroad was a long time ago, but people haven't forgotten. Racial tension is something that I don't think will ever go away in this state."

"It's too easy to separate people by skin color," Annja agreed. "Then you've got money, politics and religious preference."

Marcus grinned. "Yes, ma'am. I figure that's about the size of it. Always has been."

"Before the construction workers found the bodies," Hallinger said, "protests were already working to stop the demolition. Some groups wanted to preserve the building as a historic site. Others didn't want new business coming into the area."

A large metal sign hung on the front of the four-story building. It read Weidman Brothers Construction. Future home of Lark Shopping Center.

The young officer turned around and peered at Annja. "You're not the one on *Chasing History's Monsters* who posed for *Maxim*, are you?"

"Luis," Marcus growled.

"No," Annja said. Biting her tongue, she thought, I'm the one with an actual college degree, years of training and personal integrity.

"I didn't think so." Luis looked and sounded a little disappointed. "I saw the magazine spread she did a few months ago. She looked bigger."

Since Annja was six inches taller than Kristie Chatham, she knew the young policeman wasn't talking about height.

"No offense," Luis said quickly.

Annja made considerable effort not to unload on the policeman. After all, she'd just arrived and didn't need to make a bad impression.

"Thanks for the ride," she told Marcus as he opened the door to let her out. She missed the air-conditioning inside the car as soon as the hot wind blew over her.

Hallinger joined her. "The rest of the excavation crew is inside the building," he said.

"Who do you have?"

"Kids from the university mostly," Hallinger admitted. "A retiree who has an interest in the Underground Railroad. A few people from the historical society here and from Atlanta to help with some of the heavy lifting."

Annja didn't point out that Hallinger didn't have much skilled help. The man already knew that.

"So why did you call for me?" She hadn't wanted to ask him that question until they were face-to-face.

"Because you've got some recent experience with African culture."

"With Poulson's dig?" Annja shook her head. "That shouldn't count. I was on the ground less than three weeks before the government suspended Poulson's visa." That was still a sore point with her. She'd waited years to go to Africa, then got kicked out almost as soon as she'd settled in.

"That," Hallinger told her, "is two weeks longer than I've had. You've been exposed to the Hausa culture?"

"I've read up on it. Saw a little of it while I was in Nigeria."

Hallinger smiled. "Then you're light-years ahead of my university students and volunteers."

"I couldn't have been at the top of your list," Annja said.

"No. Nineteenth, actually. I received eighteen rejections before you accepted, Miss Creed."

Okay, that stings a bit, Annja thought as she returned his smile.

"I'm just fortunate to have called you at a good time," he said graciously. "You have an outstanding reputation in the field, Miss Creed."

Hallinger was being generous. Outside of *Chasing History's Monsters,* few people knew her. She was in her midtwenties and didn't have any significant finds to her credit. But she was good at what she did and loved the work.

"Call me Annja," she told him.

"Want to go inside?" Hallinger asked. "At least the protests and the constant roar of the helicopter rotors dull a bit."

"Sure." Annja followed Hallinger. But the distinct feeling that she was being watched haunted her. It was ridiculous, of course. She was well aware she *was* being watched by the crowd of protesters and the news helicopter.

However, one set of eyes focused on her felt predatory. She *sensed* a threat. She'd never paid much attention to such unscientific evidence as *feelings* until a few months ago when she'd reassembled Joan of Arc's sword. Her sword now.

Though it was hidden away in some *otherwhere* that she could reach into to retrieve it, she could feel the plain, unadorned hilt smooth and hard against her palm. All she had to do was close her hand, will the blade to come forth and the weapon would be there.

In front of a few hundred witnesses, Annja chided herself. Not exactly the brightest thing you could do at the moment.

She stopped at the doorway and swept the crowd with her gaze. Tapping into those inner senses she was still trying to figure out how to control, still thinking some days that they were a figment of her imagination, she tried to isolate the predator.

Annja felt the pressure fade. But she was certain that someone was out there who didn't mean her any good.

"Coming?" Hallinger asked from inside the building.

"Yeah," Annja said, and she stepped into the building.

"DID SHE SEE you?"

Dack Tatum stood in the crowd outside the warehouse and looked back at the door the woman had entered through. He thought about the way she had stopped, almost as if she knew someone was watching her. A cold thrill shot up his spine.

"Dack," the voice barked through the cell phone Tatum held.

"No," Dack said. "She didn't see me."

"Are you certain?"

Dack cursed. The speaker on the phone was his younger brother Christian. Christian had always been a worrywart. Dack turned away from the crowd and signaled Vince Retter and Brian Haggle, the two spotters he'd set up in the crowd. All of them had cell phones with walkie-talkie capability.

"I'm certain, Christian. Relax, man. I got this wired. I'm rolling heavy with manpower on this op. Chances are there were just too many eyes on her. Some women feel hinky when a guy stares at her. It's no biggie."

"It is a biggie," Christian said.

Dack was a huge man, nearly six and a half feet tall. He had dark hair shaved nearly to his skull and dark eyes that looked like gun muzzles. He was in his late thirties. For ten years, he'd been an Army Ranger. Then, when he saw he wasn't going to get the promotions he wanted and saw how much money there was to be made in the civilian sector, he'd spent the past eight years as a mercenary, for sale to the highest bidder.

He didn't usually work Stateside. But everywhere outside the United States was fair game as far as he was concerned.

Dressed in shorts with cargo pockets, a T-shirt proclaiming his love for Charlie Daniels, a skull-and-crossbones bandana and mirrored sunglasses, he looked as if he'd just driven in from the trailer park to see what all the fuss was about.

"You don't know what's at stake," Christian went on.

"So why don't you tell me?" Dack entered the nearby convenience store, which was doing a booming business in beer and Icees thanks to all the protesters, police and media in the area. He grabbed a single beer from the refrigerator unit and paid for it at the counter.

"Do you remember Horace Tatum?" Christian asked.

Dack didn't. He figured it must have been the name of a family member he'd gotten introduced to at one of the reunions. Personally, he didn't remember anyone he didn't do business with. Or didn't kill. He always remembered the guys he took out. He went to sleep every night bringing their faces up in his mind's eye. It was a relaxation technique that had never failed.

"A cousin?" Dack guessed.

"No. Don't you know anything about our family?"

"You're my brother. Our parents are dead. I don't think there's anything else I need to know."

"Horace Tatum was one of our ancestors," Christian said.

Oh, one of the dead ones, Dack thought. He wasn't going to feel bad about not remembering a dead relative. Unless it was his mom or dad. But Christian had a thing about remembering dead relatives. His younger brother had become a genealogy fiend, always tracing dead relatives farther and farther back in time.

Dack felt it was better to let dead relatives lie. Christian, however, was convinced that a treasure was out there waiting to be claimed.

"So," Dack said. "Horace, relative or not, is long dead, bro."

"Yeah. But he's the one who killed those people in that building."

"So?"

"So if people find out he's the one that killed all those slaves 150 years ago, that's going to put a kink in my plans."

Christian was planning on running for the office of the state representative next term. He was one of the wealthy elite in Atlanta. Dack knew having a murderer in the family, especially with all the attention this situation was receiving, would hurt his brother's precious image. Christian needed his older brother to get a handle on things.

Dack walked outside the convenience store and twisted the cap off his beer. He sipped, relishing the cool liquid against his parched throat.

"His father was Jedidiah Tatum," Christian went on. "The guy who owned the textile mill."

"You do remember."

Actually, Dack knew that fact from one of the news pieces he'd heard on the convenience store radio when he'd stopped in for a beer and a package of cigarettes earlier. "Yeah," he lied.

"Jedidiah kept a journal," Christian went on.

A man's word for diary, Dack told himself disgustedly. He knew his brother kept one, too. Two, actually. One that listed everything Christian did, and with whom, and the other one sanitized so that it couldn't be held against him in a court of law. Neither practice, in Dack's view, was wise or safe. Leaving the one that listed every dirty deed was just plain stupid. Even the sanitized one left holes that would be questioned by anyone who could read between the lines.

"Horace knew one of the slaves in that basement," Christian said.

"Our family owned slaves?"

"Yes."

Dack felt pretty good about that. Personally, he didn't care for blacks. Or people of color. Or African-Americans. Or whatever they were calling themselves these days. He figured they ranged from stupid and lazy to uppity and selfish.

"Jedidiah didn't just spin the cotton into goods," Christian said. "He also raised the cotton. Had big fields of it around Kirktown. Horace worked on the fields. That's how he got to know Yohance."

"Who's Yohance?" Dack took another sip of beer.

"Yohance was one of the slaves that worked on the farm. He was the one that had the Spider Stone."

Dack's head hurt. He vaguely remembered the story. Christian had always been fascinated by the story of the Spider Stone. When he'd been a kid, Christian had studied the family history at their grandfather's knee.

"What's the Spider Stone?" Dack asked.

"Horace believed it was a treasure map. Jedidiah wrote that in his journal. The night he killed all those people down in that basement, Horace looked for it, but he never found it."

"Why are you telling me this?" Dack asked.

"Because I want you to find that stone."

Dack cursed loud enough to draw the attention of a few bystanders. "I thought you wanted me to bring that building down on top of those damn busybodies," he whispered.

"I do," Christian said. "But I want the Spider Stone first."

"WE'VE GOT GENERATORS to provide power for the electric lamps we've used underground," Professor Hallinger explained as he led the way through the warehouse.

"Normally the Underground Railroad wasn't literally underground," Annja said as she followed the professor, gazing around at the history showing in every plank and joist. She loved being in old buildings that had been preserved. Stepping through their doors was almost like stepping into a time machine.

"No. It was a system of way stops used by those fleeing slavery who made their way north. Some of them went on into Canada. Usually they traveled overland through forests and swamps, off the beaten track. They used the railroad language to suit themselves. A conductor was the guide who led them out of the South along the way stops. Railroad agents were the sympathizers who hid them during the day and gave them food and supplies. But there were a few subterranean areas. Basements, root cellars, caves. This happens to be one of the latter."

"A cave?" Annja asked.

Hallinger nodded. "Beneath the building. It was used to house the furnace."

Annja surveyed the massive empty space.

The textile mills had been cavernous. Dust covered everything except the floor where pedestrians had walked it semiclean. All of the windows were boarded over, covering empty frames or remnants of glass. Empty beer cans and sleeping bags littered the floor space.

"I see the local teens didn't hesitate about claiming squatters' rights." Annja took a small digital camera from her backpack.

"No." Hallinger smiled. "A place like this must have been a godsend to preteens wanting to scare themselves with the idea of ghosts, and teenagers wanting somewhere to explore the prospects of sex, drinking and smoking."

"Not exactly a lovers' lane." Annja looked at the bird droppings that streaked the floor. Glancing up, she saw a few pigeons on the rafters.

"It was close enough," Hallinger said.

"No one found the bodies until yesterday?"

The professor shook his head as he led the way to the back of the building. "Construction workers shutting down gas mains under the building discovered a closed furnace room. I'll show you."

Annja followed him into a back room, then down a flight of stairs that led underground. Dank mustiness clogged her nose and made breathing more difficult. The only illumination came from a string of electric bulbs that led into the large basement area. Wooden shelving lined the walls and occupied the center of the room. Whatever the shelves had contained had long since vanished, either through pilfering or by decomposition.

A handful of people occupied the basement, quietly speaking among themselves as they hunkered down over ice chests with sandwiches and bottled water. They looked up at Annja and a few greeted her.

Annja responded in kind, noticing the grimy faces and casual clothing and the uneasy look most of the younger ones wore. After a brief introduction, Hallinger led Annja through a tunnel in the basement wall.

"Not exactly happy to be here, are they?" Annja asked.

"It's the bodies," Hallinger replied. "You get started in archaeology, you think your first body is going to be a mummy or a caveman."

"I know." Annja trailed the professor along the small tunnel. "My first body was less than a week old. He'd been buried at a dig site long enough to bloat and collect a number of burrowing insects."

"Where was that?"

"New Mexico. During my senior year."

"Ah, the heat. That must have made things pretty horrible."

"It was." Some nights Annja still remembered the stench.

"Who was he?"

"A grave robber. We were there helping local tribes recover artifacts, but we left the bodies intact. This guy was there collecting skulls to sell on eBay."

Hallinger scowled in disgust. "Our chosen field does attract the greedy entrepreneur looking to find shortcuts to a quick buck."

Annja agreed.

"Did you ever find out who killed your dead man?"

"No. They never even got his name. The tribal police conducted an investigation, but it didn't go anywhere."

"I'm not surprised. Desecration of grave sites won't win you any points in the Native American community."

The tunnel narrowed ahead. Timbers shored the low ceiling up in several areas. The dank smell grew stronger. Gradually, the tunnel angled upward.

"This leads to the coal furnace." Hallinger kept moving. "It was built before the basement."

"The tunnel was built to connect the new basement to the furnace?"

"I don't think so. At least, not for that reason. The furnace, the original furnace, was lost in a cave-in."

"How did that happen?"

Hallinger shook his head. "We don't know. There are signs of an explosion—soot on the walls and some blast damage. Some of the bodies were torn up in the explosion. Or maybe by people who found them later."

"If the bodies were found earlier, why wasn't something done then?"

"They haven't been found since they were buried. The entrance we came through back there had been walled over, closing off the tunnel. One of the construction workers discovered that by accident. Over the years, the mortar holding the stones together had dried out and crumbled. I don't think it was mixed well. Or perhaps the dankness of the environment contributed to the failure of the mortar. However it worked out, the team checking for gas mains discovered the tunnel. They dug it out in case there were any gas lines in there."

"Did they know what it was?"

"No. No blueprints of this building exist. It was built pre-Civil War and whatever records of the building might have been around were destroyed when General Sherman marched on Atlanta."

"Why wasn't the town razed?" Annja knew from her studies of the war that Sherman had followed scorched-earth tactics, leaving nothing standing in his wake.

"Because it was so close to the railroad. The town became the site of a Confederate military hospital in 1863. All of the larger buildings, including this one, were used in those efforts."

"Must have made the textile mill owners happy."

"I don't think it hurt them any. Have you heard of Christian Tatum?"

"No. Should I have?" Annja asked.

"Not really. He's a businessman in Atlanta now, with subsidiaries in Charlotte and Savannah. Does a lot with government contracts. Supposed to be a big deal in military engineering. He has political aspirations. His ancestor, Jedidiah, owned this building from the time it was built until he died in the 1890s." Hallinger stopped and looked back at her. He slapped the timber across the opening. "Watch your head here."

Annja ducked down a little more and stepped through the narrow opening. When she emerged, she found herself in a large room carved out of stone and filled with the dead.

2

Annja peered around the underground room. A large furnace filled the opposite wall. A coal bin sat adjacent to it. Rotting coal filled the bin and spilled across the floor. Broad coal shovels covered in dull orange rust lay on the floor.

What caught Annja's attention most, though, were the bodies strewed across the floor. The dank subterranean environment had contributed to the growth of dark mold on the bones. The clothing had largely rotted away, leaving only scattered pieces.

Sixteen skeletons lay in disarray, spread outward from the furnace as if they'd been tossed by a big hand. All of them were burned and blackened, twisted by incredible force. Rock fragments lay among them.

"Have you moved the bodies?" Annja slid out of her backpack and took out a miniflashlight. She switched on the light. The powerful halogen beam stabbed out, penetrating the darkness more strongly than the electric bulbs.

"No, we haven't touched them yet," Hallinger said as he squatted against the wall near the opening.

Annja breathed shallowly. After 150-plus years, the bacteria that triggered decomposition had done its work. All trace of a death odor was gone. But the musty thickness of the air was still filled with particulates. She took a disposable filtered mask from her backpack and fit it over her face.

"I'm not an explosives expert." She aimed her beam at the furnace. The metal sides had been warped in the explosion.

"One of the students advanced the theory that the explosion was the result of some kind of coal-gas buildup."

Annja knew coal gas was frequently the cause of mining accidents involving explosions. It gathered in pockets, and just the slightest spark could set it off. That was one of the reasons coal miners didn't carry metal objects like rings or buttons down into a mine.

"No." Annja played the beam around.

"Why?"

"With the furnace working, coal gas couldn't build up. The flames would burn it off," she said.

"They could have shut down over the weekend. Or a long holiday."

"With the South warring with the North over the textiles market with England, I doubt the mill closed down much for holidays or weekends. Time was money. Most mill owners worked as much as they could. Even if the furnace wasn't kept fed to warm the building, it would have been banked. I don't think a buildup of gas was likely."

"Do you think it was an accident?" Hallinger asked.

Annja shook her head. "I don't."

Hallinger sighed. "Neither do I. These people were murdered."

Playing the flashlight beam over the skeletons, Annja saw some of them couldn't have been much more than children. They hadn't had a chance inside the room.

Hallinger sounded tired when he continued. "It's bad enough finding these bodies after all these years, especially with them being slaves, but having to confirm to those people out there that they were murdered is going to make things even worse."

Annja silently agreed. "Why did you ask me about the Hausa people?"

Hallinger directed his flashlight beam to a large stone lying on one side of the room. The rock was as big as two of her fists together. Someone had taken time, years probably, to smooth the rock's surface until it looked polished. Then they'd carved images with a sharp point and rubbed some kind of dye or stain into them.

Drawn by the images, Annja knelt and inspected the stone. She recognized the letters. "Hausa had its roots in the Chadic language, which is Afro-Asiatic in origin."

"I knew that much. It's also an official language of several West African countries these days."

"Have you touched this?"

"No, and it's been killing me not to." Hallinger rubbed his forehead in frustration. "Everything about this place speaks of something beyond just the Civil War."

"Why?"

"These men were carrying weapons." Hallinger raked his flashlight over the bodies.

"I saw those," Annja admitted. She studied the makeshift weapons, some of them no more than hoe handles inscribed with more Hausa writing. There were also three axes, their handles marked with more of the language. Close inspection of one of the ax heads revealed that it, too, had been marked.

"Escaping slaves didn't carry weapons." Hallinger frowned. "Getting caught with one usually meant getting hung from the nearest tree when pursuers caught up with them."

The presence of the weapons told Annja what they were looking at. "This was a war party."

"I think so, too," the professor said.

Annja put the miniflashlight between her teeth and lifted her digital camera. She focused on the rock, then on the weapons, finally taking pictures of the bodies.

Hallinger waited patiently until she was done. "Can you read the writing on the stone?"

"Some of it." Annja put the camera away. "The stone tells a story of an exodus. Of a long travel, from what I gather."

"There was a slave market not far from Dakar, Senegal."

"I know. Ile de Goree. It was one of the primary contact points of the Triangle Trade," she said.

"Slaves, rum and sugar. Those are the things that built the New World. That and the search for riches." Hallinger sighed. "People think cotton is what brought the slaves to the New World, but that was only what developed out of the slave trade."

Annja knew that was true. The early Atlantic trade had started a history of hundreds of years of pain and suffering. She pushed that out of her mind for the moment, wanting to concentrate on the dig and the unanswered questions she and the professor both had. "I'm ready to start if you are," she said grimly.

Hallinger nodded. "I'll get the crew together."

THE EXCAVATION, even though there was no digging involved, was slow work. They always were. Annja had no problem with that. She loved her chosen field. As an orphan, she'd had no real sense of connection or family. As an archaeologist, she connected not only people but also years.

In a map of the past, everyone had a place. It was just a matter of finding the proper pieces, she thought.

Like the piece of the sword she'd found in France while looking for the Beast of Gévaudan. That piece had brought a number of things together. All of the other pieces of the sword that had been sought after since Joan of Arc's death on a burning pyre over five hundred years earlier had come together. Once she'd touched those pieces, the sword had reforged itself.

Magically.

She disapproved of the term, but there was no other explanation. Annja had seen it happen. In the blink of an eye, she'd held the sword—suddenly whole—in her hand. It had never been out of her reach since.

Out of that experience, she'd begun forging new relationships. One with Roux, who claimed to have witnessed Joan's death and been charged with finding Joan's sword. Another with Garin, who had at one time been Roux's protégé but now sought to kill him and take the sword from Annja. Garin was afraid that whatever power had enabled him to remain relatively ageless for those years would fade now the sword was once more whole.

Annja still didn't know if she believed her bloodline tied her to Joan of Arc. Whatever chance she might have had of ascertaining that had been destroyed during the flooding of New Orleans. The orphanage where she'd grown up had been washed away. The nuns who raised her were dead or scattered. Most of them hadn't been concerned with the pasts of the children in their care; they'd been grooming them for the future.

But Annja believed the sword had been Joan's. Now it was hers. It had changed her life. She was still learning what all that meant.

ANNJA AND HALLINGER worked well together, directing the expertise of the retired couple who had worked dig sites before, and training the university students. Using soft rope and pitons they drove into the ground with small sledges, they laid out a grid over the recovery site. Since the bodies had been scattered by the blast, the whole floor of the furnace room was designated the recovery site.

Once the grid was laid out in twelve-inch squares, Annja and Hallinger took turns working the recovery. They moved square by square, cataloging and videotaping everything they took out. The other dig workers labeled the recovered items and packed them out.

"I'm surprised the police released this site to you." Annja searched through a pocket of a shirt fragment she took from the latest square.

"Are you kidding?" Hallinger snorted and shook his head. "They didn't want this. You saw that crowd outside. As soon as the story hit the news, people poured in from Atlanta and other nearby towns. They called the university and got in touch with me almost immediately."

"You said construction workers found the bodies."

"Yeah."

"Did they take anything?"

"I asked. For a moment I thought I was going to get thrown

out. But the police chief stepped in and made it clear that my team and I were going to excavate the remains and see that they were handled with respect. The police chief reiterated my question. They said no." Hallinger shrugged. "You never know. Maybe they didn't. Most people are reluctant to touch the dead."

The pocket Annja explored yielded a folded piece of paper that had browned over the years. She didn't try to open it. That would be done under laboratory conditions to help preserve the paper and the ink.

Three coins slid from the folds of the paper. All of them were of similar design, showing a woman with braided hair under a crown surrounded by stars and a circle of wheat stalks around the words Half Cent. United States Of America circled the wheat. The dates on the coins were 1843, 1852 and 1849.

Annja dropped them in Hallinger's waiting palm.

"Liberty braided-hair half pennies," Hallinger said as he examined them. "The full penny at the time was the size of a half dollar now."

"Those were minted between 1840 and the late 1850s," one of the students said. Brian was calm and easygoing.

Hallinger glanced at his student and smiled. "We didn't cover that in class."

Brian grinned shyly. "I've been into coin collecting since I was a kid. My dad bought me a metal detector as soon as I was big enough to carry it. We spent our weekends tramping through battlefields all over the South."

"Your father was a treasure hunter?"

"Still is. Drives Mom crazy. But he's making serious money on eBay with the stuff he finds. Coins, jewelry, stuff like that. He's made enough from his hobby to buy an RV so he's not camping in a tent on weekends anymore. Mom's okay with that. She gets to work on her genealogy stuff."

Hallinger glanced at his watch. "Maybe we should think about taking a break. It's almost nine. We've been working for hours."

Annja nodded. She was still ready to work, but she knew she would be until she fell on her face. The idea that the group of men in the furnace room was some kind of war party wouldn't leave her thoughts. Where had they come from? Where were they going? Who had killed them? She was curious, definitely hooked on the mystery that had been dropped into Hallinger's lap.

But the professor and his crew had been on-site since early that morning.

Hallinger looked at her, and Annja knew he read what was on her mind. "Just a break. We'll be back." He turned to the students. All of them were covered in grime and sweat. They looked tired and hungry. "I'll even spring for pizza. I'm sure I can get the university to pick up the tab."

"Sure. Just let me get this." Annja reached for the large stone covered in Hausa writing. *A long journey.* She couldn't help wondering what that meant. Were they starting a long journey? Or coming back from one? Why had the men been armed when they knew it would mean death for them? Had they been on the same journey when they'd been killed?

Out in the hallway, someone yelped in pain.

"Get down!" a gruff voice roared. "Get down on the ground on your face and you won't get hurt!"

Annja put the rock aside as she stood. Unconsciously, she reached into otherwhere and felt her sword at her fingertips. She kept it ready but didn't pull it into the world with her. In two quick strides she reached the opening and peered out into the low tunnel.

THREE MEN in ski masks, maybe more, hurried along the tunnel. They all carried semiautomatic pistols sporting thick, stubby silencers. They blinded the students with high-intensity flashlights.

One of the students wheeled around and shoved a girl behind him. He reached for the lead invader. The masked man barely moved the pistol he held in close to his side. The muzzle-flash briefly flared in the tunnel, and only a slight coughing sound reached Annja's ears.

The bullet struck the student in the upper chest and forced him backward. Blood spattered the wall and coated the nearby electric bulb. The crimson liquid hissed and smoked for just a moment, then the bulb burned out and went dark.

"Sit down," the masked man ordered, "or I'll put the next bullet between your eyes."

The student was too stunned to move. In disbelief, he put a hand over his chest against the wound.

The masked man reached the student, shoving out a hand that hit the young man in the throat and knocked him off his feet. The young woman was screaming.

Annja held on to the sword hilt. It felt solid and sure in her hand. All she had to do was pull and the blade would be there in the tunnel with her.

And the big guy with the gun will shoot you. Or someone else, Annja thought. Reluctantly, she released the sword.

"You!" The masked man waved at Annja. "Get down! Now!"

Annja lay on the ground. Ahead of her, the young woman held the gunshot victim. He quivered and jerked, but Annja thought it was shock setting in. He was still breathing, so she chose to remain optimistic.

The masked man reached her. "Where's the stone?"

Annja kept her voice level, holding the fear and adrenaline that filled her at bay. "What stone?"

"Don't play games with me. The Spider Stone."

She chose not to answer. It's nine o'clock. Maybe it's dark outside, but these guys couldn't have gotten in here unseen. Someone has to have seen them, she thought.

The masked man pointed the pistol at the young woman holding the gunshot victim. She cried out in fear and tried to crawl away, but there was nowhere to go in the narrow tunnel.

"I'll ask you one more time, then I'll kill her. Where is it?"

"It's in the other room." Annja pointed.

The masked man stepped over her, following the pistol into the furnace room. Stepping into the room, tearing through the grid they'd strung so carefully, he stooped and picked up the stone in one gloved hand.

Annja waited for the police to arrive. She hoped they would, but she dreaded it, too. Police might mean gunplay, and gunplay could mean a lot of dead university students.

"No, it's here. I got it." The masked man looked at the stone. "It's covered in writing. I can't make it out. It's not in English."

For a moment, Annja thought the man was talking to himself, then she saw the outline of the cell phone earbud under the ski mask.

The masked man tossed the stone to one of his compatriots and turned to Annja. "Where are your notes?"

"I've got a microcassette recorder in my pocket," she said.

The gloved hand flicked impatiently. "Gimme."

Annja dug the device out and handed it over. She hated feeling helpless, and she was scared. But she didn't let the fear take over.

The masked man shoved the cassette recorder into a thigh pocket of his camouflage pants and sealed the Velcro tab. Seeing the military-style pant and thinking about the way the guy moved and wasn't squeamish about shooting other people, Annja thought maybe he was—or had been—military. The black boots looked like military issue, too.

The man's eyes focused on hers through the slits of his mask. "What does it say on the stone?"

"I don't know," Annja said honestly.

"The professor held up operations here till you arrived. Don't tell me you can't read the stone."

"I can. Some of it."

"What does it say?"

"I didn't get a chance to decipher all of it. It mentions something about a journey."

"To where?"

"I don't know. I wasn't the first choice for the job. I'm doing the best I can. We were working the room first. We were going to address the stone later."

Frustration glinted in the man's cold eyes. He swung his pistol toward one of the students again.

"I'm telling you the truth." Panic knotted Annja's stomach. Violence was something she still wasn't used to even though she'd been through quite a lot of it lately—since she'd acquired the sword—but she could deal with it. The possibility of watching the man shoot someone through the head to prove his point made her sick. "I could lie to you. I could tell you anything I wanted. You wouldn't know the difference."

"I'd know if you were lying to me," he said.

"Then prove it." Annja looked directly into those cold, hard eyes. She spoke slowly. "I haven't finished translating the stone yet. I don't know any more about what's written there than I've told you." When she finished, her heart was hammering inside her chest. Part of her knew that the student was about to die.

Then the masked man lifted the pistol. "All right. You don't know what it says."

Annja released her pent-up breath.

"But you can translate it."

"Maybe."

"That's why Hallinger brought you in."

"Yes."

"Fine. Let's go." The masked man caught Annja's left arm, yanked her to her feet and twisted her arm behind her.

Pain shot through Annja's arm, but she stubbornly refused to cry out. She also resisted the impulse to attempt to break free. While at the orphanage, she'd gotten involved in martial arts, then continued her studies in college and after graduation. When she was home in Brooklyn, she still took classes in various dojos and even did some boxing.

Wait, she told herself. Don't react until you have to, or until you can make a difference. She looked around at the students and hated seeing the fear in their eyes. None of them had signed on for what they were currently dealing with. She didn't want the men responsible for that to escape.

SHOVED AHEAD of the masked man, Annja hurried down the tunnel. In seconds they reached the warehouse. The plywood covering the broken windows didn't quite block out all the light. Enough remained that Annja knew at least some of the crowd still remained outside. There were probably even a few reporters waiting to do remotes for the last news shows of the evening.

The masked man shoved Annja toward a side door that had been boarded shut. A fine spray of sawdust showed on the scarred wooden floor.

One of the men opened the door, and Annja's captor shoved her through to the dark, narrow alley on the other side. In the alley, Annja heard car engines idling out front, letting her know the police hadn't deserted their posts, either.

A rope ladder dangled from the building opposite the warehouse.

"Up." The masked man pointed toward the ladder.

Annja went, moving along the ladder quickly. Too quickly as it turned out.

The man grabbed her leg. She looked down at him, one hand over the top of the two-story building. Moonlight shone against her hand, washing away all color.

"Slowly." The man held on to her and aimed the pistol at the center of her body. "Try anything and I'll drop you."

Annja waited until he released her leg, then she went up.

Another man with a rifle equipped with telescopic sights hid on the rooftop. In the distance in front of the warehouse, two police cars with spinning lights stood guard. Two men sat on the hood of one of the cars drinking from paper cups.

Annja tried not to feel angry with them. Someone had been out in front of the warehouse since the bodies had been discovered. She was certain everyone involved was getting tired of the duty.

In short order, the five men who had invaded the dig site joined Annja and the sniper on the rooftop. All of them were heavily armed.

"When do we blow the building?" one of the men asked.

"Now," the big man said.

Ice water filled Annja's veins. She couldn't wait any longer. Reaching into the otherwhere, she gripped the sword and ripped it free just as the first man started to take an electronic detonator from his chest pack. She swung at him even before the sword was completely in her reality.

"Look out!" one of the men yelled, lifting his pistol.

3

The sword appeared in Annja's hand as she swung it toward the demolitions man's chest pack. The man was caught flat-footed.

Three feet of naked double-bladed steel, honed to razor-sharp edges, whipped through the air. The sword was inelegant, a tool designed for bloody work, not a showpiece to be kept on a mantel somewhere. It was the sword of a warrior.

The sword tip sliced through the chest pack and nicked the flesh beneath. Annja could have killed the man where he stood. Instead, she whirled and caught the tumbling remote control in her free hand, folding her right leg into her chest, then driving it forward in a side kick.

The man flew backward three or four yards, landing in a heap. He didn't move again.

Annja was fairly certain she'd rendered him unconscious but hadn't killed him. She made it a point not to kill unless she had to.

She turned, too fast for any of the surprised men to stop her, though they tried. She shook off one man's hand, then swept the sword forward and blocked the sniper's attempt to shoot her. Metal grated on metal.

Professor Hallinger and the others had burst free of the warehouse. The shouting on the ground quickly escalated into mass confusion.

The man who'd taken her hostage took aim at Annja as she ran to the roof access door. She dodged, feeling a bullet scald the air close to her cheek. From the corner of her eye, she spotted the masked man taking aim again.

She dived forward, tucking the sword and the detonator in close, rolling to the side as bullets thudded into the rooftop behind her. Coming to her feet immediately, she raced for the access door and took shelter behind it just as a fusillade of bullets raked the front of the structure.

The screaming detonation of automatic fire told Annja the thieves no longer favored silence.

"Up there!" someone shouted.

Dropping to her knees, Annja glanced at the remote control and saw a panel on the back. Laying the sword aside for a moment, she opened the back and popped the batteries out. Placing the detonator on the ground, she picked up the sword and smashed the device with the hilt.

Footsteps sounded to her right.

The moon was behind the man. Evidently he hadn't noticed because his shadow stretched out before him, arriving well before he did.

Annja broke to her left. The roof's edge wasn't far away. Close enough, she thought, that she could make it. If she had to, she could probably jump to street level to escape.

But she didn't want to escape. These men had gone into

the warehouse, and one of them had callously shot a student as if it were nothing.

Annja didn't intend to let them simply walk away. That hadn't been her way before she'd found the sword, and it definitely wasn't her way now.

On the other side of the roof-access structure, she could see that the other men were now in full flight. They headed north across the rooftops, away from the warehouse, leaping the distance between the close-set buildings. They'd left behind the man she'd kicked. He still lay prone on the roof.

Moving quickly, Annja vaulted on top of the access structure and scrambled forward. On the other side, the shadowy man advanced around the corner, both hands supporting his pistol as he spun to face where he believed Annja was hiding.

Her shadow, caught by the moon, shot out ahead of the structure's shadow on the rooftop. The sudden appearance must have caught the man's attention. He tried to turn and bring his weapon up, stepping back to give himself room to work.

Gripping the structure with one hand, Annja swung down, angling her body so that her left foot caught the man in the face. He went down, falling backward and losing his grip on the pistol.

Annja landed on her feet, knees bent to absorb the shock. She slid naturally into a horse stance, then swung the sword and brought the flat of the blade hard against the side of the man's head as he struggled to get to his feet. He slumped on the rooftop, unconscious.

Turning, Annja set off in pursuit of the fleeing men. Her stride was immediately long and sure, eating up the distance. She had no idea who had sent the men, but it was obvious that someone felt the stone was important.

She made the leap to the next building easily, lengthening her stride again. Ahead, the men disappeared over the side of one of the buildings. Annja ran faster.

WHEN SHE REACHED the edge of the last building, Annja peered down carefully. She caught sight of the gunman stationed below just as he fired the machine pistol he held. Annja barely yanked her head back in time to keep her face from getting shot off.

Bullets ripped through the air in front of her, then chipped into the stone side of the building as the gunner tried to correct his aim. The gunfire and whine of the bullets ricocheting from the wall rang in her ears.

Farther out, three of the men ran for a white van that skidded to a stop in front of the single police car blocking the alley from curious pedestrians. The policeman took cover behind his vehicle as he shouted on his radio. The radio squawks were overwhelmed by the sound of the gunfire.

Two gunmen slid free of the van. Both of them held fully automatic weapons that peppered the police car. The lone police officer tried to duckwalk away from his vehicle as bullets cored through the police car. Before he'd taken a half-dozen steps, he pirouetted and dropped, sprawling to the ground.

One of the gunners in the van turned his weapon on the rooftop where Annja stood. More bullets tore through brick and mortar where she took cover. Frustrated, she waited out the onslaught. She had no choice.

Rubber shrieked on the street as sirens shrilled on the other side of the warehouse.

Chancing a look down, Annja saw the white van speeding

away. She also knew with the way the road curved along the warehouse district, coming back around in almost a 180-degree turn, that the thieves hadn't gotten away cleanly. She still had a chance.

She ran to the side of the building that overlooked the street where the van would have to pass along. She charged down the metal fire escape, steps banging as she made the twists and turns. She reached the final ladder, grabbed hold of it with her free hand and jumped on to ride to the ground.

Taking cover in the shadows, Annja kept her hand around the sword hilt and watched as the van came sliding around the far turn. The bright lights played over her position, then kept on moving, coming closer.

Okay, Annja told herself, this is your last chance to rethink what you're about to do. She kept picturing the innocent student the masked man had shot in cold blood. She knew that Professor Hallinger would feel responsible. She didn't want the men to get away.

Annja stepped out of the darkness into the path of the speeding van. She held the sword in both hands, up high so she could sweep the blade down.

Roux had worked with her for a time on her swordcraft, then he'd ultimately found more pleasant pursuits after spending five hundred years looking for the pieces of the shattered sword. She still practiced with the sword every day, getting to know the weapon more and more intimately as she worked.

The van's headlights fell across Annja. Shadows within the front seats moved. The passenger leaned out his window and took aim.

Annja ran toward the van, matching her speed and her stride, running toward the driver's side to make it more difficult for the gunner to track her. Bullets cracked through the air as the muzzle-flashes appeared in sporadic bursts.

At the last moment, Annja leaped, placing one foot on the van's hood and pushing off again. She arced up, twisting her body so that she flipped and landed on her feet on the van's roof. She was sure that before she'd gotten the sword she could never have accomplished such a maneuver. Now it was almost child's play.

The driver immediately took evasive action, swinging the steering wheel wildly. The van took out a line of trash cans, filling the air with the noise of tearing metal and grinding. Sparks shot out as trash cans remained stuck beneath the van.

Bullets tore through the thin metal of the van's roof. They missed Annja, who dropped to one knee and reversed the sword so that she held it point down. Using all her strength, she plunged the sword down through the roof.

Annja missed the driver by inches. The sudden appearance of the sword slicing through the van's top startled the driver. He pulled hard to the right, slamming the van into a wall in an effort to dislodge Annja.

Grimly, she hung on to the front of the van. She didn't want to let the men escape, not only for wounding the college student, but also because she wanted to know the reasons for the attack in the first place. Why was the stone so important?

Sparks cascaded along the van's side, coming in a deluge as the vehicle left scarred building walls in its wake. The grinding sound erased all but the shrill cries of the police sirens. The van gained speed.

Annja didn't know if the men could manage to escape from the police. They seemed well organized, but she didn't want to take any chances. Bullets ripped along the van's rooftop, missing her by inches.

Moving quickly, she vaulted forward and landed on the hood in a crouch. On the other side of the cracked windshield, the driver and the passenger looked incredulous. The passenger finished reloading his machine pistol and leveled the weapon.

Annja struck first, shoving the sword's point toward the driver and shattering the glass. The driver ducked, pulling hard on the steering wheel.

Already off balance from the impacts against the wall, the van slid to the left, then came up on two wheels in a slow roll. Annja jumped clear, hurling herself from the path of the sudden explosion of bullets.

Annja landed in a crouch, allowing her legs to absorb the shock of the landing. Surprise filled her for just a moment. Then she accepted what she'd just done by instinct. Having the sword or simply reforging the sword had changed her. She still wasn't sure of everything that had occurred or would continue to occur. But it no longer shocked her or scared her.

The van careened over on its side and skidded along the street. Even before it slammed to a stop against one of the buildings, the rear cargo doors opened and three men rolled free. Annja ran toward them, catching up with the first one before he got to his feet. She swung the sword and brought the hilt down on the man's head, knocking him unconscious with the blow.

Ducking the second man's attempt to pull up his machine pistol, she swept his legs from beneath him with her own, then grabbed his hair through the mask and slammed his head against the street. He went limp and the gun clattered to the ground.

The third man snarled curses at her as he pointed his pistol. Before he could fire, Annja rolled and came to her feet. She swung the sword and knocked away the pistol. The bullet missed her by inches as the weapon went flying.

Recovering almost immediately, the man launched himself at her, punching and kicking. Annja recognized him at once as she stepped clear of his attack. He was the leader, the one who'd so coldly shot the college student.

Tossing her sword to the side, Annja felt its absence as it phased back into the otherwhere. Taking another quick step back, she set herself, left forearm raised in front of her and right hand clenched at her hip. She blocked the man's attacks in rapid succession, turning aside a punch with her forearm, two kicks with her lead leg, then stepped in low to deliver a kidney blow as he tried to set himself.

He cried out in pain.

Savage satisfaction lit through Annja as she heard him. Still in motion, slipping to the man's right, she reverse kicked, bringing her foot high enough to collide with the man's face. Incredibly, he remained standing.

Okay, Annja thought, that's not good. She bounced back on her toes, setting up with her right leg forward this time, changing strong sides so he'd have to adapt.

The man spit blood.

"That's DNA evidence," Annja taunted. "Even if you got away, which you won't, the police would be able to track you down."

He snarled, "You won't know how that ends up." He curled his hands and tucked them in close to the sides of his face, elbows out to block. "I'm going to kill you," he said. Then he attacked.

Annja gave ground, knowing his weight was an advantage that she couldn't meet head-on. Her hands and feet flew, blocking, parrying, turning. Despite her skill, the impacts would leave bruises.

She escalated her defense, still giving ground but circling now. Then the rhythm changed. His breath started coming faster, his lungs sounded like stressed bellows pumps. For every three punches or kicks he threw, she threw one back, each one placed with telling accuracy, thudding into his face, his chest or his legs. She patiently allowed him to exhaust himself.

When she saw his strength was flagging, she stepped in close and swept his legs. As he fell, Annja hammered him twice in the face. He tried to get up, but she grabbed the back of his head with her hands and kneed him in the face.

His nose broke with an audible crunch. Unconscious, he rolled over on his back.

Police sirens screamed as they closed in.

Annja didn't want to be caught there. The police would have too many questions about how she had overcome a van full of armed men. She turned and ran into the night.

ANNJA LOOKED UP from the stone she'd been working on since the Kirktown Police Department had shut down all activity at the warehouse and brought everyone to the police station. Annja was seated at a borrowed desk in the detectives' bullpen.

The man standing beside the desk looked as though he was in his early thirties, with curly brown hair, dark green eyes and a square face. He wore jeans and a white snap-button Western shirt, cowboy boots and a tan corduroy blazer with leather elbow patches. He dropped a black cowboy hat onto the desk beside the stone covered in Hausa writing.

"I'm Detective Andrew McIntosh." He extended his hand.

Annja took it, feeling his flesh hot against hers in the semicooled office space. "You don't look like a detective," she said.

McIntosh reached into his back pocket and brought out a badge case. He flipped it open to reveal the badge and ID.

Annja kept her eyes on his face, studying him, but she read the ID from the corner of her eye. "It says you're from Atlanta. Not Kirktown."

McIntosh smiled. "Most people don't see past the badge."

"I do," Annja said.

"Kirktown doesn't usually find murder victims 150 years old. Or have running gun battles with terrorist weapons in their streets. Since both happened more or less on the same day and appear to be connected, the captain of detectives here in Kirktown asked for some help on this one. I volunteered."

"Are things that boring in Atlanta?" Annja was responding to the cocky smoothness the man demonstrated. The overconfidence rankled her.

He smiled, and she could see the mischievous little boy he'd probably been twenty-something years ago. His cheeks dimpled.

"Actually, that's a funny story. I'm on administrative leave." McIntosh pointed to a chair beside the desk. "Mind if I sit?"

"The police station would seem to belong more to you than to me," she said coolly.

"This is Georgia, Ms. Creed. Some of us still have manners. My momma always said it was impolite to sit with a lady without asking."

He was a charmer, Annja was amused to discover. She wondered if the down-home good-ol'-boy routine was an act. If it is, it's a good one. She was intrigued. She turned a hand toward the chair. "Please."

McIntosh sat.

Around the bullpen, several of the students and Professor Hallinger sat with detectives while giving statements.

Annja waited until he was settled. "Why am I being interviewed again?"

"You've been interviewed before?" McIntosh seemed surprised by that.

"I have been. And you know that. I just saw you talking to the detective who interviewed me."

McIntosh grinned like a kid who'd been caught with his hand in the cookie jar. "I could have sworn you were totally involved in that rock."

"I am. I could be more involved if I wasn't trying to translate it while sitting in a police station filled with people."

Leaning forward, McIntosh looked at the lettering and the pictographs. "You can read that?"

"That's what I'm trying to figure out."

McIntosh glanced at the notebook Annja had been working in.

Annja shifted just enough to shield the notebook.

Smiling easily, McIntosh leaned back in the chair. "You're an interesting woman, Ms. Creed."

"Thank you. But you didn't answer my question."

"Actually, I did. I was asked to interview you again because you're so interesting."

"How interesting?"

"Well, it's interesting that Professor Hallinger decided to call you in—"

"Because I have a little familiarity with the Hausa language," Annja said.

McIntosh nodded. "It's also interesting that the men tried to swipe that stone shortly after you arrived."

"They waited till after it got dark. Otherwise the police officers would have spotted them entering the warehouse," Annja said.

"Maybe."

Annja arched an eyebrow. "Or maybe I arranged for them to be here?"

"Someone did."

"It wasn't me."

McIntosh smiled at her. "I hope that's true. You're a good-looking woman, Ms. Creed. But you were also the one they decided to take with them when they fled the scene."

"Because I could read some of what's written on this stone."

"How did they know that?"

"While they were taking us prisoner, they asked."

McIntosh raised his eyebrows innocently. "So you just told them you could?"

"Like you, they saw my notes," Annja said, no longer concealing her irritation.

McIntosh grinned. "See? That's interesting, too."

"I escaped from those men, Detective McIntosh."

"That's what I was told."

"Then what do we have to talk about?"

"Let's see if we can come up with something," he said. Reaching into his jacket pocket, McIntosh took out a small bound notebook and a half-dozen pens held together with a rubber band.

"Why are you on administrative leave?" Annja took a sip from the cup of coffee she'd been given. It had gotten cold, but long hours at her work had accustomed her to that.

"What?"

"You said you were on administrative leave."

"I am."

Placing her elbows on the desk, Annja leaned forward and looked into his eyes. "Tell me why."

McIntosh sighed. "Are you really going to make me tell this story?"

"Yes."

"It's embarrassing."

"I like stories. Otherwise I'm going to call a lawyer in and have him ask you and the Kirktown Police Department why my time is being wasted. Not only that, but I'm going to return my producer's phone call. Maybe I can help increase the media attention you're getting here."

McIntosh feigned a frown, but Annja knew he was a natural-born storyteller. As an archaeologist, she'd learned to recognize people like that. Sometimes they helped on a dig site and sometimes they hindered. She needed to know what McIntosh was—a help or a hindrance.

"I was on stakeout," McIntosh said. "My partner and I were working a serial burglar downtown. Guy was working hotels. For a city with a lot of tourists that come in, that's not a good thing."

"I can see that," Annja said, sitting back.

"In addition to stealing valuables, the guy also had a pantie fetish." McIntosh paused. "I don't want to offend you."

"Hey. I live in New York. Talking about underwear isn't going to offend me."

McIntosh appeared to relax. "I'm gonna remember you said that. Anyway, I got the idea to use a bloodhound to track the guy. The chief has one of the best at tracking men, but the dog is one of his favorites. I kind of borrowed him without telling the chief. I guessed that maybe the thief was someone staying at the hotel. Thunder—that's the name of the chief's dog—hit on a scent almost immediately."

Annja grinned, enjoying the laconic way the detective spun the tale. The experience was even more amusing because she knew he was lying, probably making it up on the spot.

"Well, Thunder lit out. I did my best to keep up. But you have to imagine the scene. We're talking a five-star hotel here. Thunder is racing down the hallway, hits the stairwell, and down we go. He's baying to beat the band. You ever heard a bloodhound working a trail?"

Annja nodded, grinning wider now.

"I'm talking about those long, loud, *mournful* howls. If you don't know what it is, you might think somebody was getting killed. Or maybe it was some kind of monster loose in the hotel. Well now, there were a lot of people in that hotel who hadn't heard a bloodhound baying before."

"Must have really gotten a lot of attention," Annja said.

"We did. Way more than I ever wanted to. The chase ended up in the hotel lobby. The guy was there checking out when Thunder hit him. His bag popped open when it hit the floor. Jewelry, cash and panties scattered everywhere. The thief pulled a gun and shot Thunder before I had a chance to clear leather with my pistol."

"Poor dog."

"Nah. Thunder's all right. Just grazed his scalp. But it was enough to leave him scarred and gun shy. The chief wasn't happy about that." McIntosh shrugged. "So that's how I ended up on administrative leave."

"And you were the first person the Kirktown Police Department thought to call when things got out of hand here." Annja smiled in mock wonder. She started clapping, drawing the attention of everyone in the room.

McIntosh had the decency to look embarrassed. Maybe he really was, she thought. He reached over and took Annja's hands, stopping her from clapping.

Annja twisted her hands from his and leaned back, crossing her arms over her breasts. "That's the most creative load of BS I've seen someone come up with on the spot in a long time."

"What are you talking about?" McIntosh looked mystified.

"You're a Fed, McIntosh. You're using the Atlanta PD as a cover. No one around here would know you."

Some of the easygoing demeanor dropped from McIntosh's face. His features took on a distant hardness. "You *are* an interesting woman, Ms. Creed."

"One that has a job to do, and I can't do it here. So either cut to the chase or let me call my attorney."

"I'm with Homeland Security. We have power you haven't even seen. The attorney happens when I say it happens," McIntosh said firmly.

"Great. There's nothing more I like than being threatened by my own government. I get enough of government meddling when I'm on digs overseas." Annja took a deep breath. "I've been on the phone with the producer of the television show I work for every thirty minutes since I've been here." She wondered if her pseudo-celebrity status could actually be useful.

"I'm aware of your television presence," McIntosh said, sounding unimpressed.

"I've talked him out of hiring a crew out of Atlanta to cover this." Annja paused for dramatic effect. "So far. But one missed phone call, you can bet he's going to send someone in."

McIntosh reflected on the situation for a moment. "You get more interesting the more I know you."

"You should see me in action with an attorney and a camera crew, then."

"Have you had dinner, Ms. Creed?"

A glance at her watch told Annja it was almost two in the morning. "No."

"Let's get out of here and get something to eat. And I'll tell you why Homeland Security is interested in this."

"Can I bring the stone?" she asked.

McIntosh hesitated for just a second. "Sure."

4

The Clover Bee Truck Stop lay west of Kirktown along the highway that connected the city to Atlanta. The diner glowed against the darkness. Several 18-wheelers sat parked for the night in the lots outside.

"Not exactly haute cuisine," McIntosh apologized as he parked the car. He reached into the back for a slim metal briefcase. "But at two o'clock in the morning, you're not going to get much to choose from in Kirktown."

Annja slung her backpack over one arm and picked up the cloth bag holding the stone. Professor Hallinger had looked at her in surprise as she'd left with the artifact, but he hadn't asked any questions.

"Trust me. An all-night diner is great compared to having to eat powdered eggs out of a cup while holding your hand over it and hoping the dust doesn't completely wipe out the flavor. You swallow the eggs without chewing so you won't have to hear the grit grinding," Annja said.

McIntosh held open the door.

Inside the building, the convenience-store area occupied the left side, filled with spinner racks containing DVDs, books, audio books and maps. Phone-card vending machines shared space with video games and packaged, single-serving traveler's aids. Shelves in the center of the store contained everything from snacks to phone accessories to DVD players.

The restaurant area was rustic, made of large timbers and bathed in the golden glow of lamps mounted in wagon wheels. Glass tops covered red-and-white-checked tablecloths.

"Well," McIntosh said, "it's better than I'd hoped."

A short, heavyset woman led them to a booth. Even though it was dark, Annja wanted to sit by the window after having been cooped up down in the warehouse's furnace room and the police department.

McIntosh sat across from her. He put the briefcase on the bench seat beside him.

"Bowling ball?" the woman asked when Annja put the cloth bag on the table.

Annja smiled. "Paperweight."

The woman shrugged. "Must be for a big stack of papers. Do you know what you want to drink?"

"Diet Coke. Do you have breakfast?" Annja asked.

"Twenty-four hours a day, hon."

"The cook any good?"

"I eat here."

"Good enough for me. I'm ready to order." Annja's stomach rumbled as she looked at McIntosh.

"Me, too. Start and I'll catch up." McIntosh gave the menu a cursory glance.

Annja stuck with breakfast, ordering eggs over easy, hash

browns with onions and cheese and jalapeños, toast, biscuits and gravy, sides of sausage and bacon and a pecan waffle. She also asked for milk and orange juice.

The server glanced at her in surprise.

"She's not shy, is she?" McIntosh asked.

"I was going to ask how you afford to keep her." The server took McIntosh's order, collected the menus and retreated.

Annja took her notebook computer from her backpack, placed it on the table and powered it up. "You're buying," she said.

"Why?"

"Because I'm down here as a freebie, and Homeland Security has deep pockets these days. Otherwise, we don't talk."

"As long as we talk, then." McIntosh looked at the computer screen.

The screensaver showed a crude drawing of a female warrior holding a spear while standing atop a wall. She wore a gold crown and was adorned with gold bracelets and a necklace of cat's teeth, either leopard or lion. Annja had never found out which.

McIntosh pointed at the screen. "Who's that?"

"Queen Amina. Or Aminatu, depending on your source material. She was queen of Zazzau during the last part of the sixteenth century. She led her troops in battle and negotiated—at the business end of a spear—safe passage for all her trade caravans."

"I've never heard of her. Or Zazzau."

"I hadn't, either, until I went to Nigeria."

"So as an archaeologist, you don't know about all of history?"

"Do you know about every murder that took place in Atlanta? Last year?"

"I suppose that is a lot to know."

"I've got an ongoing education. It's better to accept that and move forward."

"What were you doing in Nigeria?"

"The same kind of work I'm doing here." Annja frowned. "But what I was studying wasn't the same. While I was there, I was studying the culture of a fierce, dynamic people who dominated parts of the trans-Atlantic trade routes. Here, I'm helping Professor Hallinger find out who those murder victims were."

"I thought they were slaves trying to flee along the Underground Railroad."

"They were. But they were also Hausa."

McIntosh nodded toward the stone. "That's what the stone tells you?"

"Partly. Also the signs on their weapons and some of the copper bracelets they wore. They were slaves. I don't know how long they had been in the United States. But they kept the Hausa ways in spite of their circumstances."

"How old is that stone?" McIntosh asked.

"I'll have to do some tests on it, but I think it was around a hundred years old when it went into that furnace room."

"That makes it between two and three hundred years old."

Annja nodded.

"What is the stone? Some kind of religious icon?"

"No. It's more like a—" Annja hesitated. "A book," she said.

"I guess they didn't believe in light reading material."

McIntosh's quick, offhand dismissal of what the people

in that furnace room had accomplished offended Annja. She pinned him with her gaze. "Do you know much about what a slave's life was like during those years?"

"Only what they teach you in high school," he said.

"Have you ever seen slavery? Been in countries where it still exists to this day?"

"No."

"Then don't act like this is a joke. Generations of people lived hard, small lives filled with fear, oppression and abuse."

McIntosh looked at her. "Hey, I can tell I touched a nerve here. I apologize. I didn't mean to do that."

Annja forced herself to take a deep breath. "It's not you. It was being down there with those bodies today. Not all slaves were treated harshly, but those people were. Most of those bodies in the furnace room showed fracture lines where their arms and legs had been broken. Several of them were missing fingers. The smallest skeleton down there, a boy maybe twelve or thirteen, was missing half a foot. The cut through the bone was clean."

"An accident?"

"No. Slaves who ran off usually got hobbled in some way. One of those ways was to chop off half a foot or the whole foot. I'd bet that's what happened to him."

McIntosh grimaced. "Not exactly breakfast conversation."

"You didn't bring me here for breakfast conversation." Annja didn't feel sorry for having said what she did. "I didn't come here for breakfast conversation."

The server returned with their drinks.

"What I'm trying to point out is the incredible risks those men—or whoever was responsible—took in hiding this stone." Annja reached into her backpack and brought out her digital camera. She quickly hooked the camera up to the notebook computer through a USB connection.

"What are you doing?" McIntosh asked.

"I'm going to post a few of the pictures I took today on a few of the newsgroups I'm a member of."

A troubled look tightened McIntosh's face. "I don't know if I should allow that."

Annja focused on him, unsheathing some of the anger that roiled through her. "Do you know what this record represents?"

McIntosh let out a breath. "No."

"Neither do I. Posting pictures on these newsgroups is one of the avenues I have open to me. Evidently this stone is interesting to you and Homeland Security or you wouldn't be here."

"I'm sure we have experts who could look at that stone and decipher it," he said.

"If you had someone who could do that, or one of your supervisors thought it was necessary, you'd have already taken the stone," Annja said.

McIntosh said nothing.

"You're not here because of the stone, are you?"

After a brief pause, McIntosh shook his head.

Annja studied him. "If it wasn't the stone, it must have been the men. They moved like military men. Soldiers." She let that last thought hang.

McIntosh didn't go for the bait.

"You know who they are. But you don't know what brought them here," she said, trying another approach.

Shifting uncomfortably, McIntosh folded his arms and leaned back. "You're way too good at this."

"It's just a process of elimination. I'm in a field where I

have to make educated guesses about things that happened hundreds and thousands of years ago. By comparison to millions of years of history, the present-day political atmosphere is a piece of cake. Something about those men made you—or Homeland Security—paranoid. If you want to know what I know, we need to talk."

"This is a sensitive issue," McIntosh said.

"One of the students was shot tonight." Thankfully, Annja had been told he would recover. "I'd say that was pretty serious."

"Have you ever heard of a man named Tafari?" McIntosh asked.

Annja started to say no, but then a vague whisper of memory tugged at her. "I heard the name while I was in Nigeria. He's into black market goods and drugs, I think."

"How do you know that?" McIntosh's eyebrows knitted.

"Look," Annja said, "you can ask me questions with the hope of getting information or of confirming your paranoia. But you can't do both. If you want information, it's going to be a two-way street. If you're just interested in making yourself paranoid, I'm just going to eat breakfast."

"All right. Information, then." McIntosh put his elbows on the table and pressed his hands together. His eyes never stopped roving, but they never neglected Annja, either. "Tafari isn't just a guy into black market goods and drugs. That's actually the tip of the iceberg. He's a warlord. One of the most feared in the area."

The title *warlord* wasn't just thrown around in Africa. Even before she'd gone there, Annja had known that parts of the continent were torn apart by the existence of what were basically feudal rulers. They were hard men driven by their own desires and needs.

"You're familiar with this kind of man?"

Annja shook her head. "I've never met one of them. But I've heard stories."

"Whatever you've heard, it's worse." McIntosh turned to the briefcase, flipped through the combination lock and took a thick file from inside. He opened the file on the table, using one side to block all other views.

Annja stared at the cruel face featured in the top picture. It was a waist-up shot of a powerful-looking African with beads and shells in his hair. He held an unfiltered cigarette to his lips. Blue-black tribal tattooing marked his skin, as did scars from past wounds. He wore a khaki BDU festooned with grenades and knives.

"Tafari?" Annja asked.

"Yeah." McIntosh's eyes never moved from the man's face. "This guy is a stone killer. If he decided that he didn't like you, if there was a buck to be made in the deal, he'd kill you in a heartbeat."

Annja watched as the Homeland Security agent flipped through other photographs. All of them were graphic and in full color.

"We want him for crimes against Americans." McIntosh tapped a picture that showed three dead men lying at the side of a dirt road. "Tafari has killed tourists, as well as relief workers. England wants him for the same thing. Even the United Nations wants him taken off the board."

As Annja watched, more pictures of gruesome murders were quietly turned over, building a stack in no time. "I get that he's a killer. But what does that have to do with me?" she asked.

"Not you." McIntosh flipped through the photographs and pulled one out. The photo was obviously a police mug shot, showing the man full face and in profile. "Recognize him?"

"No."

"His name is Nwankwo Ehigiator. He was one of the men in Dack Tatum's group."

"The men who invaded the dig site?"

"That's right."

Annja shook her head. "I don't know him. I don't know Dack Tatum, either." But there was something about the name that sounded familiar.

"Dack Tatum is Christian Tatum's brother."

The name struck a chord. "Christian Tatum owned the warehouse where the bodies were found," Annja said.

"At one time. From what I got from Ehigiator, Dack was here because of his brother. Until tonight, Christian had evidently been entertaining dreams of political office. Unfortunately, the Atlanta police have taken him into custody at this point and he's being charged with conspiracy to commit murder."

"Christian Tatum sent his brother to blow up the warehouse?" Annja couldn't believe it.

"Yeah."

"Why?"

"The arresting officer who took Tatum from his home said that he was there with a journal. They're going over it now. It belonged to one of the Tatum ancestors."

"Jedidiah?" Annja asked. "Jedidiah Tatum built and owned the textile mill."

"Horace," McIntosh said. He flipped through his notebook. Annja noticed the pages were covered with a strong, neat hand. "He was Jedidiah's son. The old man beat the kid and made him work with the slaves in the fields. As a result, the kid hated the slaves. He found the group in the furnace under the textile mill and dynamited them. His father nearly killed him because it destroyed the old furnace and caused a cave-in. But by that time the new system had already been built. Jedidiah decided to leave the furnace room buried to cover up his son's crime."

The cold-blooded act shocked Annja even though she'd seen the blasted remnants in the room. "Why did Horace do it?"

"To get back at the escaped slaves."

"For escaping? That doesn't make sense. He could have told his father."

McIntosh shrugged. "I don't know the particulars. Horace was eleven. You find a kid that age who's homicidal, generally they don't think much past the next thing on their list. If they have a list."

"Can I see that journal?" Annja asked.

The federal agent hesitated.

"It might help me identify the people in that furnace room."

"I'll see if I can make that happen," he said.

"You still want the translation from the stone. I can make *that* happen," Annja said.

McIntosh smiled. "Done. I'll have the book here by morning."

The waitress arrived with platters of food and quickly served it. Annja and McIntosh forgot about conversation for a moment while they dealt with the meal.

"CHRISTIAN TATUM WANTED to blow up the building in case any evidence about his ancestor's murder still existed," McIntosh said as he pushed his empty plate away. "The building was sold during the Depression. I don't think anyone thought much about it after it was boarded up in the 1970s. Then the bodies were found. So Christian Tatum called his brother."

Annja sat back in the booth. Her eyes kept straying to the stone covered in Hausa writing. Her brain picked at words here and there. She wanted to go back to her hotel room and work.

"Homeland Security got interested in what was happening here because of the other man you identified. Ehigiator. Who is he?" Annja asked.

"Ehigiator is a mercenary, like Dack Tatum. Professional soldier for hire. He's been linked to Tafari on several occasions."

"You think Tafari sent him to join Tatum's group of mercenaries?"

"No. Ehigiator has been with Dack Tatum's group for the past year and a half. During that time, Ehigiator has worked several solo assignments for Tafari. Assassinations of police and political figures who have pursued him or who have gone into the bush in an effort to get the villages he preys on to stand against him. We know Tafari was interested in something at the site because one of the snitches we use brought us that information."

"But you don't know what it was?"

"Not precisely, no. However, we do know that Tafari is interested in West African artifacts. The snitch who contacted us told us that Ehigiator had been offered a bonus by Tafari if he could recover the Spider Stone."

"Was Dack Tatum working with him?"

"No. Christian Tatum also wanted the stone."

"Do Christian Tatum and Tafari know each other?" Annja asked.

"We don't think so."

"Dack Tatum came after the stone. Otherwise he'd have blown that building apart." With us in it, Annja thought. She shivered a little when she realized how close the dig personnel had come to getting killed.

"We think he wanted it for his brother. Christian Tatum's notes in his ancestor's journals alluded to a treasure that's connected with the stone."

Annja thought about that. Many maps and artifacts came with legends and stories attached to them that suggested treasures could be found if the secret could be unlocked. Most if not all of those myths and legends were false. In fact, there were a number of artifacts said to exist that probably were as ephemeral as the stories themselves.

"Tafari wants the Spider Stone for the treasure?" she asked.

"We don't know why Tafari wants it," McIntosh admitted. "It's enough that he does. All of his life, Tafari has been interested in ways of consolidating his power base. He achieves part of that by using supernatural objects to terrorize the villagers. Hexes. Voodoo. That kind of crap."

"You can't just dismiss voodoo," Annja said quickly.

McIntosh chuckled and shook his head. "Don't tell me you believe in that stuff?"

"I maintain a healthy respect for voodoo. It's a belief system with roots deep in several religions. For those reasons alone, voodoo has power."

"Yeah, well, you can have it. My agency wants a shot at Tafari. If we can use this—" McIntosh glanced over at the stone "—to bring Tafari out into the open, we might be interested."

"Where is Tafari now?"

"In Senegal. He's never left that country. And he hasn't been caught by authorities since he was a kid. He escaped an execution squad somehow." McIntosh finished the rest of his coffee and covered a yawn. "But if he wants that stone, he'll find a way to get to it."

Despite the quiet of the restaurant, Annja again felt as if someone was watching her. She glanced out the window, but the pump area was largely empty. Only a couple of cars were gassing up.

"Something wrong?" McIntosh asked.

"Long day." Annja pushed out of the booth. "Thanks for breakfast, but if I'm going to figure out anything about this artifact, I've got to get back to my hotel and get to work."

McIntosh took out a business card and wrote on the back. "That's my cell number on the back. If you need anything, let me know."

"The journal," Annja replied. "As quick as you can."

He nodded.

Annja reached out for the heavy stone. As soon as she touched it, she felt an electric tingle. And the sensation of being watched grew even stronger.

5

The man's frightened breath could be heard if a person was patient and knew what to listen for.

Tafari practiced patience and did know. He knelt, secluded in the tall grass under a copse of twenty-foot-tall trees. Night covered the land all around him, but the moon was full and bright. And he had a hunter's eyes, trained not to look directly at something, but to look for movement or a void in otherwise natural surroundings.

He listened to the short gasps and plaintive cries as the man called on his gods to protect him. Tafari smiled. There would be no protection. There was no mercy in him tonight. He would not even grant the man a quick death. He wanted to feel the man's terror and smell the stink of it on him.

Slowly, Tafari drew the long knife from the sheath at his waist without a sound. He rose silent as a shadow and stayed low as he stalked the man through the brush and grass, tracking his prey by sound. It was a game he'd played before, with men, as well as animals.

Short and stocky, Tafari had always had a powerful build. Now he wore only a leather loincloth and the knife. His bare feet moved easily across the hard ground, protected by years of calluses. Many of the young men in his group liked European clothing and shoes. They wore those things when they were in the big cities, but Tafari didn't allow them when they were in the brush.

He had only been to Dakar once. His father had taken him when he'd finally given up trying to survive in the brush and had decided to get a job in the city. Three weeks later, his father had been killed, knifed by a stranger in an alley for the coins he carried in his pockets.

Tafari had returned to the jungle where he had been born. Only ten years old, he'd survived by hunting and stealing chickens from the villagers because no one wanted the extra burden of raising another child. Especially one who wasn't their own.

In spite of his hardships and the lack of help, Tafari had flourished. At sixteen, he had joined a Yoruba warlord named Foday who preyed on the villagers and attacked and harassed the white men who came to Senegal to hunt. They'd killed some of them outright, but others they had held for ransom for a time before killing them.

Six years ago, when Tafari had been twenty-seven, a group of British mercenaries had come to Senegal looking for Foday. They found him. They'd been hired by a family who had bought back a corpse. When the mercenaries were finished, so was Foday. They'd killed the warlord and decapitated him, taking his head as proof of his death.

Tafari had gone down in the battle, taking two rounds through the abdomen. The mercenaries had left him for dead. He'd almost died before he was able to stanch the bleeding.

But he had lived. And he'd gotten the group back together, proclaiming himself as leader. He'd only had to kill two other men who had wanted to challenge him. After that, the men realized that he was going to lead them to heights that Foday hadn't taken them. Now the group lived better than they ever had, with their pick of women and anything the villages had to offer.

Over the years, Tafari had taken in three times as many men as Foday had been willing to recruit. Keeping them fed and happy required aggressive planning. That had necessitated having more and better weapons so he could in turn control larger groups.

As a result, he had helped hide al-Qaeda terrorists, when the United States government had invaded Iraq, in exchange for assault weapons. That had earned him eternal enmity from the Americans. Occasionally mercenaries entered the brush seeking the bounty on Tafari's head.

The man he hunted now had been one of them.

Tafari's warriors had allowed the mercenary unit to get deep within the brush, then they'd taken them in the night, killing the guard and stealing the Land Rover the men had driven. On foot, the men had tried to make their way back to civilization.

For the past four nights, Tafari had hunted them, taking them down one at a time. Each night for the previous three nights, he had killed one man.

Tonight he would kill the last one.

Movement broke to his left.

Like a predator, Tafari went immediately still. Action attracted his eye and lifted images out of the darkness. He held the long knife down by his leg.

The man was white, pale against the night. He'd tried to

rub mud over his features, but he hadn't been able to conceal himself well. Big and hulking, doubtless made so by working out and the drugs that made men's muscles balloon, he looked like a monster in the darkness. Tafari had deliberately saved the largest man for last. The man wore a camouflage shirt and pants and boots that hadn't been off his feet in three days because the first night Tafari had taken one man's boots and they'd had to travel much more slowly.

Less than fifteen feet away, Tafari could smell the stink of fear on the man. The man had had no rest. Last night, he and the other man had tried to walk through the dark hours. They couldn't. At a cold camp, they'd tried to stay awake all night. Tafari had slept only a few feet away. Then he roused before dawn, walked into the camp, and slit the other man's throat, leaving him dead for the survivor to find.

The man out in the brush had awoken lying next to a dead man. He had run through most of the day, trying to use the sun as his guide because his compass and other equipment had been taken. As a result, he'd gone in a large semicircle and had exhausted himself and what little water he'd carried.

During the day, Tafari had slept and rested, looking forward to his final night of hunting. Taking a fresh grip on the knife, he moved stealthily after the man. He came up on him from behind, levering an arm across the man's forehead and yanking his head back to expose his throat.

"You are dead," Tafari told the man in English. He'd learned the language piecemeal over the years, from other warriors, as well as the Europeans he did business with. In West Africa, English was the chosen language of drug dealers, traffickers in human slavery and the black market.

"No!" the man shouted. He struggled to get free, but Tafari wrapped his legs around the man and rode him like a beast.

"You came here," Tafari said, "to my place. To take *my* life. That is unforgivable. Now you will pay for that with your life."

"Don't! You can't do—!"

Tafari rested the edge of his blade against the man's throat. "I can. You can't stop me."

Squealing in horror, the man tried to run, aiming himself toward a tree.

Taking gleeful pride in the man's fear, Tafari rode him, hanging on despite the man's efforts to pry free the arm around his head. The man's teeth gnashed as he tried to bite his tormentor. He grabbed for the knife. Tafari raked the sharp edge across the man's palm, slicing it to the bone. Blood sprayed everywhere, slung off by the man's exertions.

The man howled again and rammed Tafari into the tree. The impact hurt, but Tafari only drew himself more tightly to the man and laughed in his ear.

"Now," Tafari snarled, "you will die." He clamped his teeth on to the man's ear, tasting the man's blood. When his victim reared his head back to try to tear away from the teeth, Tafari slit his throat and felt hot blood cascade over his hand and arm.

Tafari rode the man to the ground as he died, never once letting him forget who had killed him. When it was over, he stood and hacked the dead man's head from his shoulders.

Holding the man's head by the hair, Tafari stood and presented his offering to the dark gods he worshipped, telling them this was a sacrifice he had made in their honor. If a man had to sacrifice to the gods, Tafari believed it had to be in blood. There was nothing else so precious.

At that moment, a large pharaoh-eagle owl glided across

the round face of the silver moon. The bird's tawny, white-and-black feathers gleamed in the light. A dead mouse hung from its talons.

"Both of us were successful hunters tonight, brother," Tafari told the owl. He felt certain the bird's presence was an omen, a promise of good things to come.

The winged predator made no response and quickly disappeared from sight.

Kneeling, Tafari wiped his knife clean on the dead man's clothes, then stood and gave a loud whistle. In the distance, an engine started and headlights sprang to life. He walked toward them, holding on to the head.

The driver pulled the jeep to a stop in front of Tafari. Three other men, all young and armed with assault rifles, sat in the back. Most of them wore tribal tattoos and necklaces of gold and ivory. They flaunted their wealth, because in West Africa wealth meant power.

"You've finished your hunt," Zifa stated. He was young and hard, a man not to be trifled with, though most didn't realize that until too late. Scars covered his arms and there were a few on his handsome face. When he had been younger, in his teens, he had fought with knives for prize money in Dakar. To lose was to die. He had never lost, but he had been cut several times.

"I have." Tafari plopped the dead man's head on the front of the truck. The other heads he'd taken were already tied there, all of them bloated and turning black from the heat. When he was done with them, he intended to have them returned to the man who had hired them.

One of the men in back clambered out with elastic ties. He quickly secured the head to the jeep's hood, then stood back and admired his handiwork.

Tafari waved the man into the jeep. He pulled himself into the passenger seat. "Have you heard from Ehigiator?" he asked the driver.

They had communications equipment at their base. Some of the younger recruits had been to college and had learned about such things. Tafari prided himself on being able to use the knowledge they had for his own agenda.

"No." Zifa put the jeep into gear and pulled around in a tight turn. Then he was following his headlights, using the vehicle's bumper to chop through the brush. There were few roads in northwestern Senegal. Most of the ones off the main thoroughfares were trails villagers used to get from one market to another.

"Perhaps it is too early." Tafari studied the landscape.

"Perhaps." Zifa drove easily, at home with the vehicle as it crashed through the brush. "There is another matter."

"What?"

"The Hausa village to the north."

Tafari knew of the village. Over the past few weeks, the people living there had become a thorn in his paw. "What about them?" he asked.

"They continue their rebellion."

Tafari thought about that. In the overall scheme of things, the village wasn't much. It was like a raindrop in a monsoon. But it had the chance of becoming something much bigger if those who lived there persisted in their defiance of him.

"Why haven't you dealt with this?" Tafari demanded.

Zifa didn't react to the anger in his voice. He focused on his driving, and that angered Tafari further. He had placed Zifa second in command, had killed a man who had been with him longer but didn't have the cunning Zifa did. Failure in that position wasn't an option.

"Jaineba is there," Zifa said. "You said you wanted to deal with her."

Tafari cursed and spit. He didn't want to deal with the old woman. Nor did he want anyone else to deal with her until he knew for certain how he was going to handle her.

"She is there now?"

Zifa nodded.

A trickle of fear seeped through Tafari's bowels. He still didn't know what to do about the old woman, but he couldn't put it off. He glanced at the line of heads bouncing on the jeep's hood. He'd made his offering to Ogun, chief among the *orisha*—the sky gods—and appealed to that god's sense of vengeance, praying that all of his enemies might be struck down in the days to come.

Still, Jaineba was a person of power. Ancient and withered, the old woman was tied to Africa in ways that Tafari still didn't understand.

But he couldn't put off dealing with her if she was getting in his way.

"Take me there," he commanded.

Zifa brought the jeep around, churning dirt as the wheels chewed into the earth.

Reaching back over the seat, Tafari took the Chinese assault rifle one of the men on the rear deck handed him. If he had his choice and the situation demanded it, he would rather kill the old woman with the knife. But she commanded magic. He wasn't too proud to use the rifle if it came to that.

His thoughts strayed to the Spider Stone, wondering if Ehigiator had been successful in wresting it from the Americans and the police. The Spider Stone was important. Especially if all the myths about it were true.

THE PHONE RANG.

Seated in bed at the hotel Professor Hallinger had arranged for her, Annja grabbed the phone by reflex. She pressed the talk button and put it to her ear.

"Hey, Annja."

She recognized Doug Morrell's voice at once. Her producer at *Chasing History's Monsters* had a distinctive New York accent. "Doug." She glanced at the hotel clock. It was almost 4:00 a.m. "You're up late or early," she said.

"Both," Morrell replied. "I'm sneaking home after picking up a girl at Dark Realms."

Annja knew Dark Realms was a Goth bar in Manhattan that her producer liked to frequent. In the nightclub, he was a count and high in the pecking order of wannabe vampires. Although he wouldn't admit it, Doug liked playing a vampire and hanging with the night crowd.

The bar was owned by Baron Riddle, a mysterious millionaire who'd gotten rich with the five Goth clubs he'd built around the United States. There was a waiting list for memberships.

"Sneaking home isn't exactly the gallant thing to do after a tryst," Annja pointed out.

"It wasn't a tryst," he protested. "More like an exchange of fantasies. We did the biting thing. A little playacting with ropes and interrogation—"

"Stop." Annja sat up straighter in bed, trying to work out the kinks she'd developed while working on the translation of the stone.

"What?"

"Too much information. I really don't need to know all the details of your little fang fest. You called at this hour for a reason?" she asked wearily.

"I just heard about you on CNN. The thing down in Atlanta. So I thought I'd give you a call and see if there's anything in it for us."

Annja answered immediately. "No."

"Aw, come on," Doug whined. "This could be big."

"You just want to jump on the coattails of the CNN coverage." Annja couldn't believe the story had made national news. Must be a slow news night. Or maybe they were wanting something off the beaten track, she figured.

"It is an opportunity," Doug replied. "Ratings matter."

"There's nothing for you here. No monsters. Those people were killed 150 years ago by a kid with a grudge and a racial issue."

"We could work with that. Any chance that the warehouse is haunted?"

"I thought you hated ghost stories," Annja said. Every time she had advanced the idea of pursuing a story and had to cite spectral manifestations as the only lure, Doug had shot it down.

"I do hate ghost stories. We're not *Ghosthunters*. We chase monsters."

"No monsters here," Annja said.

"Are you sure about that?"

She reached for the cup of coffee on the nightstand. "I'm sure," she said.

"I'll take a ghost if I have to," Doug said. "Maybe we can parlay it into something else."

"This is legitimate archaeological work." Annja said that slowly, willing it to sink in. Ever since she'd picked up the job at *Chasing History's Monsters* so she could have travel expenses paid for trips to places that she couldn't get to on her own, she'd worked hard to keep her real work separate from the sensationalism the television show demanded. "It's not television fare."

"CNN seems to be running with it. They're even playing you up in the piece. Professor Annja Creed. Don't tell me you haven't seen it."

Annja glanced at the armoire on the other side of the room. She hadn't even opened it. "Haven't even turned the television set on."

"You should."

"It's been a busy night. Maybe you missed the part about us almost getting blown up."

"You almost got blown up?"

Annja sighed. Doug had a tendency to hear only what he wanted to hear. "I guess you didn't call to see how I was doing," she said.

"How are you doing?" Doug asked.

"I'm fine. But I've got a lot of work to do."

"What work?"

"Translating the stone we found."

"What stone?" He sounded excited.

Annja had to smile. Doug Morrell truly had the most one-track mind of anyone she'd ever met. "I need to get back to it. I'll talk to you later."

"I should have asked how you were first, huh?"

"It would have been nice, but it wouldn't have been you."

"I do care that you're all right."

"I know."

"Friends?"

"Friends."

"So if you find out the warehouse was haunted…?"

"Good night, Doug." Annja closed her cell phone. Reluctantly, she got up from the bed and walked to the window.

From there she could see the top of the warehouse. The lights of the police car whirled in the darkness.

She walked to her notebook computer and logged on to the hotel's WiFi link. Once she was on the Internet, she opened up the archaeology newsgroups she favored. She'd placed pictures of the Spider Stone and some of the history of the site in the forums under Spider Stone less than an hour earlier. She hadn't expected much, but there were already three responses.

She opened up the first one and began to read.

6

Caught the story on CNN tonight. You're one hot-looking babe. Married? Looking for a cheap fling with a guy who can talk three languages?

Great, Annja thought. And you probably sound just as charming and irresistible in all three languages. She hoped the other postings weren't as juvenile. She skipped the rest of the entry and moved on to the next one.

I blew up the pictures of the stone, hausaboy@africanskys.org wrote. The digital camera you're using is freaking awesome. Wish I could afford one.
That looks like the Hausa language, unless I'm way off base here. Saw the story on CNN and got intrigued.
From what I've been able to translate so far, the stone describes a journey from the author's homeland to America back in 1755.

Okay, Annja thought, I'm evidently dealing with someone who's better versed in the Hausa language than I am. She checked the writer's e-mail and saved it off to a working file.

The date caught her attention. If the stone was dated as being from 1755, it had been one hundred years old before it ended up in the warehouse furnace.

Wait, she chided herself. You're tired. The story might have a date in it, but that doesn't mean that's when the stone was inscribed.

The post continued.

Have you translated the writing? If not, I might be able to assist. I'm Nigerian. Currently going to school at USC. Majoring in computer arts but have an archaeology jones I just can't shake.
If you can shoot the rest of the writing in sequential order, I'd be happy to help.

Even though archaeology relied on discipline, skill and exposure, Annja knew that luck couldn't be beaten. She got her camera out and shot the stone again, overlapping the pictures so the writing could be viewed continuously.

Once she had them finished, she posted them to a Web site she maintained as a clearinghouse for projects. She created a page just for the Spider Stone images.

Then she wrote a note to hausaboy@africanskys.org.

Here are the pics. Thanks for your time! Would love to compare notes when you get something ready.

The third posting was from mythhunter@worldoflegends.net.

Just caught the pics you posted. Can't help you with the language, but maybe with some of the myth behind the stone.
Are you familiar with Anansi? He was an African god. A trickster. His legend crossed to North America when slaves were brought over. He's still a major folklore presence in the Caribbean.
Don't know if the rock you're looking at has anything to do with Anansi, but the spider pic is totally cool.

Annja was familiar with Anansi. As a trickster god, Anansi had been a neutral figure, working always for his own ends as much as for the gods or men. According to legend, Anansi was the son of Nyame, the sky god, and taught mankind the skills of agriculture. He also negotiated rain, which put out wildfires that ravaged the countryside. One of his chief duties was acting as intermediary for mankind with other gods.

From what Annja had managed to translate from the stone, Anansi was praised as being an intermediary for whoever had told the tale.

She wrote a quick thank-you note and closed out of the newsgroup.

She stood, took a deep breath and went through a few tai chi forms to loosen up. Go to bed, she told herself. Get some sleep. You've got a full day tomorrow.

She retreated to the shower long enough to soak for a few minutes and clear her head. When she returned, feeling refreshed and more tired at the same time, her cell phone rang.

She scooped it up from the bed, checked the caller ID—

thinking it might be Doug Morrell with a new angle and plea—and saw that it was Bart McGilley. She answered.

"Annja?" Bart was a homicide detective in New York. He was also a good friend and resource. He was always there when she needed a date to go to a function in New York. She sometimes reciprocated for him at police functions, allowing both of them to mix and mingle without getting hit on. Annja realized his recent engagement put an end to that part of their relationship.

"Hey," Annja said.

Despite what was going on in his life or the lateness of the hour, Bart McGilley always sounded positive. If Annja didn't know him so well, didn't know that that was just how Bart was, she would have been instantly suspicious. In fact, when she'd first gotten to know him, she had been suspicious. No one could be that well adjusted. Especially not in New York.

"You called," Bart pointed out.

"I did."

"You said the time didn't matter."

"It doesn't," Annja said.

"So what's up?" For Bart, he sounded tired.

"I take it you haven't been watching CNN," Annja said. The story was already cooling off on the news network, but it was still being given a quick mention in the roundup.

"No. Got called in on a multiple homicide between rival gang members. There are some new players in town who haven't learned that they can't lean on Russian *mafiya* territory. Have to tread easy with this one—otherwise the media will play it up and we'll have terrorist stories on everybody's radar again."

"Oh." Annja didn't know what to say. Their professional

worlds were like oil and water until she needed background information on someone shady or until Bart had a case that involved art or collectors of artifacts.

"You didn't call to find out about my day," Bart prompted.

Quickly, Annja outlined her situation. As always, Bart was a good listener, never asking questions until she'd finished.

"What can I help you with?" Bart asked.

"I just want to make sure McIntosh is who he says he is." Working as an archaeologist meant double-checking every scrap of information that turned up. She'd learned in the early years that she couldn't always trust people. Some lied intentionally, but others assumed they knew the truth or tended to say what they wanted others to hear or hoped to pull someone into line with their thinking.

"I can do that." Bart paused. "But what you're involved in could be dangerous. Any time you throw the race issue into a volatile environment, it doesn't take much to set things off."

"I know. You should try working a dig site when you've got a couple countries interested in whatever you find. Getting torn between the British government and the Roman Catholic Church is no picnic." That had happened while she'd been working near Hadrian's Wall in England, causing days of delays. The find had turned out to be mildly exotic, the grave of a celebrated Roman general who'd disappeared into history and was at first believed to be the source of the legend of King Arthur. That hadn't turned out to be true, but it had been exciting at the time.

"Yeah, but at least they aren't trying to kill you," Bart pointed out.

They talked for a little while, enjoying the easy camaraderie of their friendship. After making tentative arrangements to meet when she got back to New York, they hung up.

Worn out, Annja glanced at the clock. It was almost 5:00 a.m. She set the alarm for eight o'clock and turned out the light. She slept well, but a spider kept weaving webs throughout her dreams, trying to trap her. Thankfully, she had her sword and managed to cut her way free.

ANNJA WOKE before her alarm sounded. That wasn't unusual. When she was on a dig she never slept for long. She was ready to go again.

She dressed in casual clothes and took a look outside the hotel window. The protesters had returned to the warehouse. There was no sign of the media yet.

She checked the archaeology message boards. There were several new messages. Most of them addressed the mythological nature of Anansi. Annja wasn't too interested in that aspect of the puzzle yet. At best, myths and legends only told part of the story.

But there was a new e-mail from hausaboy@africanskys.org dated only a few minutes earlier.

This isn't the stone you should be looking for. According to the writing on the stone you currently have in your possession, there is another. It is the more important stone. It has a map or something on it. This one is just a record and a false lead, IMHO.

In my humble opinion. Annja decided she would take that. The part of the text and pictographs she had deciphered had alluded to something like what hausaboy was describing.

Looking at the time on the e-mail, she decided to take a

chance that he might still be online. She quickly drafted an e-mail to him and sent it.

Are you still on-line?

After a few seconds, an offer to go to instant messaging popped up on her screen. Annja accepted immediately.

Good morning, hausaboy wrote.

I was hoping you would still be on, Annja typed.

I've got class in a few minutes, but I'm cool for now, he replied.

I don't want you to be late.

No sweat. I'm setting the curve in the class.

Annja smiled at that. There was nothing wrong with getting a brainiac for a resource.

Good for you! Let me know when you need to go.

Okay. I looked you up on the Internet, too.

Annja didn't know how to respond to that so she didn't. She never paid attention to what was written about her. She had contributed several articles to different Web sites about archaeology. She wondered if he'd read some of them.

Found out about *Chasing History's Monsters.* That surprised me.

Not my best work. *CHM* allows me to go places I want to go without paying for it, Annja typed.

That's cool. Checked out a few of your articles. You know your stuff. If I'd thought you were just out looking for freebie research, I'd have taken a pass.

Thanks. Archaeology is what I do. *CHM* is part of what it takes to get to do it more.

I can respect that. Anyway, what I've translated so far is that there are at least two stones. The one you sent me pictures of and another one.

The smaller one you mentioned, Annja wrote.

Yeah. I think it's the key to this stone or something else.

Annja was intrigued. Why do you think that?

Because of some of the symbols copied to the large stone. It's like whoever inscribed the large stone knew someone else would expect them to be there. They're on there out of context.

Explains why I was having problems with the translation.

LOL. Probably. Bunch of gobbledygook the way it's written now. You kind of have to read between the lines.

Thinking of the war party that had accompanied the Spider Stone, Annja wrote, Do you know who might have been looking for the stones?

No. The text just mentions the enemies of the people.

The people?

The tribe the stones belonged to, hausaboy explained.

According to what I was able to translate, this Spider Stone was a gift of the gods, Annja typed.

Right. A gift from Anansi. You're familiar with him?

Spider god. Trickster. The myths about Anansi got integrated with a lot of cultures in North and South America.

Exactly. Anyway, this smaller stone was supposed to have been given to this tribe by Anansi. It was a promise.

A promise about what? Annja asked.

That they would always exist. That they wouldn't be destroyed.

That thought settled uneasily in Annja's head. It was a big promise, and one that hadn't been kept. For the stone to have come to the United States meant that at some point that village had been invaded by slavers who had stolen the people away to sell on the slave blocks. It made her sad, but slavery had centuries of sadness tied to it.

Have you ever heard of a stone like this? she typed.

No. But I did a search for it last night. You probably did, too, her translator wrote.

Annja felt chagrined.

No, I didn't. I had to deal with the police last night. Never even thought about it.

She hadn't thought about it. The idea that other people knew about it had never occurred to her.

Look at this Web link, hausaboy wrote.

Annja clicked on it and another page opened up. The header immediately identified the Web site as a collector's market specializing in West African artifacts.

Several pictures showed statues of warriors, gods and animals from different cultures like a four-hundred-year-old wooden Igbo maiden mask, a two-thousand-year-old Nok ceramic sculpture of a lion, colorful *djembe* and *dunan* drums, a Benin copper funerary mask almost eight hundred years old and several ivory carvings, as well as wooden ones.

Annja looked for the stone but couldn't find it.

I don't see the stone, she typed.

No pic. Look under Searching For.

Halfway down the page, Annja found a listing for art pieces that collectors were searching for. The entry read:

> Looking for Anansi Stone. Hausa design. The stone has an image of a spider (Anansi) on it. Some refer to it as Anansi's Promise.
> Information leading to the piece will be rewarded.
> Contact Yousou Toure
> (yousou.toure@artforms.senegal)

The instant-messaging box beeped for attention as a new message cycled into it.

Did you find it?

Yes. Just looking at it. The stone's been buried for over 150 years. That means someone has been looking for it for at least that long.

Some families get it into their heads to collect stuff their ancestors were looking for. This could be a case of that.

Annja silently agreed.

Anyway, I thought you might be interested, hausaboy wrote.

I am. Thank you.

Okay, gotta go. I'll keep working on these pics.

Do that. If something comes to fruition out of this, I'll hook you up for a finder's fee, Annja typed.

You don't have to do that, but if you want to, feel free. Tuition isn't getting any cheaper.

Thanks! Annja shut down the instant-message block, then closed her computer.

ANNJA'S PHONE RANG when she was in the hotel lobby. She paused, shifted her backpack and retrieved the device from a side pocket. "Annja Creed."

"Did I wake you?" Professor Hallinger's voice sounded chipper and alert.

"No, I've been up for most of an hour."

"So have I. I couldn't sleep anymore, so I finally gave up and came to the dig. Where are you?"

"Leaving the hotel. You'll see me in a few minutes."

"Have you had breakfast?"

"Not yet."

"If you'll stop at Wally's, the small café across the street from the hotel and pick up two breakfasts, I'll buy."

Annja smiled. "You've got a deal, Professor."

"It's the least I can do after everything I've gotten you involved with," he said.

"Are you kidding? I live for this kind of thing."

"Still." Hallinger cleared his throat. "I've got something to show you when you get here."

"Taunt me like that and you may not get breakfast. I may come straight over. Curiosity often gets the better of me."

"You'll want breakfast. *I* want breakfast. We may work straight through lunch."

"All right. I just finished swapping e-mail with a guy at USC, a student, who knows the Hausa language."

"He's studying it?"

"No. He's from Nigeria and he has an interest in history."

"How fortunate," the professor said.

"Not fortunate," Annja said because she'd seen other information come by way of the newsgroups. "That's just the World Wide Web at work."

Hallinger sighed. "I step into the cyberworld with extreme reluctance. Sometimes I wonder what archaeologists a thousand years from now are going to think of our culture."

"We've got more written for them to study than at any time in history. Just the personal information on MySpace.com and other places would more than fill the library at Alexandria. Much of what we know about life in Restoration England during the seventeenth century comes from the diaries of Samuel Pepys. He covered what happened during the plague as well as the Great Fire of London."

"Yes, but what if an electromagnetic pulse were to strike the earth?" Hallinger asked. "Either from a solar flare or from a smart bomb? All those computer records could be wiped out in the blink of an eye. Everything would be lost. To that future archaeologist, it would appear that we were a culture of wastrels, producing diapers and plastic bottles that will last a thousand years."

"Let's concentrate on what we have here now," Annja suggested.

"You're right, of course." Hallinger sounded embarrassed. "What did your cyber colleague tell you?"

"I'll tell you when I get there." Annja folded the phone and put it away. But before she'd reached the door, she heard someone call her name.

"Miss Creed."

Turning, Annja discovered an old woman sitting in one of the chairs in the hotel lobby.

She was black and looked to be seventy or eighty years old. Dressed in a yellow print dress and wearing thick glasses, she reminded Annja of the nuns who'd raised her at the orphanage. She held a thick bound book against her chest, arms crossed over it protectively.

"Yes?" Annja stepped toward the woman.

"I wanted to talk to you," the woman said. "About the people found in the basement of that building." She paused. "I think I know who they were."

7

Jaineba sat cross-legged in the small hut and breathed in the smoke of the white *ubulawu* coming from the small brazier hanging from the iron chain connected to the spit over the fire. She wore a loose-fitting grand *bubu,* a big dress popular in Senegal, and a scarf that held her cotton-white hair back from her face. The acrid smoke burned her nasal passages for a short time, then it came easier.

White *ubulawu* was also called the dream root. A botanist Jaineba had once guided through the savanna had told her the root was called *silene capensis.* Jaineba had no need for the names educated men gave things. She practiced her magic as her grandmother had taught her. Too many things changed in the world, and it had been that way since she'd been a little girl.

Sometimes when the young children of the villages saw her for the first time—that they remembered, anyway—they tried to guess how old she was. Even Jaineba was no longer certain. No one had marked the year of her birth. They only remembered who had been around when she'd been born. She guessed that she was eighty or ninety. An old woman by anyone's standards.

But her job was not yet done. Sadly, she had no granddaughter to pass her craft to. Some days she found great sadness in that. But the gods were good to her. No matter the sadness, every day she found something to rejoice in. Even after all that she had seen, wondrous and miraculous things like a child being born or a lion passing by her without offering any threat or a desert transforming into a beautiful flower garden during the rainy season, there was always something new. Or she could borrow the new eyes of the young and exult in the discoveries children made.

She breathed in the smoke and chanted. She wanted to slip into the dreamworld. That seemed easier these days, as if that world paralleled hers now instead of meeting occasionally like forbidden lovers.

The white *ubulawu* aided her in her visits to the dreamworld. The smoke's magic also held at bay the evil spirits that feasted on the unwary.

She hunted for the dreams she'd been having, hoping to see more this time. Still, they eluded her.

You're being too selfish, she chided herself. Only seldom do the gods allow you to peek into what they have planned for the world. You can't demand more than they are willing to give.

Footsteps sounded in the doorway.

Jaineba breathed out, releasing her hunt for the dreamworld. She opened her eyes and blinked at the rectangle of harsh morning light. It framed the woman standing there. But she was not the woman Jaineba had seen in her dreams.

This woman was black. The one in the dreams was white.

Her visitor was tall, several inches taller than Jaineba's own five feet, and young, probably no more than thirty. She had clear brown eyes and wore her hair cut short. Her face was slender and strong, an easy face to get to know, and one that turned the heads of men when she passed by. She had a woman's full body, though Jaineba felt the woman was on the thin side. She wore jeans, hiking boots and a white pullover that contrasted sharply with her dark skin.

She was British, speaking in that clipped and rapid accent and having only a few words of the Hausa tongue. Jaineba knew her name was Tanisha Diouf. She was an engineer working for the Childress Corporation exploring for oil.

"Little mother," Tanisha said quietly. "Am I interrupting?"

The young woman's formal manners had surprised Jaineba. Most European, Arab and American people who spoke to her had a habit of dismissing her out of turn because she was old or because they'd heard that she practiced magic.

"No." Jaineba waved her into the hut. "Come. Come."

Hesitant, Tanisha entered the hut.

Jaineba waved to an area on the other side of the fire.

Tanisha sat and quietly waited.

That was another quality that Jaineba liked. The young woman knew how to offer respect.

"Are you well?" Jaineba asked.

"I am. And you?"

"The gods watch over me, child. You need not concern yourself over my welfare."

"I know. But I do." Tanisha smiled. "Without you, I could not get the things done that I need to do."

"You are blessed. I have told you that."

Tanisha smiled. "I know. But some days I don't feel so blessed."

“How are your children?”

The woman had two sons, healthy sons, which would make her a wealthy woman in most villages. They were six and eight, and boys in the truest sense because they were unafraid of exploring their new environment. When their mother wasn’t around, which wasn’t often, the boys talked of hunting lions with the other boys of the villages. Jaineba knew their mother would panic if she only knew.

“They’re fine. I didn’t bring them with me this morning,” Tanisha said.

“That’s too bad. I would have enjoyed seeing them.” Jaineba fanned the embers of the dream root. They burned quickly, putting another small cloud of smoke into the hut.

“They won’t be happy when I tell them that I saw you without them. They enjoy your stories.”

“Of course they do. All children enjoy my stories.” Jaineba looked at the younger woman. “The stories belong to them, too.”

Tanisha didn’t respond to the statement.

Jaineba was used to that. The mother doesn’t feel the kinship with the land that her children do. She was all right with that, and she understood it. Children’s senses were so much more alive than an untrained adult’s.

Since they had met, Jaineba had told Tanisha that her home was here, in Africa. Not in England. Despite her own denial, Tanisha Diouf was one of the Hausa people, one of those whose ancestors had been sold on the slave auction block.

“Why did you come here?” Jaineba asked.

“To see you.”

“Have you eaten?”

“Yes.”

"You can eat again. You are too skinny." Jaineba stood, grabbing hold of her gnarled walking staff and pulling herself to her feet. She shuffled to the door of the hut and looked out.

Tanisha's Land Rover had caused a stir in the village. Children stood around it in fascination, admiring and touching the vehicle with hesitant but curious fingers. Most of them had never seen anything like it up close. The village was normally a place travelers passed by. No one ever stayed there.

Jaineba called to one of the women and told her to bring food. Then she turned back to her guest. "Why did you come to see me?"

Tanisha frowned. "Last night someone tampered with the trucks and the equipment at the camp."

"It was no one at this place." Jaineba settled herself on the pile of furs the village women had given her to rest her bones.

"I didn't think so. But I need to find out who it was, and I need to find a way to get them to stop."

"There are many who don't want to see the white man's machines tear through our lands."

"The refinery that Childress is going to build will provide jobs," Tanisha said.

Jaineba heard the timbre in the other woman's words. Tanisha Diouf believed what she was saying. "Those who oppose you don't feel they need jobs," the old woman said.

"They may say they don't want the jobs, but they'll make a big difference to the people who live here," Tanisha said.

"Working for the outsiders changes everyone's life. Change is not always something people want. Often it's not even good."

"This could be good. It could mean health benefits for families. There would be more food. No one would have to go to bed hungry."

Jaineba looked at the foreign woman for a time. She liked her. Tanisha Diouf was a strong-willed woman who made her way in a man's world. Jaineba understood that. With her magic and her ability to heal, she walked in a man's world, as well, taking up the mantle of leadership. Too few women did that.

"I hear what you are saying, child," Jaineba replied in a calm voice.

"It would help if you would talk to these people."

"Not everyone wants to listen to an old woman."

"You could make them listen," Tanisha implored. "They do listen to you."

"Perhaps," Jaineba said. "But let me ask you a few questions."

Tanisha waited. A sense of urgency burned in her eyes.

"Does everyone in your country get enough to eat? Do all the children have full bellies before they go to bed?"

Uncertainty made Tanisha's face heavy. "No. But the opportunity is there. It's just that not everyone takes advantage of the programs that are available."

"Does everyone have a job?"

"All the people that want one have a job," Tanisha said.

Jaineba felt compassion for the younger woman as she made excuses for her country and her way of life. "Does everyone who has a job have the job they wish?"

Tanisha sighed. "That would be too much to ask."

"Is it?"

"The opportunity is there."

"But the opportunity for servitude at a job or a corporation also exists. Even the men who work for Childress Corporation are not all happy working here. They would rather be somewhere else. Yet they are here. Away from their families and the way of life they're familiar with."

Tanisha fell silent.

"What you offer, what your employer offers, is not a bad thing." Jaineba felt compassion for the younger woman. So young, and so certain she had all the right answers. "But the changes they would make in our land would be permanent."

"It's progress."

"Africa," Jaineba stated quietly, "is familiar with progress. We have had it since the Europeans first began trading with our country. In the north and in the south. *Progress* is forced on us at every turn. Our people have died as a result of the diseases they have unleashed there. I have seen whole countries abandoned by the Europeans and Americans when it suited them. They took away the jobs and all the money they brought into those countries. But they left their sicknesses, their vendors selling products families could no longer truly afford, and the feeling that nothing Africa had to offer was good enough. Do you know what it's like to live without hope?"

Sadness darkened Tanisha's eyes. "No. Not to that degree."

"Women in this village have buried their children," Jaineba said quietly. "They have seen their husbands and sons lured away to big cities like Dakar. They have seen their friends and daughters taken by the warlords, to be used, then cast aside or killed." She was silent for a moment. "And all of this has come about because of *progress*."

"It doesn't have to be that way," Tanisha said.

"Africa," Jaineba said, "has its own pace. We are the

cradle of life. Most scientists believe humankind began here. We had, until all the genetically modified crops were pushed on our farmers, more plant diversification than any other place in the world. Did you know that?"

"Yes."

The woman whom Jaineba had sent for breakfast stopped in the doorway. She held bowls of *uji,* a thin gruel made from cassava. Her daughter held pieces of a fresh mango.

Jaineba nodded.

The woman and her daughter entered the hut respectfully and served the breakfast. Tanisha was polite and made certain to thank both, meeting their eyes with her own.

The little girl, no more than six or seven, smiled shyly. Jaineba thought perhaps Tanisha was the first foreigner the little girl had ever seen.

The mother scolded her daughter for staring, then apologized to Tanisha in her own language. Of course, Tanisha didn't understand. That was one reason she'd sought Jaineba. She needed an interpreter.

"What's she saying?" Tanisha asked.

"She wants you to forgive her daughter," Jaineba explained.

"For what?"

"For staring and being impolite."

Tanisha smiled reassuringly at the mother and daughter. "Please tell them that I took no offense, and that her daughter should be curious."

Jaineba did.

Reaching into her pocket, Tanisha took out a small vial of lip gloss. She applied it to her lips, then offered it to the little girl.

The little girl hesitated, looking up at her mother. The

mother looked at Jaineba. The old woman nodded. With her mother's permission, the little girl took the lip gloss and awkwardly put it on her lips, looking pleased with herself.

Tanisha laughed, and the sound within the hut was infectious. "I love my sons," she said as the mother and child departed, "but I would have loved to have a daughter."

"It's not too late," Jaineba pointed out. "You are still young."

"No way." Tanisha used the wooden spoon to eat the *uji*. "I have a career. I don't have time to have another child."

"So you're trading a dream of yours for your own personal progress?"

"Two boys are almost more than I can keep up with," Tanisha said. She frowned. "In fact, I often feel torn between them and my job. I was fortunate Mr. Childress was generous enough to allow them to come with me."

"If they had not come, where would they be?"

"At my mother's."

Jaineba knew from past conversations that Tanisha's husband had been a soldier and had been killed three years earlier.

Tanisha popped a piece of mango into her mouth, chewed and swallowed. "The problem with the attacks on the equipment remains."

Jaineba finished her *uji* and set the bowl to one side. "You must be patient."

"I can't afford to be patient. If I don't find some way to stop the attacks, the security teams are going to start taking more punitive action."

"What will they do?"

"Mr. Childress hires mercenaries," Tanisha said. "Not all of them are good men. In fact, I'd say most of them aren't good men." She shook her head. "I don't know what they'll do, but I know they won't sit back quietly. Mr. Childress isn't paying them to do that."

"What are you afraid these men will do?" Jaineba asked.

"Go into the bush after the men who are damaging the equipment."

"That will be dangerous for them."

"They know that. I think several of them are looking forward to it."

Jaineba breathed in deeply. Some of the smoke from the dream root remained. She closed her eyes for a moment and reached for the woman in her dreams. For just a moment, Jaineba sensed the woman. She's close, she told herself. She already has the trail. She will be here soon.

"Did you hear me?" Tanisha asked.

"Yes." Jaineba opened her eyes. "Things will work out, child. You must believe that."

"Someone is going to get hurt if this keeps up. I can't sit by and do nothing."

"There is nothing you can do. These men will clash, and some will be hurt. Possibly even killed. Surely you knew that when you took this job."

"No." Tanisha spoke quietly. "No, I didn't. Or maybe I didn't want to believe it."

"You are coming to a crossroads, and you will have to make a choice. I'm sorry. I wish that your way could be easier, but it isn't. This is the path the gods have put you on."

"I can't accept that there's nothing I can do," Tanisha said.

"You're not responsible for this."

"I'm working as lead on the engineering team. I have to assume some responsibility."

"What about Childress? Shouldn't he share some of the responsibility, as well?"

"Mr. Childress is responsible to the shareholders in the corporation. He has to regard their interests first."

"He will do nothing when fighting breaks out," Jaineba stated.

"I don't know. He's put a lot of his own money into this venture. He wants to see the oil refinery turn a profit."

Jaineba nodded, knowing she shouldn't take any of this on but unwilling to leave Tanisha alone with her distress. "I will see if there is anything that can be done," she said quietly.

"Thank you. I hoped you would say that."

"I can't promise anything."

"I know."

The roars of straining engines sounded outside.

"Was anyone with you?" Jaineba asked.

Tanisha shook her head.

Reluctantly, dreading what she felt certain she would find, Jaineba pulled herself up along her staff. Her bones felt weak and fragile. She swept a hand over her dress, smoothing out the wrinkles. She walked outside as the engines growled a final time and died.

A military-style jeep sat alongside Tanisha's Land Rover, which proudly proclaimed Childress Construction, Inc. on its sides. The English vehicle was a rolling billboard for the corporation.

Several warriors of the village gathered. They stood in pants and shirts, most of them barefoot. Some of them had weapons, mostly machetes they had brought with them from the farms where they worked, but a few of them had pistols and old single-shot Enfield rifles. None of them stepped forward to challenge the intruders.

The women sent the young children to the huts. The

village was built on the eastern side of the hill. Most people coming from Dakar along the old trade roads didn't know the village was there unless they were already aware of its existence. As soon as the children were inside the thatched huts, they stuck their faces to doors and windows.

The man in the passenger seat of the jeep climbed down. He was in his late thirties. The sun and elements had weathered and darkened his skin. Tattooing and scars marred his face. Even without the additions, he wasn't a handsome man. He looked brutish, like something only half-made. Gold hoops dangled in his ears. The leather loincloth hung from a leather tie around his hips to a few inches above his knees. A silver headband inlaid with garnets and ivory glinted in the sun.

A long knife, almost a machete, hung in a scabbard at his side. A bandolier containing extra magazines draped his chest. He carried an AK-47 in one hand with the muzzle pointed at the ground.

"Who is he?" Tanisha asked.

"His name is Tafari," Jaineba answered. Too late, she realized that she should have had the Englishwoman remain inside the hut. Already Tafari's hot gaze had locked on to her. "He is a very bad man."

8

"My name is Mildred. Mildred Teasdale."

Annja held her hand out to the old woman. "It's a pleasure meeting you, Ms. Teasdale."

"Thank you." The woman's grip was solid and sure, but dry and papery. Her palms were lined with calluses, marking her as a woman who had worked hard all her life.

"You said you thought you knew who the men were in the furnace room?"

Mildred nodded. "Because of an ancestor of mine. A man named Franklin Dickerson."

"I'm sorry, but we haven't identified any of the men in that building," Annja admitted.

"Franklin wasn't one of those men, Miss Creed. But his younger brother, Moses, was. My family's been wondering what happened to young Mose ever since he disappeared all those years ago."

Annja was intrigued. "How do you know your ancestor was one of those men?"

"Because we kept a family history." Mildred's hands tightened on the book she held. "Franklin Dickerson was one of the slaves who learned to read and write. He took his life in his hands by doing that. If his masters had found out, they'd probably have killed him. Black men weren't supposed to learn how to read back in those days."

"I know," Annja said.

"Some of them learned anyway," Mildred went on. "In secret. They prepared themselves for the day they could steal away north on the Underground Railroad. They'd heard a black man who could read and write could get himself a good job in the North."

Mildred nodded. "I come from Augusta, Georgia," she said. "None of my family ever really escaped to go north. We thought Mose might have been the only one. But we knew something must have happened to him because he would never have stayed away from Franklin. Those brothers were close in everything but their politics. The rest of the family stayed here through the worst of everything. But Franklin Dickerson kept his precious journal. In the beginning, that record wasn't anything more than a collection of tattered papers."

Annja didn't mean to look impatient. In fact, she hoped that she didn't look that way. But she felt it. She searched for the best way to excuse herself.

"I know you have things to do, Miss Creed," Mildred said, "and I know there are a lot of people waiting to hear what you people find out today. I'm just trying to help make it easier. And to get some sense of closure for my family. I think I can help you identify those men."

Annja thought of the crowd of protesters standing out in front of the warehouse. Anything that shows some forward movement is going to win everyone over, she thought.

"Can we sit?" Mildred asked. "So I can show you this book? I promise I won't take any more time than you can give me. If you don't think I have anything useful, I'll just go on my way."

Annja agreed.

Mildred led the way to the chairs and found two side by side. She waved Annja to one of them, then sat in the other. She opened the big book.

Neatly arranged printing filled the first page: "A Slave Dreams of Freedom. By Franklin Dickerson."

"Not exactly the most original title someone could come up with," Mildred said, "but Franklin had poetry in his soul. If you took time to read the book, you'd see that."

"I'm an archaeologist, Mrs. Teasdale. Most of the documents I study aren't perfect. Reading the journals of Lewis and Clark as they explored the Louisiana Purchase taught me that knowledge of the language isn't a prerequisite for intelligence."

"My father was a fisherman," Mildred said. "He always said that a man who tried to make a living wasn't any better than the net he could cast. He wasn't a man of letters, either, but he was a storyteller. He knew his way around a metaphor. In keeping with that, Franklin's net had a lot of holes in it, but it was big. He captured a lot of the slave's experience in his writing."

The television in the lobby was tuned to CNN. A quick update on the situation in Kirktown flashed on. Looking at the screen, Annja realized that more protesters had gathered at the warehouse and that the media had returned.

"Franklin could only print," Mildred said with a note of embarrassment in her voice. "That was one of his regrets. He liked the flowing hand that some journal keepers had."

Annja understood that. She kept journals herself, and her handwriting and illustrations were points of pride for her.

"This book was rewritten from the texts that Franklin Dickerson wrote," Mildred continued. "I've got most of the original papers, but some of them have faded over the years. This book wasn't prepared until just before Franklin's death in 1886. He was buried on five acres of ground that he managed to buy and raise a family on." She smiled. "I've had offers from universities that want this book."

"I can imagine. It's quite an impressive document," Annja said.

"It's about my family. That's why I'm not giving it up. But I've allowed copies to be made. They tell me it's not the same as having the original."

"It's not," Annja replied. "There's a lot you can read from the original document that a copy just won't reproduce."

"Anyway, let me show you the parts I wanted you to see." Mildred thumbed through the book. On page thirty-two, neatly numbered in the upper right-hand corner, she stopped.

An illustration in the center of the page drew Annja's attention immediately. The drawing showed a stone with a spider on it. Unconsciously, Annja reached for the drawing, tracing the spider with her finger as her mind jerked into high gear. The paper felt thick and grainy and had yellowed considerably with age.

"Is this it, then? Is this the stone the rumors say you found?" Mildred's voice tightened in excitement.

Annja studied the stone, noticing only then that it rested in someone's palm in the illustration. Judging from the comparison she was able to make, the Spider Stone was about the size of her thumb.

"Is that the stone you found?" Mildred repeated.

"No," Annja said, thinking of hausaboy's announcement that the stone she'd asked about was a copy of another stone. "It was much bigger than this one."

"This was the original stone, according to Franklin," the older woman said. "The second stone, the larger one that you found, is a copy of the true stone."

Annja didn't let her excitement betray her. She knew that sometimes when archaeologists interacted with someone who had a story to tell, that person would elaborate or guess at what the listener wanted to hear. The storyteller wouldn't knowingly lie, but could embellish or twist the truth. "Why was the stone copied?" she asked calmly.

"Because people had heard of it. Once people started talking about the Spider Stone, a second one had to be created. In the early days, no one knew. But as Yohance started to pull others to his side and give them their histories, more people knew about the Spider Stone."

"Do you know what the Spider Stone is?" Annja asked.

Mildred looked at her. "In this book, Franklin says that the Spider Stone has magic. An old magic given to the Hausa people by an African god."

"Anansi."

Mildred nodded and smiled. "The spider god. Now, I don't believe in such foolishness myself. I'm a Christian. I go to the Baptist church right down the street from my house in Augusta. But I'm reminded that sometimes God works in mysterious ways. I believe that He could have revealed Himself to Yohance's people in another way. And God has been making promises since the Ark of the Covenant."

"Was there anything specific the Spider Stone was supposed to do?" Annja asked.

"It was supposed to protect the Hausa village that it was

given to. Not protect them from the things that happened to them, but make sure that village would never die. Not as long as the stone existed. That's what Yohance told Franklin."

"Who was Yohance?"

"Well, now," Mildred said, "that's a story."

TAFARI STRODE toward the old witch woman. Some called her a healer and a seer, and believed she did only good things with her powers. A thrill of fear wormed up his spine. He stopped fifteen feet away when he'd intended to walk up close to her and make her back away fearfully.

Jaineba didn't move.

In fact, Tafari's approach also caused the woman standing beside the old witch to step forward. He stopped and grinned, lifting the assault rifle meaningfully.

Most of the villagers drew back at the gesture, but a few of the men stood their ground and held their weapons. A handful of others took a step forward.

"Stupid woman," Tafari spit. "You tempt the gods with your foolishness. My trouble isn't with you. I've no wish to kill you." But he wouldn't hesitate to kill her if it became necessary.

The younger woman said nothing, but her eyes remained focused on him. She was afraid. Tafari saw that in her. She was afraid but she didn't give in to her fear.

"She doesn't understand you." Jaineba's voice was calm and held no hint of trepidation.

Tafari took in her clothing. "She's a foreigner." His words dripped with disgust.

"She's my friend," Jaineba declared.

Those words, Tafari knew, were intended as a warning.

"As my friend, she is also under my protection." The old woman fixed him with her fierce gaze.

Tafari held up a hand. In response, the gunner in the back of the jeep aimed the light machine gun mounted on a tripod at the two women.

The handful of men who'd found the courage to act moved forward again and started objecting to Tafari's presence. The machine gunner swept his weapon toward them and fired a line of bullets into the ground at their feet. Tafari had specified that no one was to be hurt unless he ordered it or they were attacked. He wasn't afraid of the men of the village, but he was afraid of the witch.

The foreign woman caught the witch's arm and tried to drag her back. With surprising strength, Jaineba resisted. The woman looked confused.

"You can't stay here," Tanisha said.

"I will." Jaineba never took her eyes from Tafari. "He will not hurt me. And he will hurt no one in this village, either."

Tafari smiled. "You're too sure of yourself, witch."

"I know how to treat a carrion feeder."

Anger stirred inside Tafari, but he made himself stand steady when he itched to curl his finger around the assault rifle's trigger and blow the witch's head from her shoulders.

Only he couldn't be sure that even that would kill her.

All his life Tafari had heard stories about Jaineba's powers, how she had made the dead live, though not in the same fashion as the *bokors* who practiced voodoo and made the living dead walk. Jaineba's grandmother, the one she had learned her skills from, had risen from the dead three times after drowning, being shot by a white man and being struck by lightning. She hadn't died until she'd decided her granddaughter was fully trained.

"You're an American," Tafari told the woman in her own tongue.

"I'm not. I'm English."

"I am Tafari." He was smug about himself, trusting that the name would leave an impression on her. He wasn't disappointed. Fear glinted a little more sharply in her eyes.

"What are you doing here?" the woman demanded.

"Tanisha," the witch said, "let me handle this. He is here to see me." Jaineba locked eyes with Tafari. "Aren't you?"

Tanisha. Tafari committed the woman's name to memory. She was a beautiful woman. He had left beautiful women dead and dying behind him.

"I am," Tafari agreed. "You're involving yourself where you're not wanted."

"I do what I want," Jaineba declared in an imperious voice. "No man may ever tell me what to do."

"Maybe you're protected by the gods, witch," Tafari said in his own language so the people of the village would understand, "but the people you're turning against me aren't."

"They are protected by me."

"Even when you're not there?"

Jaineba stepped forward, leaning on her staff.

Tafari resisted the impulse to raise the assault rifle and fire. His second impulse was to step back from the woman. He stood his ground, but he was aware that he leaned back from her.

"Harm any person under my protection and I will place a curse on you, Tafari. By the bones of my grandmother, I promise you that. You will never know peace. You will never know a time when you are not in fear for your life." Jaineba drew a calm breath and never blinked. "Do you understand me?"

Everything in Tafari screamed at him to break eye contact

and look away from the old woman. She had powers that he could only guess at. He believed that. She had the power to curse a person.

An ivory poacher she had crossed paths with a few years ago had laughed in her face and shot a young warrior who had tried to avenge the disrespect. As Jaineba held the dying warrior, she cursed the poacher. Three days later, the poacher was killed by a leopard in an area where the big cats hadn't been seen in years. Leopards didn't usually attack men. It was later found and killed, but by all accounts it was far north of its usual hunting grounds.

Even before that had happened, people who knew Jaineba told several stories about the powers the witch wielded.

"You can't save everyone, witch," Tafari said.

"That remains to be seen," Jaineba snarled. "Don't presume to threaten me. I won't permit it."

Tafari searched her for fear. He couldn't see any, couldn't hear it in her voice and couldn't smell it on her the way he could with so many men who feared him.

"Your time is almost up," Tafari said. "You're old. You never had children of your own. Your last apprentice died from a sickness you failed to cure in time." He shook his head and smiled. "After you, there is no one to carry on your traditions." He smiled again, wider this time. "Perhaps I can wait."

She had no reply to make.

Leaving her standing there, Tafari walked back to the jeep that had brought him, pulled himself into the passenger seat and sat with his assault rifle across his knees. He was still afraid of the witch, but he felt certain that would soon pass. When it did, he would kill her.

He told Zifa to get them out of there. As Zifa turned the jeep around, Tafari looked at the Land Rover. It was nearly new, an expensive piece of equipment. He couldn't read the lettering on the side, but was familiar with it from past experience. Childress Construction, Inc. seemed to be everywhere these days.

But now he knew where to find the woman, if he ever wanted her. Sharp hunger rose up in him as he glanced back at her.

Like the other villagers, the woman couldn't stay under the witch's protection forever.

"THE BOY WHO BROUGHT the Spider Stone to America was named Yohance," Mildred said.

"I thought you said the boy your ancestor talked to was named Yohance." Annja took notes in her hardbound notebook. It was five inches wide and ten inches tall, fitting comfortably in her hand. That was important because often when she was out in the field at a dig she didn't have a desk or even a flat surface to write on.

In her loft, she had scores of notebooks. Most of them had been scanned onto disks and placed into storage. Even then, she hadn't been able to get rid of the original notebooks. They represented her work, her time and her love of what she explored.

The book she worked in now was new, but already she'd filled up several pages with notes, questions and illustrations. Several of the pages had tabs stuck to them, marking areas where she'd devoted a large amount of time to wrapping her brain around something.

"Franklin knew a Yohance," Mildred explained. "But all of the Keepers were named Yohance, even when that hadn't been the birth name their mothers had given them. They changed their names when they became the Keepers."

"Who were the Keepers?"

"The Keepers of the Spider Stone, of course. It's covered here in Franklin's book." Mildred turned the page and found a drawing of a young boy in chains. He looked scared but determined.

"Franklin was quite an artist," Annja said.

"You should see the pictures he's drawn in here." Mildred's eyes gleamed with pride. "This book, it's the most precious thing I own."

"This Yohance was a slave?"

"He wasn't born into slavery like the rest of the Keepers were." Mildred gazed at the small boy. "The first Yohance came from West Africa. His village was destroyed by Arab raiders."

"When did that happen?"

Mildred shook her head. "I don't know. It's not written in this book. I don't think Franklin knew."

Annja wrote, "First Yohance?" then added, "Check slave rolls." Over the years, databases had been created that listed some of the slaves who were brought over on the slave ships. There was a chance the boy might be listed there. Of course, she was well-aware there was also the chance that the ship's captain had simply renamed the boy when he'd sold him.

"The Keeper was supposed to protect the Spider Stone," Mildred went on.

"Slaves weren't allowed possessions except those given to them by their masters," Annja said.

"Yohance hid the Spider Stone."

"How?"

"He swallowed it. The Spider Stone was small enough to permit that. When he excreted it, he would clean it and swallow it again." Mildred looked at Annja. "Can you imagine what that must have been like?"

"No," Annja answered. She honestly couldn't.

"When the first Yohance realized that he wasn't going to live long enough to escape, he groomed another boy to be the next Keeper."

"Any boy?"

"It had to be a Hausa boy," Mildred replied. "Franklin wrote that the first Yohance kept track of bloodlines. He tried to keep the stone in the hands of the purest Hausa he could find, someone who had a link to his village. Otherwise the Spider Stone's power would be lost, you see."

Annja nodded, fascinated with the story.

"As I said, Franklin and Mose were close. They were lucky enough to be kept on the same plantation not far from this town. Farther to the south. I've been out that way and walked over the fields they used to farm when they were boys." Mildred smiled and shook her head. "It made me feel closer to them, made me feel like I almost knew those two boys. Like I could just reach out and touch them. But I'm sure that was just my imagination."

"I don't know," Annja said. "Sometimes when I'm at a site, I can close my eyes and almost hear the people who once lived there. That could be a thousand years ago."

"Maybe we just both have overactive imaginations," Mildred said.

"And maybe we're just sensitive to things other people miss," Annja replied. Since the sword had come into her possession, she'd discovered that sometimes those feelings within her were even stronger.

"It was Yohance who separated Franklin and Mose when nothing else would do it," Mildred said.

"What happened?"

"Franklin sought Yohance out. By this time, Yohance—the Yohance Franklin and Mose came to know—had gathered men to his side."

"Who were the men?"

"Other slaves. But they were all of the Hausa bloodline. As were Franklin and Mose."

"You're of Hausa blood?"

Mildred nodded. "I didn't know that till my daddy read Franklin's book to me when I was a little girl. It wasn't until I was in college that I was even able to look up the Hausa people and find out who they were."

"They were traders," Annja said. "During their time they were fierce, noble and intelligent."

"I know. I take a lot of pride in coming from people like that. But it doesn't matter to my kids. I tried to introduce them to the history of the Hausa people, but they didn't care. They told me they had to live in this world, and it wasn't such a good place." Mildred shook her head. "None of them live around here anymore. I guess they all finally followed the North Star out of here."

"How did Yohance separate Franklin and Mose?" Annja asked.

"Yohance and his bodyguards—"

"Bodyguards?" Annja was startled.

"Franklin called them Yohance's protectors in his book. Yohance had another name for them, but Franklin didn't even try to spell it. He used protectors, and you can tell it was a young man trying to show off his vocabulary. Anyway, they had decided that they were going to try to escape the plantation. This was in 1861."

"The Civil War was starting," Annja said.

Mildred nodded. "It was. Franklin had kept up his reading. He'd read several abolitionist papers that said the North would have an easy victory over the South. Franklin believed that. Yohance believed that the early months of the war would provide the most confusion and they could take advantage of that to slip away."

"They were on a plantation owned by Jedidiah Tatum," Annja said.

Mildred looked surprised. "How did you know that?"

"The textile mill where the bodies were found," Annja explained, "was once owned by Jedidiah Tatum."

"I didn't know that."

Annja decided not to tell the woman that Horace Tatum had dynamited the men in the underground furnace. Eventually that news would come out, but the longer that was kept out of the news, the less complicated things at the dig would be.

"Yohance wanted to escape," Annja prompted.

"He did. He believed that they could reach Canada, and from there they could join a ship bound for West Africa."

"Why would he want to go there?"

"Because of Anansi's promise. Yohance had been told by the Yohance before him, and so the story had been told, that their village would rise again if the stone found its way home."

"By magic?" Annja asked.

"Well," Mildred said, "there was some talk of a treasure, as well."

9

"I thought you weren't coming."

Annja handed one of the takeout food containers to Professor Hallinger. She was later than she'd wanted to be. She felt as if most of the morning had escaped her, but the conversation with Mildred Teasdale had left her with excitement thrumming in her veins.

"I hear we have quite a crowd out there again." Hallinger sliced into a thick stack of pancakes.

"We do." The darkness in the furnace room was complete. Only the lanterns strung along the wall allowed the dig crew to work.

"You'd think the possibility of getting shot would have scared some of them out of it," the professor said.

"Not necessarily," Amber, one of the college students, said. "It brings out the gawker gene."

Hallinger looked at her and smiled in confusion. "What?"

Amber shrugged. "Call it the stupid factor if you want. It's the same thing that happens when there's a car wreck or a really bad tornado or fire. People just naturally wander out to see what's going on, never realizing that they could get swept up in it."

"The gawker gene," Hallinger repeated. "I like that."

"Do I get an A?"

"No."

"Bummer." Amber frowned theatrically and went back to helping restring the grid. Most of it had already been replaced.

Annja looked around. "We lost some students."

"The one who was shot, naturally. And three others. Their parents arrived in the night to claim them and take them home from the police station."

"I missed that," Annja said.

"I'd heard you were out having breakfast with the dashing young detective from Atlanta."

Annja glanced at the professor.

Hallinger held his hands up as best as he could while laden with the breakfast container. "Don't shoot the messenger. People talk."

"Kind of goes along with the gawker gene," Amber said. "They gawk. They talk. So how was breakfast? That guy looked totally hot."

"For one, he's not a detective. He's Homeland Security." Annja didn't want to hold back any of the information she'd discovered. They all deserved to know as much as she did so they could make informed decisions.

"Why would Homeland Security be interested in our dig site?" Hallinger asked.

"They're not. They're interested in the mercenaries. One of them turned out to be connected to a West African warlord who's interested in the Spider Stone."

Hallinger frowned. "That puts a different spin on things, doesn't it? I don't want my students in the line of fire," he said.

"I don't think we're going to have any more problems," Annja said. "Besides that, we've got Homeland Security peering over our shoulder now."

"Still—" Hallinger looked uncomfortable.

"Professor," one of the other students said, "there are more cops out there today than there were yesterday. I think they imported." He looked around at the other students. "I don't know about anyone else, but I got into this field for the opportunities to get a better look at the past. Maybe this isn't digging up a pyramid in the Valley of the Kings, but this is as close as I'm going to get right now. I'm not going to leave unless somebody orders me out."

"I could do exactly that," Hallinger threatened.

Annja said nothing. They needed the help, but Hallinger was in charge.

None of the students looked as if they were going to go without a fight.

They're drawn to the potential danger as much as the mystery of who these people are, Annja realized. She knew the feeling. When she'd found the thief's corpse out in New Mexico, that same mixture of feelings had been a siren call to her. They still called out to her whenever she worked a dig.

"All right," Hallinger relented. "You can stay. But we leave the site tonight before it gets dark."

The students had no problem with that.

"I know who these people are," Annja said. She quickly relayed the story she'd been given by Mildred Teasdale.

When she was finished, one of the students said, "If that

woman has all the names of the slaves that were caught down here by Horace Tatum, we don't need to do anything else." He sounded disappointed.

"That's not true," Annja said. "Most archaeologists approach a dig with expectations they believe will be met. Mysteries come along, but they're usually small ones. What we're going to do here is verify the story I was told this morning."

"How?" a student asked.

"By examining the artifacts they left behind," Hallinger answered. "That's what archaeologists do. That's what we'll do."

"We're ahead of the game," Annja said. "We've got an actual record to match up against." She pulled out her notebook. "Besides names, I've got descriptions that will help in most instances." She returned the notebook to her backpack. "But to spice it up a little, so we'll literally leave no stone unturned, I'm going to tell you this. We're looking for another Spider Stone. This one will be about the size of the ball of your thumb."

"What's so important about it?" one of the students asked.

Annja grinned, knowing the answer was going to spark another round of excitement. "It's a treasure map," she said.

For a moment, silence reigned in the basement furnace cave, as if everyone present had taken a collective breath and was now holding it.

"Totally freaking cool," Amber whispered, grinning.

"Yeah," Annja admitted. "It is." Archaeologists were only about a step removed from fortune hunters.

THE BASE OF OPERATIONS Tafari had established was in a collection of hide tents that blended with the surrounding brush and trees. Even if a helicopter searched for them, either from Dakar or from one of the American or European corporations, he was sure they wouldn't be found.

Zifa pulled the jeep under a net that had been woven into the surroundings. A live carpet of greenery covered the net.

A man walked from the tent that held the communications gear. Even though they'd muffled the generator that powered the satellite uplink and computers as much as they could, the sound remained steady and constant. Tafari hated it but could do nothing about it.

"I have some bad news." The man was young, one of those Tafari had enticed away from Dakar. He knew how to use computers. His name was Azikiwe. He wore brightly colored shorts and an NBA tank top. He spoke French—the official language of Senegal—better than he spoke the Yoruba dialect.

Tafari couldn't remember what the NBA was. It was an American or European thing that he had no interest in.

"I'm in no mood for bad news," Tafari warned, choosing to speak in Yoruba.

Taking heed, Azikiwe switched languages. "The man you sent to get the Spider Stone is in jail. His lawyer called to let you know."

"Tell the lawyer to get him out."

"He's trying, but that doesn't seem likely."

"Why not?"

"There are other outstanding charges against him."

Remembering that was true, Tafari reconsidered his options. "Did the lawyer say if the Spider Stone was there?"

"Yes. Ehigiator saw it himself. For a moment, he had his hands on it."

That irked Tafari. He had been so close to his prize. "Where is the Spider Stone now?"

"The archaeologists have it."

"Where?"

"I don't know."

Tafari walked past Azikiwe and into the tent. It was much cooler inside than outside because a large window air-conditioning unit sat on crates. The young men who knew computers claimed they needed it to keep their machines cool and operational. Tafari suspected they wanted it to keep themselves cool.

Rubber sheets that didn't conduct static electricity covered the ground. Three workstations containing the computers that connected the outpost with the rest of the world were spaced around the area inside the big tent. Each workstation also had a small television.

Azikiwe hurried forward and shut off the television on his desk. Seeing the mostly black men running up and down the floor while bouncing or throwing a ball reminded Tafari what the NBA was.

Azikiwe tapped the keys on his computer, then pointed at the screen. "That woman is the one who found the Spider Stone," he said.

"You're sure?" Tafari asked.

"Yeah." Azikiwe plopped down into the chair in front of the computer. "I downloaded the CNN footage of her. The stuff that was aired last night, as well as other files I found. I even got a couple of episodes of *Chasing History's Monsters.*"

"What is that?"

"A television show."

Tafari had never understood how so many people could simply sit and watch television.

But he understood the draw of electronics. People everywhere wanted electronics. His black market operations kept trading in electronics, mostly things he didn't even know the nature of. It was enough that others were willing to trade for them because he could use the artifacts and ivory they traded to sell in Europe and America.

"The woman is supposed to be very smart," Azikiwe said. "Her name is Annja Creed."

"Smart?" Tafari asked.

"She's an archaeologist."

"Another bone rattler," Tafari said, thinking of Jaineba. "I've had my fill of them today."

The television screen filled with images of the woman walking through a cavernous vault.

"She's walking through a German mausoleum," Azikiwe said. "She was searching for some mad Nazi doctor who was rumored to still be alive and be behind a rash of killings."

"Was he?"

Azikiwe shrugged. "Annja Creed never found him. She went through the records of several homeless people and those needing psychiatric care, but she never found any proof. The thing that saved this particular episode was her knowledge of German history. She had fascinating stories about gargoyles that were built."

"What is her interest in the Spider Stone?" Tafari asked.

"I don't think she intended to find it." Azikiwe rested his elbows on the arms of the chair and steepled his fingers. "According to the news story, she was called there to help identify the corpses found under the building."

"What bodies?" Tafari hadn't been told about the bodies. Ehigiator had only mentioned the presence of the Spider Stone. That had been one of the items he'd told all his people to look for. Ehigiator was one of the go-betweens the warlord used to ferry around the black market artifacts he shipped to America.

"Slaves," Azikiwe replied. "They've been there for 150 years or more."

That explained why the Spider Stone dropped from sight. Tafari watched the news footage until it showed the Spider Stone.

"Stop it there," Tafari ordered.

The screen locked on to an image of the Spider Stone. A policeman held it and explained in English that they weren't sure what it was, but he knew it had been found in the furnace area under the building, and that the mercenary team had wanted it.

"The men Ehigiator was with wanted the Spider Stone?" Tafari asked.

"Yes." Azikiwe nodded.

"But this," Tafari said, "isn't the Spider Stone."

"What do you mean?" the young computer tech asked.

"I mean that there is another Spider Stone. This one is only similar. It's far too large." Tafari peered more closely at the screen. "No, this was made as a decoy, or perhaps to honor the original Spider Stone." He looked at the tech. "Get my nephew on the phone. He is in Atlanta. I will talk to him."

ANNJA WORKED slowly and carefully. It was the only way to work in archaeology. So much could be—and had been—lost by those who hurried through a site.

In the early years, when the fortune hunters had plundered the Egyptian tombs seeking only gold and jewels, a number of clay tablets containing invaluable records, histories and insights into science and religion had been lost. Greed had plunged men through shelves, returning those tablets to the dust from which they'd come.

"You're smiling."

Annja looked up at Hallinger. "I shouldn't be," she admitted.

The professor handed her a bottle of water. "Tell me. Anything that can make you smile while we're down in this dungeon has got to be worth a moment's diversion."

Annja took the bottle and twisted off the cap. The water wasn't cold or even cool, but it was wet and she felt parched. Her shirt and pants were drenched with perspiration, and grime crusted her exposed skin and had managed to slide down inside her clothing. She was uncomfortable physically, but mentally she was on her game. They were making good, if slow, progress.

"I was thinking about your comment earlier, about the fragile nature of the digital information storage we now have."

"Yes?"

"I was thinking of the clay tablets the Egyptians, Babylonians and other cultures used. How they were destroyed by tomb robbers, earthquakes and floods. If Atlantis truly existed and wasn't just something Plato made up, then it sits somewhere at the bottom of an ocean and probably most of those records are destroyed, as well."

Hallinger grimaced. "You haven't exactly been thinking happy thoughts."

"What I'm saying is that each culture that cares to make records does the best it can with what it has. Think about the oral historians used by the Native Americans along the northwest coast of the United States and Canada. They didn't have a written language. Oral historians were inviolate and had to be at every peace conference and war that took place. If one of them was inadvertently killed by another tribe, the offending tribe had to give one of their young boys to be trained as an oral historian by the tribe that suffered the loss."

Hallinger slipped his glasses back on. "I see your point."

"We do what we can. Right now, the digital format is better than anything we've ever had," Annja said.

"I know." Hallinger sighed. "I also know how much we've possibly lost over time."

"Professor Hallinger!" Excitement rang in the student's voice. "Over here! I think we found it!"

Annja tossed her empty water bottle into the trash bag they'd set up to handle refuse so it wouldn't get mixed up with what they were handling. She stood, feeling the painful burn in her thighs and calves from squatting for so long. Carefully, she stepped through the grids.

The team had cleared over half of the room, taking the skeletons from the site one bone at a time when they had to. Most of them had been identified by descriptions of personal effects and old injuries Franklin Dickerson had recorded in his memoir. Only two of the skeletons hadn't been identified, and with all the names given in the book, that probably wouldn't be too difficult.

Everyone had crowded around the find, but they pulled back long enough to allow Annja and Hallinger to close in. The student who had made the find directed a flashlight beam at a small stone, plucking the object from the dank shadows under the skeleton's thin hipbones.

Even lying on one side as it was, Annja could still see the distinctive spider design that had been carved into it. They'd found the real stone.

10

The stone was about the size of the ball of Annja's thumb. It was striated, with differing layers of sedimentary formation that showed brown and gold with threads of red.

"A tiger's eye?" Hallinger asked.

Annja asked for her camera and it was quickly handed over. "Maybe." She took pictures from different angles, catching the stone from the best views possible before it was moved. Covered by dust as it was, the stone was difficult to see. But once seen, the spider carved into it was unmistakable.

"Anybody know what tiger's eye is?" Hallinger asked. "Any geology minors in the room?"

"Me," a student replied. "Tiger's eye is a chatoyant gemstone."

"Oh, that really helps," someone said.

Despite her excitement at the find, Annja smiled and paused. Even though one of their number was still in the hospital, the students had remained enthusiastic.

"Chatoyancy refers to the reflective ability of the stone," the student went on. "If the stone has a fibrous structure or fibrous imperfections, it's called chatoyant. It's a lot like single-crystal quartz."

"Is it from Africa?"

"It could be. But tiger's eye is found in a lot of places, including the United States and Canada. This rock could have been mined or found right around here."

Handing off the camera, Anna reached through the skeleton's bony pelvis and plucked the stone from the ground. She turned it over, holding a mini-Maglite on it.

A scarlet spider showed up instantly.

Utter quiet fell over the group. Only the buzz of the electric lanterns was audible.

"That's the Spider Stone," someone whispered.

"Yeah," Annja whispered. "It is." She rolled the stone over her palm, taking in the smooth chill it held.

"I guess this is Yohance," another student said.

Annja flicked the light over the necklace the skeleton wore. She checked the image of the river splitting the mountains against the image she'd copied into her notebook. "This is Yohance," she said.

"I thought he was a boy."

"The first Yohance supposedly came over to America as a boy," Annja corrected. "The Yohance in Franklin Dickerson's narrative was in his late teens or early twenties. The same age as most of you."

"We could have checked out at the same age he was last night," someone said.

"We didn't," someone else said.

"Did he just drop the stone there?" a student asked. "I don't see a purse or pocket he was carrying it in."

"He wasn't carrying it in a purse or pocket," Annja said. "He carried it internally."

"What do you mean?"

"He swallowed it, then defecated it and swallowed it again."

"Eww," Amber said. "That's just gross." She wrinkled her nose in displeasure.

"I'm sure he washed it in between," one of the students said.

"That's how all the Yohances carried the Spider Stone," Annja said.

"And that doesn't gross you out?" Amber asked.

"No," Annja said. "It's just the way it was." She shone the mini-Maglite on the tiger's eye. "After the flesh rotted away, the stone was left behind."

"It sank through the body?"

"Unless it was released when he voided himself after dying. That could have happened, too."

Despite the situation, Annja couldn't help taking a little perverse enjoyment in the discomfiture of the students. You people have a lot to learn about the field of archaeology, she thought.

"What's wrong with the skeleton's ribs?" someone asked.

Handing the stone to Hallinger, Annja studied the skeleton. Something *was* wrong with the ribs. They looked as if they'd been cracked, but she knew that wasn't the case because the fractures weren't spaced as they would have been from a blow, or even several blows.

She reached out and felt the cracks, realizing at her touch that they were notches. Upon closer inspection, she saw that they were of different depths. "Those were caused by a knife." Annja shone the light around and found a rusting knife near the hand of a skeleton sitting up against the wall. The knife had a heavy blade, one that had been made by a skilled craftsman. "There," she said.

"That looks like a bowie knife," someone said.

"It's a fighting knife," one of the male retirees said. "It looks like whoever that is spent some time gutting Yohance."

Annja silently agreed. "Maybe the explosion didn't kill them all at once. Whoever that was may have tried to cut the Spider Stone out of Yohance. But either he couldn't find it in the darkness or the stone had already entered the intestines."

"He tried to do that in the darkness?"

"We didn't find a lantern that seemed to survive the explosion." Annja directed her beam at one of the nearby lanterns they'd found in the room. The glass was shattered and the frame was bent. "I think he tried to do it in the dark. By feel."

Someone made gagging noises.

"Committed," Hallinger commented.

"Very," Annja agreed. She glanced at the Spider Stone again. What secrets do you hold? She took a deep breath and forced herself to relax. "Okay, we've got a few more hours before it gets dark. We found one of the things we came down here for, but there's still more we need to do. Let's get it done."

More quietly than before, and maybe a little enthusiastic about their find, the group started sifting through the rubble.

"What about the treasure?" one of the students asked.

"That story is hundreds of years old. I doubt it's still there," Annja said. But she realized that didn't mean everyone else who knew the legend of the Spider Stone felt the same way.

11

"You don't look like an African prince."

Icepick leaned across the table in the club and smiled at the young blond woman seated across from him. "And what does an African prince look like?" he asked.

The blonde gave him a cool look, as if she were merely humoring him. "Like Eddie Murphy."

Icepick grinned. The young woman had a sense of humor. He liked women with a sense of humor. When he scared it out of them, they were more docile than women who worked out of anger.

"I am an African prince," he told her. "I promise."

He thought he could have been a prince, too. He was tall and well built, with a shaved head and tribal tattooing that marked his arms, the back of his neck and his shoulders. He wore black jeans and a turquoise T-shirt that fit him like a second skin. A black leather jacket hid the SIG-Sauer semiautomatic pistol he had snugged into a shoulder rig. A gold Rolex watch, gold chains and a gold cap on a tooth completed the ensemble. His dark skin was flawless except for the tattoos.

The blonde looked like a professional, an executive or a lawyer. She looked sleek and beautiful in her business suit.

At another time, Icepick would have been more willing to chase her. But he was at the club on business. He glanced around, taking his eyes from the woman for the moment partly to make sure his men were paying attention and partly to remind the woman that she wasn't the only female in the room.

Terrence and Pigg sat at another table nearby, flirting with women. All of them looked as if they had money, so attracting women was no problem. Terrence, tall and rakish, would have attracted attention anyway. Pigg was a solid, blocky mass of a man with a vicious underbite that had helped give him his name.

The club was small but successful, a new business growing red-hot by word of mouth in Atlanta. It was called Nocturne which had something to do with night, Terrence had told Icepick. Terrence had been to college.

Icepick was part owner of the club. He'd been a silent investor when it had opened. He didn't invest because he'd expected it to be successful, but because it was a good place to sell drugs—his main business. He'd hoped to create a market where he could deal directly with a younger crowd and so he could move his operations off street corners. He hadn't expected the club to become successful and start drawing some of the new money in Atlanta.

Then Lyle, whom Icepick had met on the streets, looked at how much money he'd started making at a legitimate business without selling the drugs he'd helped sell for the past five years on street corners. Now he seemed to think he was too good for that business.

Icepick was there to remind Lyle that he had a past and a commitment that wouldn't go away.

"You don't seem like royalty," the blonde told him.

"What do I look like?" Icepick asked.

She considered him for a moment. "A drug dealer," she said.

Icepick put a hand over his heart and grinned. "You wound me."

"Or maybe a government assassin."

"Is that a step up? Or a step back?" Icepick loved playing the game with women who thought they held all the cards.

"Sorry. I just call them as I see them."

"What would it take to convince you I'm an African prince?"

"A crown."

"My father doesn't let me take it out at night," Icepick joked.

The blonde thought. "Maybe a royal bodyguard."

Icepick pointed to his men.

"They look like thugs," she said.

"And how is it a royal bodyguard should look?"

"I don't know. Royal?"

Icepick knew the woman was rounding the corner from humor to sarcasm. "I'll show you something." He waved to Hamid, one of his bodyguards.

Hamid came over at once, carrying a sleek briefcase that was chained to his wrist.

"Put it on the table and open it." Icepick didn't glance at the briefcase. He knew what it contained. He'd put it there.

Producing a key, Hamid opened the briefcase. Inside, in specially cut foam inserts, lay a mask made of gold and crusted with rubies, topaz and diamonds.

The jewels caught the woman's eyes at once. She reached for the mask, then pulled her hand away. "Did you steal that?"

"No." That was the truth. The mask was going to be a bribe for another deal he was working on.

"What is that?"

"A funerary mask."

"What's a funerary mask? Like something made after a person's dead?"

"Yes."

"That's a really ugly mask."

Icepick knew the woman was lying. She'd been captivated by the jewels and the gold. And now that he knew he had her hooked, he also knew he could trump her with guilt. "It was my grandfather's." Of course, that was another lie.

"Oh, I'm sorry." She looked embarrassed and shocked.

Both of those emotions were weaknesses, as far as Icepick was concerned. "You couldn't know. After all, you don't believe I'm an African prince." Icepick waved Hamid away.

The man closed the case and returned to his seat just a short distance away.

"What are you doing with your grandfather's death mask?"

"I'm taking it back to my country. It was loaned to the Jimmy Carter Library and Museum in Atlanta. It was part of the exhibit 'The African-American Presidents: The Founding Fathers of Liberia, 1848–1904.' It was released back into my custody this afternoon. Now I'm flying back home in two days. But first I wanted to see more of this city. I've only been here a few times. I'm visiting family on my mother's side."

Icepick had lived in Atlanta for many years, though he had been born in Senegal. His mother had never left that country.

"I'm really sorry," the woman said.

"It's all right."

She shrugged. "It's just that, you know, I'm a woman here by myself. I get hit on a lot when I go to a bar by myself."

"That's totally understandable. If I were so inclined, I would hit on you."

"You're not?" she asked.

"At first, I just thought I would get to know you. Now..." Icepick shrugged. "Of course, if you find my interest in you unwelcome, all you have to do is say so."

"No. That's all right."

"I'm glad."

"So," the blonde said, "what country are you prince of?"

Returning his attention to the young woman, Icepick said, "Nigeria. West Africa," Icepick told her. "Right on the coast of the Atlantic."

She nodded and sipped at her drink, but Icepick thought that was just to let him know it was empty again.

Icepick waved a server over and ordered another round.

"You're a prince of Nigeria?" the blonde asked.

It would have been easy to simply say yes, but Icepick had learned to be elaborate with his lies. People believed an elaborate lie wrapped around a hint of truth more often than a simple lie.

"No," Icepick said. "Nigeria is made up of what used to be several African empires. Have you heard of the Yoruba people?"

She shook her head.

At that moment, Terrence stood and attracted Icepick's

attention. He nodded toward Lyle, who was walking through the club with a couple of his own bodyguards in tow.

Lyle was tall and dapper, in his early thirties. The dark blue suit he wore looked expensive. Icepick had good suits back home in his closets. Despite the darkness filling the club, Lyle wore sunglasses and looked like a young Ray Charles.

Irritated with Lyle's timing, Icepick stroked the back of the blonde's hand. "The Yoruba are a proud people," he said.

"How long did you say you were going to be in town?" the woman asked.

"A few more days."

The blonde smiled. "Maybe we could get together. I could show you around."

Icepick smiled. "I'd like that."

"Do you have a card?"

Icepick hesitated.

Then the woman shook her head. "That was stupid. You're not from here. Why would you have a card?" She rummaged in her tiny purse and produced a business card. "That's me. Sandra Thompson."

"It says attorney-at-law."

"That's right. I specialize in corporate law. Mergers. Tax shelters. That kind of thing."

"You must be very smart to do something like that."

"I like my job and I'm good at it."

Lyle walked into his office, never looking around. He was totally secure in his environment.

Icepick was about to change that. "If you'll forgive me, I've got something I need to attend to," he said.

"Sure." The woman glanced at her watch. "Actually, I'm about to turn into a pumpkin. I've got to go." She swept her purse from the table and flashed him a smile. "You have my card. Call me." Then she was gone, and the heads of several men turned in her direction as she crossed the bar.

Icepick watched her all the way to the door. Then he got up and walked toward the office. Terrence, Pigg, Hamid and three other men fell into step with him. By the time they reached the office door, all of them had suppressor-equipped pistols in their hands.

Nodding to Terrence as they stopped at the door, Icepick stepped to one side. Terrence lifted his pistol and fired into the locking mechanism. The muzzle-flashes were lost in the light show, and the sound of the bullets crunching through the lock was covered by the music.

Icepick kicked the door open and shoved his head and shoulders through.

The office was small and filled with electronics. Monitors showed pictures from a dozen different angles inside the club, and each of those rotated through still other cameras.

Lyle sat at the big desk in front of the monitors. His two bodyguards occupied chairs on either side of the desk. Both of them were on their feet and trying to draw their weapons, no doubt alerted by the monitor system.

Icepick shot the first man through the head twice. Before the corpse had time to topple backward, Terrence shot the second guard through the chest and neck. The second man took a little longer to die, but he was dead within seconds.

Lyle stood, throwing his hands high. "Don't shoot! Please! Don't shoot!"

Crossing the room, Icepick grabbed Lyle's suit coat and shoved him back into the chair. Terror widened Lyle's eyes. Then Icepick closed them when he pistol-whipped the man across the face with his gun. Without a word, he pressed the pistol barrel into Lyle's throat, pinning him against the chair.

"Move and I will kill you." Icepick ripped Lyle's sunglasses from his face. The man's pupils were pinpricks, advertising the drugs in his system.

"Don't kill me," Lyle whispered. "Please don't kill me."

"You've been cheating me," Icepick said.

"No!" Lyle shook his head desperately. "No! I haven't been cheating you! I swear!"

"I've got someone in the club. You've been skimming."

"That's a lie!"

"It's not a lie." Icepick slapped Lyle with the gun butt again.

Lyle's cheek opened up and blood ran down his face. He whimpered and tears spilled from his pinprick eyes. "I'm sorry! I'm sorry! I'll pay you back!"

"Put your hands on the table, Lyle."

"No." Lyle's refusal came out as a whimper.

"Put your hands on the desk or I'm going to blow your head off."

Reluctantly, Lyle put his hands on the desk.

Reaching into his jacket, Icepick took out an ice pick.

"Don't," Lyle pleaded. "Please. Please don't."

Without a word, without mercy, Icepick plunged the ice pick through Lyle's right hand and impaled it on the desk.

Lyle cried out in pain.

Icepick plucked the handkerchief from Lyle's jacket pocket and shoved it into his mouth.

Still sobbing, Lyle fell forward when Icepick released him. He reached for the ice pick. The handkerchief in his mouth muffled whatever sound he was making.

"Don't touch that," Icepick ordered. "You try to pull that out and I'll kill you."

Lying on the desk, staring in agony at his maimed hand, Lyle cried.

"I helped you get where you are today, Lyle," Icepick said. "I talked to my uncle for you. He agreed to set us up in business. He fronted the money you spent on this place. He expects a return on his investment. Not to be ripped off. Do you understand?"

Lyle nodded.

"If we have to have this discussion again," Icepick promised, "I'm going to ship your head to my uncle."

"It won't," Lyle gasped, "happen…again."

"Good." Icepick released the club owner and stood. He looked around the office. "Get this place cleaned up. Quietly. I don't want any of this rolling back on me. If my ankles get covered from now on, I'm going to bury you in whatever I'm looking at during that moment."

Turning on his heel, Icepick walked to the door. He shoved the SIG-Sauer back into the shoulder leather. Pigg opened the door without a word.

As he left the club, Icepick's cell phone rang. He fished it out of his jacket pocket and flipped it on. "Yeah."

"Nephew," Tafari said in the Yoruban language, "I need you to do a task for me."

"Of course. All you've ever needed to do is ask."

"There is something I want in a small town outside Atlanta," Tafari said.

"Anything," Icepick answered, but he was thinking about his uncle. Tafari was a hard man. He wouldn't have let Lyle live. But somebody had to get rid of the bodies, Icepick reasoned.

Almost twelve years ago, Tafari had sent his sister's only son to Atlanta to start managing some of the illegal trade in

African artifacts that brought in so much money. Icepick had shown resourcefulness and an understanding of the criminal economy that his uncle had been pleased to discover. Icepick had negotiated a small drug-dealing business, then shipped the drugs to Tafari. Once the drugs reached Senegal, Tafari sold them to merchant ships in Dakar. The crews in turn took the drugs to other ports of call.

Everybody made a profit. It remained a constant source of revenue for them.

"The Spider Stone has been found," Tafari said.

Outside Nocturne, Icepick froze, caught in the glare of the neon signs. Cars passed in the street, but he hardly noticed them. The whole time he'd been growing up out in the savannas, his uncle had talked of many things. Legends and myths, and tales of gods. But one of the most repeated legends had been the one of the Spider Stone. The Hausa village that had possessed it had been said to have been blessed in trade. Supposedly, there was a treasure trove awaiting anyone clever enough to find it.

"Where is it?" Icepick asked.

"In a small city outside Atlanta. A place called Kirktown. Can you get there?"

"Of course," Icepick replied. "I can be there before morning."

"Do that. It would be best to work under the cover of night."

It would, Icepick thought. Ever since he'd left Africa, then changed his name to his current one, he'd been aware of the magic in the night. Predators thrived there.

And he was one of the best predators his warlord uncle had ever reared.

12

"What have you gotten yourself involved in?"

Bleary-eyed and tired, Annja really wasn't in the mood for any remonstrations. Especially not from the man currently connected to her by cell phone.

Roux was the only name she had for the old man. At least she thought "Roux" really was his name. He sometimes used others and "Roux" might have been just as false.

"Nothing." Annja straightened her back, stiff from being in a cramped, bent-over position for hours. She and Hallinger were working together in a small warehouse not far from the old textile mill. Other units in the warehouse were rented out as garages and paint-and-body shops, and the stink of the chemicals filled her nose.

The university had hired a small security service from Atlanta. The men sat around the archaeologists drinking coffee, reading gun magazines and reliving past postings with each other.

Having the men there didn't make Annja feel particularly safe. She felt more invaded than anything else.

Body bags containing the remains of the slaves who had been killed in the furnace room lay on the floor. Hallinger and Annja had commandeered tables for use in studying the various artifacts they'd recovered.

There were a few artifacts, most of them related to the Civil War. But the thing that caught their attention now that the slaves had been identified was the Spider Stone.

Roux snorted.

Annja sighed. Despite having spent months around the man, she truly didn't feel that she knew Roux any better than she had when she'd first met him. There was so much that he hadn't told about himself, and probably most of it he would never tell.

How could you live five hundred years and not have left traces of yourself everywhere? she wondered. How could you keep all those stories bottled up?

None of that made sense to her.

Garin—who also went under other names these days—was easier to understand. He was a self-motivated person, and all she could truly count on him to do was look after his own interests. Garin had tried to kill her shortly after he'd found out that she had the reassembled sword. He was convinced that he was going to start aging at any time now that the sword was whole and in Annja's hands.

She didn't know what was going to happen. She was very aware that she had been changed by the sword's power, but she didn't know if those changes had been completed. She had no idea if they'd affected whatever spell or force or cosmic happening that had allowed Roux and Garin to live for five hundred years.

"Getting yourself killed isn't an optimum career choice," Roux groused.

"That didn't happen," Annja argued. She knew he was only worried about what might happen to the sword. *If something happened to the sword—or to me—are you afraid you'll be held accountable again?* It was a question that always hummed in the back of her mind whenever she talked to Roux.

"According to what I saw on CNN a few minutes ago, getting killed was a near thing," Roux said.

"That was yesterday."

"So today is better? You're safe?"

Annja looked around at the bored security guards. "Yeah. I'm safe."

"Good. I don't want worrying about you throwing off my game."

You're worried about me? That thought warmed Annja for just a moment, then she reined in those feelings. They were just the remnants of being raised in an orphanage.

Roux wasn't exactly a fatherly figure, but there was something demanding and dependable about his presence. If they were on the same side in something, she knew he would never abandon her. He'd proved that when she'd first found the sword and had to fight to keep it. But he'd let her go her own way after that.

Still, the sword somehow bound them and she was distinctly aware that both of them knew it. Neither of them was happy about it, but it was interesting.

"I doubt you'd worry too much about me," Annja replied.

Roux snorted again. "All of this is over people who've been dead for the last 150 years?" he asked.

"Not completely," Annja admitted. "Do you know much about the Hausa people?" She knew that Roux had a vast knowledge of many subjects. She always learned something new whenever she talked to him.

"Which empire?"

"What do you mean?"

"There were several empires. Come, come. You're supposed to be the archaeologist. I'm just a dabbler with an interest in old things."

With five hundred years' experience, Annja thought. No archaeologist I know is going to be able to put together that kind of résumé.

"I don't know which empire yet." Annja knew there had been several Hausa trading empires.

"Then what are you dealing with?"

Annja gazed at the tiger's eye stone that Hallinger was observing under a computer-assisted magnifying glass they'd borrowed from the university. From time to time, the professor took digital captures of the stone's surface. They were slowly mapping the intricate Hausa language written on the surface.

"A stone," Annja answered.

"Doesn't sound interesting to me."

"It's supposed to be a treasure map."

Roux laughed. "Treasure maps litter history. Even those a hundred or two hundred years old usually turn out to have been part of some con man's game."

Someone called in the background. The voice was soft and young.

That irked Annja a little, though she knew it shouldn't have. She knew Roux had a fondness for young women. Every time Annja had visited the old man at his rambling mansion outside Paris, he'd always had a woman with him. None of them ever stayed long.

"I'm going to have to go," Roux said. "Someone requires my attention."

Randy old goat, Annja thought. But she said, "Sure."

"You may send me a few pictures of your latest hobby. If you wish. Perhaps I could help."

"Are you sure I won't be taking up too much of your time," Annja said.

Roux huffed. "There's no reason to be persnickety, Annja."

"I'm not being *persnickety,*" she argued.

Hallinger looked over his shoulder at her, then quickly returned his attention to the Spider Stone.

"You sound it to me," Roux said.

"Maybe you should have your hearing checked."

"Why? Everything else seems to be functioning well. I don't get any complaints," Roux said.

Now that's an image I don't need, Annja thought.

The soft voice called again, sounding more needy this time.

"Send me the pictures if you've a mind," Roux invited.

"Maybe." Annja was unwilling to commit to anything.

"On that note," Roux said, "I'll say goodbye. Stay well, Annja. I wouldn't want anything to happen to you."

He hung up while Annja was still trying to figure out how to react. Roux cared about her. Somewhere inside, she knew that, but caring about her exposed him to a lot of hurt. For five hundred years, he'd watched anyone he'd grown close to grow old and die. If they managed to grow old.

Except for Garin. During most of that time, Roux's ex-apprentice had tried to kill him whenever they were around each other. Finding Annja and the sword had brought them together briefly. She knew their relationship was complicated.

Annja put her cell phone in her pocket. Roux cared about her.

Maybe it's hard for you to accept that, she told herself. She'd walled herself off from most people. She had some friends, good ones. And even a few who tried to mother her, the way that Maria Ruiz, the owner and chef of Tito's, her favorite Cuban restaurant in Brooklyn, did.

But there had never been anyone like Roux in her life.

"You okay?" Hallinger asked.

"Yes." Annja stepped over to the coffeepot in the corner and poured another cup.

"Your dad?"

Annja frowned and shook her head. "Definitely not."

"Sorry. Sounded like you were talking to your dad."

"He's just…just a guy I know."

"Oh." Hallinger looked away, clearly feeling awkward.

Annja suspected the professor thought she'd been talking to someone she felt romantic about. "It's not like that," she said.

"It's really not any of my business."

"No," Annja said, feeling flustered, "I mean it. It's not like that."

"I believe you."

Get a grip, Annja told herself. But she couldn't let it go. She suspected maybe it was because she was tired. "He's a…mentor."

"A professor?"

And didn't that just bring up the lovely subject of star students crushing on professors? Annja let out a breath. "You know, I just don't want to talk about it."

"Okay." Hallinger didn't look at her.

Maybe it would have helped if he had. Then she could have known what he was thinking, and maybe he would have been thinking that nothing she said was any of his business and that would have been the end of it.

But he didn't look up.

"He's just this guy. A really *old* guy." Annja described Roux that way because that fact seemed important. "He knows a lot about history."

"A historian?" Hallinger asked.

"More or less."

"That's a good field. I've always been interested in history myself." Hallinger shrugged. "I guess it's a natural spin-off from archaeology. Reading other people's interpretations of an event or a person."

"He just called to check on me."

"That was thoughtful."

"He's not really that thoughtful."

Hallinger continued working.

"He knows a lot that I would like to know," Annja said. "Except he won't tell me. He says I need to find out some things for myself."

"My dad used to tell me the same thing," Hallinger said. "He was an archaeologist, too."

"The guy I was talking to isn't my dad."

"You said that already."

Annja sighed and gave up. There was no explaining Roux. She couldn't even explain the man to herself. Whatever tied them together wasn't going away, and she didn't know whether to feel glad or threatened by that.

Hallinger glanced at her. "Are you really all right?"

"Yes," Annja replied, folding her arms and sealing off the confusion of emotions that ran through her. *No.* She really needed a good night's sleep.

"Ready to work?" he asked. "I think I've found a map."

"YOU THINK they got enough Five-O there?"

Icepick gazed from the shadows of the alley across the street from where the woman archaeologist was supposed to be holed up with whatever she had found. Three police cars sat out in front of the building.

He looked at Terrence. "We don't have a choice about this. My uncle sent me to get this thing."

Terrence nodded. He knew Tafari, and he knew the warlord would not allow them to back off just because of the police.

The men were pumped on speed, tense and wired up, ready to take action. Dressed all in black, the members of the small army held assault weapons and were connected by walkie-talkie headsets.

"What we need is a distraction," Icepick said. "Send Pigg and a couple of others to the bank we passed on the way into town. Have them plant some of the explosives we brought, like someone's trying to break into the bank, then wait for my signal. That's far enough away to buy us time to take down the warehouse, get the stone and hit it. By the time everything gets sorted out, we'll be gone."

Terrence nodded and turned to make things happen.

Crouched with his back against the wall, Icepick took out a small vial of cocaine. His uncle didn't like him using the hard drugs, but Icepick kept his use to a minimum. They were just for times when he needed an edge.

He shook some of the cocaine onto the back of his hand, then snorted it. He licked the back of his hand and felt his tongue grow numb. The cocaine was good, expertly cut.

New energy blossomed within Icepick. He forced himself to wait although his nerves jangled for him to be up and moving.

He reached under his leather duster and took out the

Glock 18C machine pistol. The weapon looked like a normal semiautomatic handgun, but it was configured to fire through a 17-round or 33-round magazine in a single pull of the trigger.

The pistols were usually employed by American law-enforcement agencies, but Icepick had negotiated the purchase of a few dozen. The weapon had been featured in one of the *Matrix* films and *Terminator 3*. After seeing the Glock there, Icepick had decided he had to have one.

Several 33-round magazines filled the deep pockets of the duster he'd had specially made. It was like something Neo from the *Matrix* movies would wear, too. He also wore a Kevlar vest. It was bullet resistant and would stop most rounds. He'd take a vicious beating from the blunt trauma, but a few bruises were a small price to pay. But he didn't plan on getting shot at all.

Icepick inserted one of the 33-round magazines. High capacity meant that his team didn't have to be accurate. They just had to be careful not to shoot each other.

Pigg and the two men Terrence had chosen drifted away into the night.

Crouching, zinging inside, Icepick whistled tunelessly while he waited.

HALLINGER *HAD* FOUND a map.

Annja shifted through the images the professor had taken and fed into the computer. The digital images could be dramatically blown up.

"Do you see it?" Hallinger asked.

"I do." Annja manipulated the image. "The map's unmistakable."

"But we have no reference points." Hallinger sounded tired. "It could be anywhere in Africa."

"West Africa," Annja said. "We know that because of the Hausa language."

"The Hausa were once scattered across a far larger part of Africa than they are now," Hallinger pointed out. "Where this map is depends a lot on how old this stone is."

"Not the stone," Annja said. "The carving."

"Agreed." Hallinger leaned a hip against the table and looked disgusted.

"The carving is exquisite work." Annja studied the lines. "There's not a misplaced line in the map."

"The Hausa worked in stone."

"But whoever made this was a gifted craftsman. That's going to narrow the field a bit."

"I shouldn't allow myself to be disappointed," Hallinger said. "It's not like we're going to get to go look for the treasure."

Annja looked at him and smiled. "Is it the treasure you want?"

"If the Hausa put gold and ivory away for a rainy day, you can bet they put away more than that. That place, wherever it is, could also be a library containing records, histories and a real look into the Hausa culture during those days. Some of the oldest empires of civilization are in those areas." Hallinger rubbed his jaw. "I wouldn't mind being remembered as the guy who found something like that."

Neither would I, Annja thought. She turned and leaned against the table, too. She was aware that some of the security guards were watching and listening to their conversation even though they were trying to be subtle.

"Maybe we can get a shot at doing that," Annja said.

Hallinger stared at her.

"My producer on *Chasing History's Monsters* has wanted in on this," Annja said. "So far I've kept him out of it. The last thing we needed was a film crew leaning over us."

"Agreed. But you think he might be interested in this?"

Annja smiled. "An ancient map to a lost treasure of a people protected by a spider god? He'd go for it in a heartbeat. There's only one catch."

Hallinger lifted an inquisitive eyebrow.

"We'll need a monster. Or a legend of a monster."

"We haven't found any monsters yet that weren't of the human variety," Hallinger pointed out.

"We could play up the Anansi angle. Anansi wasn't always a good god. He's believed to have come from the Ashanti people. Maybe there's something there."

"If you're talking about Africa, and especially West Africa, you're talking about *voudoun* and zombies."

"I think my producer may finally be as sick of doing stories about zombies as I am." Annja thought about it. "Maybe we could work with the cult aspect of the *bokors*. They lean toward the dark side of *voudoun*."

"They create the zombies."

"Without getting into the whole zombie litany," Annja said.

"With the Islamic influence, we also have the jinni."

"Weak." Then Annja reconsidered. "Actually, we haven't done anything with jinni that I know of."

"Several of the African cultures also believe in lycanthropes," Hallinger said.

"But we don't have a specific monster. Or person who was thought to be a monster. A general story about werewolves wouldn't fly."

"That makes a difference?"

"Can you believe it?"

"I have to admit," Hallinger said, "I've seen the show. I wouldn't have thought there was much criteria for acceptable monsters."

"There is," Annja said.

They both fell silent for a moment.

"What about vampires?" one of the security guards volunteered.

"Vampires," Hallinger said.

Annja shrugged. "My producer loves vampires. He hangs out at vampire clubs and plays a count."

"Terrific," the professor said dryly. "You know, this is a sad statement on our profession that we even have to sit around discussing such subjects."

"It's all about acquiring funding," Annja replied. "You have to get creative when you're going after funding."

"In 2002 and 2003," the security guard said, "they had a bunch of vampire attacks in some country. Killed a governor and a bunch of other people. Started a riot."

"Malawi," Annja said.

The guard snapped his fingers and pointed at her. "That's it."

"Only one person was killed during the riot. Four other people, including the governor, were stoned but lived. The citizens thought the governor was in league with vampires." Annja had been offered the story at the time. She'd passed. Kristie Chatham had accepted the story, negotiated a fat bonus for the travel, then proceeded to run screaming through the streets of Blantyre, Malawi.

No vampires had ever put in an appearance. There was no mention of the hominid remains and stone tools that dated back more than a million years. The episode had still gotten one of the highest ratings in the history of the show.

"Maybe we just need to sleep on this," Hallinger suggested. "By morning, we could have a new take on what we're doing."

Before Annja could say anything, a loud explosion sounded outside.

"What the hell was that?" one of the guards shouted.

No one had an answer. They all stood and put their hands on their weapons.

Apprehension triggered Annja's personal early-warning system. She put her hand out and touched the sword but didn't draw it from the otherwhere. There were too many people around. But she had the definite sense that something very wrong was happening.

13

Icepick cursed. The sound of the explosion at the Executive National Bank could be heard throughout all of Kirktown.

"Done." Pigg's voice over the earpiece sounded distant.

"How much of that damn plastic explosive did you use, Pigg?" Icepick demanded.

"Enough, man. That bank's front door is in splinters. There's alarms going off everywhere."

There was no arguing that. Even where Icepick was, with the echo of the explosion bouncing around inside his skull, the strident wailing of the alarms screamed through the streets.

"We're haulin' ass," Pigg advised.

"Get clear." Icepick took a fresh grip on his pistol as the three police cars in front of the warehouse burned rubber getting into motion. He supposed that every cop dreamed of catching a bank robber.

In seconds, the police cars had disappeared, roaring toward the other side of Kirktown.

"All right," Icepick said, "let's move." He led the way across the street, closing in quickly on the warehouse door they'd figured was closest to the area where the archaeologists were working.

Annja Creed. He rolled the woman's name in his mind, enjoying the sound of it. She was a good-looking woman, and his uncle hadn't said he had to keep his hands off of her. It was always better to ask forgiveness than to ask permission, he thought.

Terrence came up behind him and took the other side of the door. One of the other men came forward with a shaped charge. Icepick took care to surround himself with capable people when it came to killing. The killing itself could be learned on the spot, but getting into areas rapidly took special skills.

"Back," the man said. He'd once been part of a special-forces unit, trained by the military to do exactly what they were doing now. Urban assault, he called it. "Fire in the hole."

In the next instant, the door lock exploded and was driven into the room beyond. The door bounced in the frame, letting Icepick know that it was free.

He grabbed the door with a gloved hand, feeling the incredible heat the detonation had left, and yanked it open. Embers spilled out in an arc.

Icepick went into the room with the Glock held before him. A lot of television shows had military and law-enforcement personnel holding their side arms in two-handed grips. Icepick had never done that. He'd learned his gun skills on video games, and the lessons had translated easily to real guns on the street.

A small lobby equipped with a desk and a phone led into

the large work area behind it. The lobby door opened and a heavy-set security guard stepped through.

Squeezing the trigger, Icepick put the first two rounds through the man's belt buckle, then felt the gun rise through the next six. The security guard's shirtfront turned red, and he fell backward into the next room.

Icepick went after the man, moving into alignment with the doorway the same way he would in Halo or any of the James Bond video games. Another guard lifted his weapon and fired from ten feet away. At that range, missing Icepick was almost impossible.

Two rounds struck the Kevlar vest, slamming into Icepick's chest and causing him to stumble back. He cursed but brought the Glock up anyway, triggering a spray of bullets that caught the guard at the ankles and stitched their way to the top of his head.

Terrence was beside him as he ejected the empty magazine and slammed another one home. Terrence took aim, but two security guards fired first. Their bullets went wide of Icepick but took out three of the men crowding into the doorway. At least one of them was dead, hit between the eyes.

Then Terrence opened up and dropped both security guards. He wasn't pretty when he shot, but the reflexes were there.

Looking across the room, Icepick saw the archaeologists running toward the back door. He grinned. They weren't getting away—they were running straight for the rest of Icepick's group.

ANNJA HELD on to Hallinger's arm and ran toward the back door. She had no idea who the black-clad men were, but she knew that hanging around to ask questions was a bad idea.

Bullets whipped along behind her, smashing into the body bags lying on the floor. A light exploded overhead, then dropped free of its moorings and smashed against the concrete floor in a shower of glass.

The back door started to open, alerting Annja to the fact that someone was entering from the alley. She slammed against Hallinger, catching him midstride and knocking him into the wall. The air went out of him in a rush and he dropped to his knees just as bullets chopped into the wall. He ducked all the way down.

Annja went airborne as she neared the door, then crashed into it in a flying kick. The impact slammed the door hard. Two men tumbled to the ground, but four more pushed the door open in a split second.

Annja knew she couldn't run. There wasn't enough time. She pushed herself to her feet, sprang forward and grabbed the first man's arm as he took aim. Controlling the arm, using the limb as a lever and her body as a fulcrum, she wheeled and hip tossed him. The man flew across the alley and slammed awkwardly into the wall.

The man's neck snapped on impact. The brittle, crunching sound reached Annja's ears even over the sound of gunfire coming from inside the warehouse.

Annja hadn't intended to kill the man, but for the moment she was just grateful to be alive. She threw herself to the left of the next man as he fired. The flaming muzzle tore away the darkness in the alley for a moment. Bullets cut through the space where Annja had been standing. If she hadn't moved, she'd have been dead.

Holding her curled fists beside her face in a defensive position, Annja swung her right leg around in a roundhouse kick. Time seemed to have slowed down slightly as it sometimes did when adrenaline spiked her system. She knew she was really moving fast. The surprised looks on the faces of the men gave that away.

The man she kicked went down as if he'd been hit by a truck. His pistol skidded from his hand.

"Now you gonna die!" another man yelled.

Annja didn't try to figure out who spoke. Both of the remaining men were dangerous, and Professor Hallinger was still inside the building.

She took two steps and vaulted up onto a Dumpster behind the warehouse. The men turned toward her, chasing her with their bullets, knocking pieces of broken brick from the wall.

Still on the move, Annja leaped up and somersaulted in the air. She reached for the sword and the weapon filled her hand. She swung the blade at one man's pistol, knocking it from his hand in a shower of sparks.

Then she landed behind the second man. Desperate, alarm stamped on his face, the second man tracked her, firing along the warehouse wall and up into the air. His pistol emptied before he could bring it back down, but he swung it at Annja's head.

Blocking the blow with her left forearm, Annja snap-kicked the man in the groin and took the fight out of him. While he struggled to remain standing, she brought the sword hilt crashing into his forehead. He fell to the ground.

Annja turned and surveyed the alley. All of the men were down. More shots sounded from inside the warehouse.

She released the sword, dropping it back into that unknown space, then scooped up two of the pistols from the ground. Both of them had extended magazines that made them look slightly cartoonish.

Annja had taken gun-safety courses on revolvers, semi-automatic pistols and rifles. She was good with firearms but preferred not to use them. Bullets didn't recognize friend from foe, and she didn't have control over them like she did the sword once they were unleashed.

Stepping back into the doorway, she peered around the corner. Professor Hallinger had his hands lifted over his head and was slowly getting to his feet.

The African-American with the shaved skull who appeared to be the leader was talking, one hand pressed to an ear.

Radio communication, Annja realized. She knew he'd be aware that he had lost the team outside.

Two other men approached Hallinger, trailed by a third.

"Get your hands up!" the third man ordered. "Keep them up where I can see them!"

Obviously shaken, Hallinger stood his ground and kept his hands raised.

The two men closed on him. Annja let them, wanting them close enough that there could be no mistake.

"What's your name?" the man asked.

"Hallinger," the professor responded.

"Do you have the Spider Stone?"

Annja was surprised, although she couldn't think of any other reason for the men to raid the building.

"No," Hallinger replied.

Annja felt the weight of the stone in her shirt pocket. She'd grabbed it instinctively, remembering the times when dig sites she'd been on had been raided by bandits or fortune hunters.

"Where is it?" the man asked.

"I have it," Annja said as she swung around the doorway and dropped the pistols into position.

All three men tried to respond to the threat, but they were too late and they knew it.

Willing herself to be cold, remembering how the invaders had shot the security guards without warning, Annja squeezed the triggers. The pistols erupted in her hands like live things trying to escape traps. They climbed steadily as bullets tore into the three men, driving them backward in quick stutter steps. The final bullets tore into the lights, knocking two of them down in crashing heaps.

The man with the shaved head dived to the ground, followed by the two other men who remained of his attack group.

Throwing down the empty pistols, Annja caught Hallinger's arm and got him moving.

"You killed them," the professor said incredulously.

"They didn't give me a choice." Annja pushed Hallinger through the door just ahead of the fusillade of bullets that slammed into the wall after them.

In the alley, Hallinger froze for just a moment, looking down at the men Annja had left in disarray. He looked up at her. "*You* did this?"

"Those men are coming after us." Annja shoved him toward the street. "*Go.*"

Hallinger lurched into a run, then put his heart into it. His feet slapped against the pavement.

Annja reached for the sword and it was in her hand. She took up position behind the Dumpster, crouching so she couldn't be seen. Her heart thudded in her chest.

At the end of the alley, Hallinger had reached the street and was running for his life. He turned and was out of sight just as their pursuers rushed from the doorway.

Annja watched from the shadows, letting the first man

pass her by. Then she lunged to catch the second man, hoping it would be the man with the shaved head. If she could get her hands on the leader, maybe the other two could be controlled.

It wasn't him. Annja caught the man's jacket with her left hand and slammed into him hard with her left forearm. The air left his lungs in a rush and he doubled over. Annja pushed him backward into the leader, sending them both down in a heap.

Twisting, knowing how precarious her position was, Annja went for the first man. He was only a few feet away, already firing at her. Quick enough to dance between lightning strikes, Annja dodged to the side. She brought the sword up in both hands with blinding speed, slapping the flat of the blade against the man's temple. Out on his feet, the man slumped to the ground.

Annja turned quickly, moving toward the last man.

He pointed his pistol at her as he got to his feet. "You're finished," he growled.

Without a word, Annja brought the sword down in a glittering arc. The keen blade smashed the pistol's body. The weapon fired, but the bullet struck the sword blade and ricocheted into the warehouse wall.

The man cursed in disbelief, staring at the ruined barrel. He tried to fire again, but the pistol had jammed. He suddenly remembered the pistol in his other hand and drew it up.

Annja gripped the sword and spun, bringing her foot arcing down on the man's wrist. Bone broke and the man cried out in pain as the gun flew from his fingers. Before he could move, Annja swept the sword around, slicing neatly through his Kevlar vest as if it were cheese.

The man looked down at the gaping cut as if expecting to see his intestines come tumbling out. They didn't. Annja knew she'd missed his body by less than an inch. She'd intended to.

"Now," she said, "would be the time to surrender."

Moving with surprising speed, the man turned and ran toward the other end of the alley. He got just enough of a jump that Annja didn't catch him until he'd reached the corner.

"Come get me! Come get me!" the man yelled.

Annja knew he was communicating with the rest of his team. As she reached the corner, she saw a big dark luxury sedan hurtling down the street. The lights pinned the fleeing man and the driver stepped on the brakes. Rubber shrieked and the vehicle slewed sideways as the driver tried to control it.

The man slowed, anticipating catching a ride.

Annja never broke stride. Her quarry turned at the last moment, his hand on the car's front fender. His eyes widened as he saw her.

She leaped, letting the sword slip away, and crashed into the man, driving him back across the hood of the oncoming car. They slid across the hood and smashed against the windshield, turning it into a frosted glaze of cracks. They rebounded and tumbled over the side.

For a moment, Annja was stunned. She wasn't strong enough to body block moving vehicles. But her quarry had fared worse. His face was a bloody mess and his right arm was bent unnaturally behind his back.

He wasn't trying to get up.

Annja struggled to get to her feet as the driver got out of the car with a pistol in his fist.

"Icepick! Man, I couldn't stop, dawg!"

"Shoot her!" Icepick ordered hoarsely.

The big man took aim.

Annja dodged, leaving the street just as the bullet scarred the pavement.

Three gunshots rang out in quick succession. The big man jerked backward. Puzzled, he glanced down, seeing the blood pouring from his mutilated neck. At least one of the rounds had torn out his throat. He slumped to his knees and fell forward.

A harsh voice boomed out, "Homeland Security! Drop your weapons! Now!"

A flashlight beam blazed out of the darkness and splashed over the car. The two men inside threw their weapons out the window.

"Ms. Creed, are you all right?"

Annja recognized McIntosh's voice then. "I am. What about Professor Hallinger?" she asked.

"He's safe. We've got him."

McIntosh closed in with three other men who were dressed in street clothes. Swiftly, they took the men into custody.

"Do you normally tackle guys into cars?" McIntosh asked.

"Kind of seemed like the thing to do at the time," Annja said. "They killed the security guards in the warehouse." She looked down at the man at her feet. "I couldn't let them get away with that."

McIntosh looked at her silently for a short time. "No. I suppose you couldn't."

FOR THE SECOND NIGHT in a row, Annja sat in the Kirktown Police Department. She sat in one of the straight-backed chairs with eyes closed.

"Hey," a soft voice said beside her.

Blearily, Annja glanced up.

A gray-haired detective with his tie at half-mast looked down at her and held out a cup of coffee. "I would have let you sleep, but McIntosh asked me to make sure you were awake. I think he's going to want to talk to you in a little while."

Annja took the coffee and gazed out the window. Full morning had dawned. Puffy clouds floated by in the blue sky outside.

"Thanks," she said.

"You're getting to be quite a celebrity," the detective said. "The guys around here are thinking about giving you an honorary police commission. You've collared more violent criminals in the last two nights than most of them have their whole careers."

"Not exactly what I'd intended to do here."

"The Homeland Security team says you tackled that guy Icepick. Put him up against a moving car."

"Who?" Annja looked at the man.

"Icepick." The detective frowned. "You didn't get his name?"

"There wasn't a lot of time for introductions."

The detective smiled. "Lady, you're about as tough as I've seen them."

"Thanks." Annja sipped her coffee and found it hot and bitter. "I think."

"It was meant as a compliment," he assured her.

"You called him Icepick."

"That's his street tag. His real name is Gani Abiola."

After a moment of reflection, Annja shook her head. "I don't recognize the name."

"He usually hangs in Atlanta," the detective said.

"What's he doing here?"

"He hasn't said. McIntosh has been with him since we brought him in. The guy lawyered up almost immediately, but he's in the system. We're not starting from scratch on this one. We'll get answers. Guys like that can't run and hide for long."

Looking across the room, Annja saw Hallinger asleep at a desk. As archaeologists, both of them had learned to sleep anywhere and any time they had the chance.

"The prof's doing okay," the detective said.

"Good. We both got lucky. But the security guards didn't."

"Looks like two of them are going to pull through," the detective said.

Part of the acidic knot in Annja's stomach came undone. "I thought they were all dead."

"So did the EMTs and our guys when they first arrived on the scene. But they weren't. That's a good thing. You learn to take those when they come." The detective looked toward the back of the room. "Here comes McIntosh."

Turning in the chair, Annja looked back and saw the detective making his way toward them. McIntosh looked frayed. He carried his cowboy hat and jacket in one hand. His pistol stood out prominently on his hip.

"Hey," he said when he reached Annja.

"Hey."

"Want to get out of here?"

Feeling more claustrophobic in the detectives' bullpen than she had down in the furnace room, Annja stood. "I do."

"Let's collect the professor. I've got a deal for the two of you."

Suspicion filled Annja. McIntosh started toward Hallinger at once.

"What kind of deal?" Annja asked.

"The two of you are really interested in that treasure map you found on that stone, right?"

"Are you interested now, too?"

"Me?" McIntosh smiled and shook his head. "Not me. I don't believe in fairies or treasure maps."

"The map is real," Annja said.

"I believe you believe that, but from what you've said, you don't even know where to find that area on that rock."

"Not yet. But that doesn't mean we couldn't."

"That's what I told my boss." McIntosh stopped at Hallinger's side and gently shook him awake. Hallinger sat up slowly, reached for his glasses and put them on.

"Why would you tell your boss that?"

"Because he needed to know that you guys could probably find it."

"Why did he need to believe that?"

"So he could appropriate the money to send us there."

Annja stared at McIntosh.

"Your boss is sending us where?" Hallinger asked.

"To West Africa," McIntosh said. "Wherever you want to go." He looked at Annja. "If you're interested."

14

"Let me get this right," Doug Morrell said. "You're going to West Africa to go chasing after this Spider Stone?"

"I really can't talk about it." Annja pulled on her backpack and grabbed her suitcase. She'd packed light to come to Atlanta. Now she was paying for it because she didn't have everything she wanted from her Brooklyn loft.

"You can't talk about it," Doug repeated.

"That's right." Annja took a last look around the hotel room, then stepped through the door.

"Annja," Doug whined, "this is me. You can't hold out on me."

"I can. I am."

"That goes against everything our relationship stands for."

"We don't have a relationship." Annja stopped in front of the elevators. "We have an arrangement."

"That's cruel," Doug said.

The elevator doors opened and Annja entered. She hoped

she'd lose the phone signal, but she didn't. "You had first dibs on sending me to West Africa," she stated.

"West Africa is big," Doug said. "Where are you going in West Africa?"

"You're not thinking of sending Kristie there." Annja wanted to scream because she knew that was *exactly* what Doug Morrell would be thinking.

"Hey, there's a story here," Doug insisted.

"No monsters."

"It's Africa. There's gotta be zombies."

"I thought you said zombie stories are out with the show."

"We got zombies and an ancient treasure map in this," Doug said. "That's really cool."

The elevator opened and Annja stepped out into the lobby. McIntosh stood near the checkout desk with four men in plainclothes. They looked like an NFL offensive line.

"Annja, you gotta let me in on this," Doug whined. "You're all over the news. CNN. Fox News. MSNBC. I've even heard Larry King is trying to get hold of you."

"Larry King?" That stopped Annja for a moment. She liked watching Larry King, but she couldn't ever imagine meeting the man, much less being interviewed by him.

"That's what I was told. You're major news right now."

Those were the magic words. *Right now.* Annja knew several archaeologists who had enjoyed momentary fame during unusual finds or when some popular legend or myth caught the attention of the public. It never lasted.

"You can't buy this kind of advertising," Doug said.

Annja knew that, but she was thankful for it, too. She liked living her life out from under the microscope. Obscurity was a good thing. She didn't care for the limelight despite the pieces she did for *Chasing History's Monsters.*

Those were a means to an end, and she felt they gave her the opportunity to at least teach a little about what she knew and loved.

"Did you hear me?" Doug asked.

"I did." Annja walked to the checkout desk.

"I already took care of the paperwork," McIntosh said, taking her suitcase and handing it to one of his agents. "We're ready to roll. Finish your call."

"I don't think you're seeing the opportunity that you have here," Doug said. "This is freaking huge."

"Is that the television producer?" McIntosh asked.

Annja nodded.

"Let me have the phone." McIntosh radiated impatience. He held out his hand.

Pushing aside the immediate resentment she felt, Annja handed over the phone.

"Doug Morrell," McIntosh said in a voice that crackled with authority. "This is Special Agent McIntosh of Homeland Security. This conversation is over." He shut the cell phone and handed it back to Annja. "Let's go. We're going to have to hurry if we're going to make the flight out of Atlanta to Paris."

Annja was about to put the phone away when it rang. McIntosh shot her an irritated look. She answered the phone because of the look more than anything else. She wanted the relationship with McIntosh clarified. *I'm here because I want to be.*

"Hello."

"Is that guy really a special agent from Homeland Security?" Doug asked.

"Yes."

"Man, that is so awesome! Annja, seriously, you can't just shut me—"

Annja ended the call and turned the phone off.

McIntosh took the lead. As soon as they walked through the hotel's front door, they stepped out into a crowd of reporters. Annja stopped for just a moment, staring out in disbelief.

Hallinger stepped up beside her. "McIntosh kept the media out of the hotel," he said.

Voices filled the immediate area as television reporters began their spiels. A phalanx of Kirktown police parted the crowd. McIntosh took Annja by the elbow and led her to the second dark sedan in a five-car convoy of similar vehicles.

"Is it true you're going to find a lost treasure?" a female reporter asked.

"No comment," Annja answered automatically. You've been watching too many movies, she told herself.

McIntosh stopped for just a moment and turned toward the reporter. "Where did you get that information?"

The reporter immediately responded with another question. "What are you going to do with the treasure when you find it?"

"No comment," McIntosh responded.

Annja slid a pair of sunglasses from her backpack and looked at McIntosh. What are you up to? she wondered.

One of the special agents opened the car door and McIntosh folded her inside, sliding in to join her. She was sandwiched between McIntosh and another Homeland Security agent. Hallinger was put into the front passenger seat. The reporters and other members of the crowd pressed in against the windows.

Annja placed her backpack on the floorboard between her feet. She unzipped one of the pockets, took out a sheet of paper and handed it to McIntosh.

"What's this?" McIntosh asked.

"A list of books I'm going to need."

"Books?"

"Reference books. History books. Maps."

"Is this going to be expensive?"

"Probably. Most of those are textbooks. They're not cheap. I already have most of them in my loft, but you'll have to have someone purchase those for us along the way."

Hallinger reached into his pocket and came out with a folded piece of paper. "I made a list, too."

Reluctantly, McIntosh took the professor's list, as well.

"If there are any duplicates," Hallinger said, "just cross them off."

"Actually, make sure we get two of each," Annja said. "It would be better if we had our own books to search through."

"Well," Hallinger said, "that is true. What with notes and possibly needing to consult the same book at the same time."

"Didn't you learn anything while you were getting your degrees?" McIntosh asked.

"Archaeology isn't like law enforcement," Annja said pointedly. "We don't get an updated list every day of who the bad guys are and what steps to take when we find them. There are thousands of years of human habitation to learn about, and millions of years before that. A lot of archaeologists specialize. But some of us, like Professor Hallinger and myself, understand that archaeology and the study of civilization is a lifelong pursuit. Even your doctor hands you off to a specialist when things get to be unfamiliar. That specialist is just like us. He or she will open a book, get on the Internet or call a colleague to get more information."

McIntosh held up his hands. "Point taken." He handed the lists to the agent on the other side of Annja. "Call it in."

The agent made the call, told whomever he was talking to that the books needed to be delivered to Charles de Gaulle Airport in Paris and started reading off the book titles.

Annja focused on McIntosh. "Do you want to tell us now why Homeland Security has agreed to fly us to West Africa?"

McIntosh grinned at her. "For the treasure hunt, of course."

Annja just looked at him.

"I thought a little humor might help," McIntosh said.

"Two security guards died last night," Annja said. "I'm not in the mood for humor."

McIntosh sobered.

Despite his devil-may-care attitude, Annja could see that he was tired, too.

"Actually," McIntosh said in a more subdued tone, "you're going to be bait."

"GANI ABIOLA, the guy from last night that you came to know as Icepick," McIntosh said, "is the nephew of Tafari."

"The West African warlord you mentioned," Hallinger said.

Annja sat at the table in the small security room McIntosh had arranged at the Hartsfield-Jackson Atlanta International Airport. She picked at the breakfast tray the security personnel had delivered right after they'd arrived.

"Right," McIntosh agreed. "Tafari has become a person of interest to Homeland Security."

"You mentioned that he had ties to al-Qaeda," Annja said. "That he'd provided training camps for them."

McIntosh nodded and tapped a button on the notebook computer that had been delivered with the meal. Someone had put together the file he was now using. "The department has reason to believe that Tafari's exposure to al-Qaeda goes deeper than that."

Pictures scrolled across the computer screen. Several of them showed scenes in the African savanna lands, filled with short trees and scruffy brush. They were obviously surveillance shots taken with long-range lenses.

"Intelligence suggests that Tafari has been part of a biological-weapons research effort on behalf of al-Qaeda," McIntosh went on.

"What makes them think that?" Annja asked.

"That's classified information, Ms. Creed."

"You said we're being used as bait."

"To draw Tafari out. Not al-Qaeda."

"And if we just happen across a biological-weapons research center while we're out in the bush?" Annja asked.

McIntosh shook his head and looked very confident. "You won't be anywhere near al-Qaeda."

"You can guarantee that?" Hallinger asked.

"I feel very confident about that," McIntosh replied.

"That's reassuring," Annja said.

"Look," McIntosh said, "I understand the sarcasm. I really do. Personally, I didn't want to put you people in the field." His eyes turned harder. "You're civilians. You're not trained for this. If I was in charge of this expedition, neither one of you would be going. We've got other people that we have access to that have some training. Enough to save themselves." He looked at Hallinger. "You've got no experience at all when it comes to this."

"I'm not going to argue with you," the professor responded.

"And you." McIntosh looked at Annja and took a deep breath.

Annja returned his challenging gaze full measure.

"You tackle guys in the path of oncoming cars," McIntosh grated. "Not exactly the brightest thing I've ever seen. There's a certain lack of subtlety in something like that."

Annja resisted the impulse to fire a rejoinder.

"Whether you go with us or without us," McIntosh said, "you know that Tafari is interested in that Spider Stone you found. Going over there by yourselves—if you could find someone to pick up the tab—isn't a good idea, either. No matter what you do, you're going to be dealing with him. You're better off letting us deal with him. That's what we're trained to do."

Silence hung in the room for a moment.

"You know," Hallinger said quietly, "Special Agent McIntosh has a valid point."

Reluctantly, Annja agreed.

Someone knocked on the door.

"Enter," McIntosh said.

One of the agents posted outside opened the door and stepped inside. He held up a hand. "Five minutes until we board."

McIntosh nodded.

The agent stepped back into the hall.

"Okay," McIntosh said, looking back at Annja and Hallinger, "it's show time. Are you in or out?"

ANNJA WOKE on the plane. It was dark. For a moment she didn't remember where she was and she knew she was very tired. She traveled a lot, but there was something about flying at night that she found unnerving. A heavy book rested on her lap, and she shifted it to a more comfortable position.

"I could put it in the overhead compartment."

McIntosh sat on her left. He held out a hand.

Annja memorized the page number and passed the book over to him. He stood long enough to put the book away.

"Pillow or blanket?" he asked.

"No. Thanks."

McIntosh dropped into his seat. "You okay?"

"Yeah."

"Looked like you were sleeping okay."

"I shouldn't have slept," Annja said. "There's a lot I should be doing."

"You're tired." McIntosh shifted in his seat until he was comfortable. "When you're tired, you're supposed to sleep."

"I slept a little in Paris." They'd had an eight-hour layover in the City of Lights. Everything was hurry-up-and-wait.

While they were in Paris, Annja had thought about Roux. She'd almost given in to the temptation to call him, but she didn't know what she'd have said. Trying to figure out where Roux fit in her life was confusing.

"You slept maybe three hours in Paris," McIntosh commented.

"I've slept less."

"The night before was no picnic, either. It catches up to you after a while. You're not going to do yourself any good if you're dead on your feet when we get to Dakar."

"I'll be fine by the time we get there." Annja lifted the window cover.

A silver quarter moon hung over a bed of fluffy white clouds. The sky was indigo above the clouds but quickly deepened to black.

"How far out are we?" Annja asked. She'd been immersed in one of the books containing topographical maps that had been delivered to de Gaulle and hadn't noted the time.

McIntosh glanced at his watch. "About two hours. You still have time for a nap."

They were scheduled to land in Dakar at 8:15 p.m. local time.

Annja closed the window cover. "You've got a fixation on naps, Special Agent McIntosh."

"I just wish I could sleep. I never can on an airplane," he said.

"Why?"

McIntosh shrugged. "I never have been able to."

Annja looked over her shoulder, spotting Hallinger and the other Homeland Security agents. McIntosh had assured her that most of the men with them had come out of the CIA and had previous experience in West Africa. Most of them, Annja had noted, were also African-American. They looked like grim, competent men.

"Nobody else seems to be having a problem." Annja resettled in her seat.

"Yeah, well, I wish I wasn't."

"You're not quite living up to the big, bad special-agent image, McIntosh."

"This isn't exactly what I set out to do."

"You didn't want to be a spy guy?"

McIntosh's lips curled into a smile. "I wanted the babes. Don't get me wrong there. I grew up on James Bond movies. But after you reach a certain point in your life, you realize those are just movies."

Annja smiled back. She liked that McIntosh could be honest, and that he'd seen the world differently as a boy. Some men never grew up.

"Then how did you get to be a spy?" she asked.

"I'm not a spy. I'm a federal agent."

"There's a difference?"

"I think so. I chase threats to our country. It's an important job. My dad was a cop. I was, too. He did Vietnam. I did the first Gulf War. After that, cop work made sense. I was good at what I did. Made detective in Atlanta pretty quick. I liked the work. Putting bad guys behind bars. I thought that's what I'd do until I retired, then maybe join my dad's security agency. He started that up when he pulled the pin."

"Then why the change to Homeland Security?"

McIntosh was quiet for a moment. His eyes didn't meet hers. "My mom and dad had never been to New York City. They'd always talked about going. My mom more than my dad."

Dread knotted Annja's stomach. She was certain she knew what was coming, but she couldn't stop it. She'd elicited this by trying to question McIntosh's motivations.

"They went to New York," McIntosh went on in a voice that was devoid of emotion. "They were inside the World Trade Center the morning it came down. We were on the phone, Dad giving me grief about something. Just like usual. Then…they weren't there anymore." He was silent for a moment. "After that, when the Department of Homeland Security was formed, it made perfect sense to me that I be part of it. So I've been working out of the Atlanta PD ever since."

Without a word, Annja reached over and took his hand. She felt the calluses under her fingertips. "This isn't the hand of a guy who just rides a desk."

"No." McIntosh squeezed her hand gently, accepting the support she offered. "I have a small ranch. I do a lot of the work myself." He looked at her. "You know, I've been partnered with a lot of guys who would tackle a perp onto the hood of a moving car, but I wouldn't want them holding my hand."

Annja laughed, and in that, with the return of the humor, the melancholy was put in abeyance. At least for the moment. She was sure it returned regularly.

"So tell me," Annja said.

"What?"

"Why are you scared of sleeping on planes?"

McIntosh smiled. "I was on a plane that went down, barely survived the crash."

She looked into his eyes. "You're lying."

"I have episodes of missing time on airplane flights."

"Fear of alien abduction?" That was an urban myth made popular by *The X-Files.* Annja shook her head and rolled her eyes.

"Don't believe that one, either?" he asked.

"I'll know the truth when I hear it."

McIntosh took a deep breath. "You ever watch *The Twilight Zone?*"

"Sometimes. The Rod Serling version or the later one?"

"The classic episode with William Shatner."

"The gremlin on the wing?" Annja laughed, and it felt good to do that. For the moment, they were thirty-five thousand feet in the air and Kirktown's violence and the danger coming with their arrival in Dakar seemed a million miles away.

"Hey," he protested. "That's not funny."

"Yeah, it is."

Then McIntosh's eyes crinkled as he smiled, too. "Yeah, I suppose maybe it is." He was quiet for a moment. "In all seriousness, Tafari is a dangerous man."

"I kind of got that the first time he almost killed us. I learned clue-gathering from watching Scooby-Doo as a little girl."

McIntosh shook his head. "I can't imagine you as a little girl."

"I was. Once."

"Where did you grow up?"

"New Orleans."

McIntosh grimaced. "Not a lot of good things have happened there lately."

"No."

"But you live in Brooklyn now."

"I see somebody did a background check," she said.

"I did an Internet search, too. You beat Kristie Chatham hands down when it comes to archaeology."

Annja cocked an eyebrow, waiting for the rest of it. McIntosh didn't say anything more. She kept looking at him.

"What?" he asked finally.

"That's all you're going to say?"

"If I said anything else, I think I'd be in trouble. No matter what I said. And I really don't want to jeopardize the hand-holding because it kind of helps on the whole gremlin thing."

Smiling, Annja leaned back in her chair. "Wise move, Special Agent McIntosh." She closed her eyes and slept.

15

Annja stood as the plane door was opened and the passengers were allowed to start filing out. McIntosh handed down her book, then grabbed his own kit and waited.

"We'll let everyone else deplane first," he said. "Then we'll move as a group."

"Doesn't that mean they'll get us all in one concentrated burst?" Annja asked.

McIntosh frowned at her, but his eyes still held a twinkle. "You've got a demented mind."

"Ever wonder why Scooby and the gang separated every episode?"

"I'd always thought it was so they could get confused over who was who under the sheets. If it had been an armed engagement, somebody would have gotten killed."

"Okay, that takes the fun out of it," Annja said.

"I just want us to stay safe."

Annja took out her cell phone and turned it on. There were nineteen missed calls. Eighteen of them were from

Doug Morrell. The other was from a number that surprised her.

Annja punched in the number and waited.

"The producer?" McIntosh asked.

Annja shook her head, but she didn't bother to explain.

"Ah, Annja, you decided to return my call." Garin Braden's voice was deep and guttural, reflecting his German heritage. The voice fit the man. Garin stood six feet four inches tall and had broad shoulders and a powerful build. His long dark hair matched his magnetic black eyes. A goatee usually framed his mouth and gave his face a roguish cast.

"I did," she replied.

"And what would Roux say if he knew?"

"To stay away from you and not trust you, I imagine," Annja replied easily.

McIntosh looked at her.

Annja shook her head and listened to Garin roaring with laughter.

"You do amuse me. I appreciate that."

"What did you need?"

"Nothing. I just happened to see the footage of you in that small town in Georgia—"

"Kirktown."

"Whatever it's called. Anyway, I saw it and I thought I'd give you a call and see how you were faring."

The plane was emptying slowly, but most of the passengers were now off.

"I don't have a lot of time," Annja said.

"I won't take up much of it, then. Are you well?"

"Yes."

"Good."

"Were you worried?" Annja asked, immediately suspicious.

"Not really," Garin admitted. "You've always shown yourself to be a woman who could handle herself." For a moment, an awkward silence stretched between them.

"Was there anything besides checking on my health that was on your mind?" Annja asked.

"A warning, perhaps. I take it Roux hasn't been forthcoming with everything you can expect now that you have the sword in your possession."

For just an instant, Annja felt the sword hilt press against her palm. She didn't know if the sword felt threatened or she did. Maybe it was both.

"I get the feeling there's a lot he hasn't told me," Annja said.

"The news reports mentioned a Spider Stone. According to the legend behind it, the stone was supposed to be some kind of gift from a god."

"Anansi."

"Ah," Garin said. "The spider god. There's a lot of power in an entity like that."

Entity? Annja thought. Not mythical being?

"Dealing with something like that, if the stone truly was given by Anansi to the person who carried it, could prove decidedly dangerous."

"I'll keep that in mind," Annja said.

"Do so. There will be powerful men after an item such as that."

"Do any particular names come to mind?" Annja asked.

"No, but I do know there are evil men in the world. I don't want you to come to any harm until we meet again."

Because you want to harm me? Annja wondered. A chill ghosted up Annja's spine. She remembered how Garin had attacked her in her loft. Then they'd turned around and had breakfast with Roux, who'd also come calling, and then he'd loaned them his private jet while she finished up the bloody business relating to the Beast of Gévaudan.

Like Roux, Garin Braden was a confusing man.

"I would like to see you again, Annja," Garin said. "Call me. We'll do lunch anywhere in the world that you want to."

"Sure," she answered casually. She wanted to see him again, too. Not because he was good-looking and rich, though that would have been enough for most women. But because he might talk and reveal some of what he'd seen and done during the past five hundred years.

Roux would never do that.

"Be safe, Annja," Garin said. "If you need anything, call me."

While Annja was trying to figure out how to respond to that, Garin broke the connection.

"THE CITY'S DIFFERENT than I thought it would be," McIntosh said.

"How?" Annja studied the Dakar sights through the tinted window of the rental sedan the Homeland Security team had secured.

"It's bigger. A lot bigger. And modern."

Annja smiled. "Don't tell me you were expecting grass huts."

"No, but I just didn't expect *this*. It seems like any city in the United States. Except for all the French advertising."

"French is the national language," Annja said.

Neon lights splashed over the car's windows. The downtown area was still throbbing and active. Pedestrians filled the streets as they walked from bars and taverns. The Atlantic Ocean was only a short distance away to the west.

"Over two million people live in Dakar," Annja went on. "A lot more come into the city to work at service jobs in hotels, bars, tourist areas. The architecture of the newer sections of the city looks like any other large city. But if you see the older sections, like the Kermel Market, you'll see colonial houses that date back to the mid-nineteenth century. The big market, Sandaga, is located in a neo-Sudanese building that is absolutely wonderful to walk through."

"Fond memories?" McIntosh asked.

"I read it in the travel guide," Annja said, laughing.

"Probably won't be a lot of time for sight-seeing," McIntosh informed her.

"I know."

"Who are we meeting here?"

"Jozua Ganesvoort," Annja said.

"He's an archaeologist?"

"No. He owns an import-export business that's been in Dakar for over two hundred years."

"Why are we meeting him?"

"Because he's an armchair historian who has access to ships' logs that date back to the early years of the slave trade."

"And you need the ships' logs?"

Annja looked at him. "Yes."

"Why?"

"To see if we can find a reference to Yohance. The first Yohance. The one whose village was razed and who was taken into captivity and sold as a slave. If we find him listed, there may be some mention of where he was from. Once we get close enough, the map carved on the stone should be enough to get us the rest of the way."

"You don't have to do that," McIntosh said.

Annja felt slightly irritated. "Yes, we do. That's what Professor Hallinger and I came here to do."

"You're going to be exposed if you start traipsing around all over this city."

Her irritation grew. "Hallinger and I didn't come here to sit around as bait."

"We can't guarantee your safety unless you follow procedure."

The car stopped at a light. Shadows bumped and moved across the windows. McIntosh reached for his pistol under his jacket.

Annja looked at the men and women, young and old, lurching at the car. Many of them were maimed, missing fingers and hands and eyes, their faces horribly scarred. Their skin was mottled with leprosy or ashen-gray with illness.

"Calm down," Annja said. "They're just beggars. The city is full of them."

The beggars pleaded in a number of languages, all of it sounding sad and hopeless.

Annja reached into her pocket for some money. Quickly, she pressed money into the hands before her.

When the light changed, the beggars backed off.

"It's not a good idea to give them money," the driver said. "Once they find out you'll do it, they'll stay after you."

"You've been here before?" Annja asked.

"A few times." The man looked at her in the rearview mirror as he pulled through the intersection.

"Then you know that those people can't do anything else but beg," Annja said. "They live outside the city in cardboard huts and sleep three and four to a room. They have to get water from a standpipe every day and sometimes stand in line for hours to do that. Then they have to walk or crawl or drag themselves into this city every day in hopes of begging for just enough money to do it all again the next day."

The driver looked away.

Annja leaned back in the seat and settled into the shadows. Neon colors continued to slash across the windows.

"Sorry," McIntosh said. "I guess I overreacted. For a minute there I could have sworn we'd been overrun by zombies."

"They're just poor and sick," Annja said. "They can't fix that. Someone has to help them. That's one of the things I hate about traveling. No one seems to care about the poor. Governments don't want to deal with the issue because it's too expensive. And tourists feel like their vacations are getting interrupted." She took a deep breath. "There's so much history in these places, but all the resources have been tapped out, or they haven't been able to compete in world markets." Annja sighed.

They rode the rest of the way to the hotel in strained silence.

Annja felt guilty about that, too. She wasn't being fair. McIntosh and the other agents hadn't known what they were getting into.

She'd overreacted because she'd almost allowed herself to forget.

ALONE AT LAST, Annja stripped off her clothing and stepped into the deep bathtub in her hotel room at the Novotel Dakar. The hotel was located near the business district. Her room was at the front of the building, facing the Atlantic Ocean and the Ile de Goree.

The scented bath smelled divine, and she could already feel the heat from the water penetrating her muscles. Lying back, she luxuriated in the bath, letting it soothe away the aches and abrasions from the fights she'd had. In Atlanta, she'd only taken showers, always in a hurry.

Tonight it was comfort time.

She loved baths. She'd had a large tub installed in her loft when she'd signed her first contract with *Chasing History's Monsters.* In the beginning, she'd thought the show—and she—would only last a season. She wasn't an actress and the show—in her opinion—wasn't very promising. So she'd splurged on the tub and tried not to feel guilty.

Taking a deep breath, she submerged, sliding under the water and letting the heat soak into her. She closed her eyes, feeling almost weightless in the water.

Don't go to sleep, she warned herself. More than once she'd woken in cold water, undoing all the good the hot bath had done.

In an effort to stay awake, she thought about McIntosh.

She was certain that he'd put her in the big suite on purpose, and she doubted that Hallinger or any of the Homeland Security agents had matching accommodations.

The room's a peace offering, she realized. She wondered if she needed to apologize for the episode in the car on the way over. After that, her mind wandered to other thoughts of McIntosh that were entirely healthy and not exactly conducive to relaxation. She decided to push all of that out of her mind and concentrate on the puzzle of the Spider Stone. That's what you're here to do, she reminded herself. You're not some kind of bounty hunter for terrorists.

Unable to hold her breath any longer, she regretfully

surfaced. The knots of tension that had tightened her back and shoulders had, for the most part, disappeared.

Reaching over the side of the tub, Annja dried her hands and arms on a towel and reached into her backpack where she'd placed it on a small folding table. Working in the tub wasn't new to her. Her mind was too busy to properly soak if she didn't occupy it. She took the Spider Stone from one of the pockets and held it up to the light.

Amber gleamed like cold fire along the striations.

Hallinger had enlarged photos of the stone in his room, claiming that he'd rather work with them. Since he didn't know the language, he was working with topographical maps of Senegal, trying to overlay the map on the stone onto the country.

While she'd been on the plane, Annja had worked through most of the message, but she wanted to check her findings. There was only one place to do that.

She got out of the bath, wrapped herself in a bathrobe and set up her computer. When she was online, she logged onto the message boards.

There were several messages. Evidently the people on the board had figured out who she was. She usually logged in with a different name on each project and sent private messages to people she'd worked with in the past who had proved reliable.

Most of the messages were from teens with out-of-control hormones, or men who were old enough to know better. Interestingly enough, there were also overtures from females, which was really different from the normal responses.

She scrolled through a number of propositions and jokes looking for anything that might be useful. Finally she came across a private message from hausaboy. Annja opened it.

Hey, Annja. I got most of the message translated. Cool stuff. Lotta work. Here's the story, and I say "story," even though Hausa believers might consider that term sacrilegious, because that's how this tale comes across to me.

Sometime years ago, one of the earliest ancestors of this particular Hausa village—think the name translates into "Falson's Egg"—was under attack from fierce enemies. He prayed to Anansi, who was the chosen god of his people, and asked that his village might be spared.

Unfortunately, that was one of Anansi's less responsible days. He was off on his own pursuits and ignored the pleas of the villagers he'd chosen to adopt as his own people. That happened sometimes with any of the gods of whatever mythology you want to ascribe to.

The village was destroyed by fire or lightning—I can't be sure of the translation. Something like that.

Annja had struggled with the same translation. Fire and lightning were interchangeable in some instances.

When Anansi returned to the village, he was sad. He promised the people who had survived that they would be safe from that point on. The villagers had to travel far away. Anansi had to find them, but he did.

Anansi gave the medicine man the stone. The location of the new village was drawn on the stone's surface, as was Anansi's likeness. It was his promise that they would be taken care of.

As you know, Anansi wasn't around the night the slavers ransacked the village.

There's also some mention of a curse against anyone not of the village who might come into possession of the stone.

Great, Annja thought. All I need is to be cursed.

Thought you might want to know that last part. Personally, I don't believe in curses.

Annja quickly typed out a response.

Hey, hausaboy, thanks for all your help. I'd come up with pretty much the same thing. If there's anything I can ever do for you, please let me know.

After she sent the e-mail, Annja went back to her bath. The water had chilled slightly while she'd been busy. She turned on the hot water and opened the drain at the same time. Almost immediately, the water began to warm.

She thought about the possibility of a curse as she studied the Spider Stone. Curses were old. They depended on local belief systems and chance. If enough people believed in a curse, it didn't take much coincidence to make believers out of everyone around. As a result, curses were generally the first line of defense for grave sites.

Reaching for her backpack, she rooted for the topographical maps of Senegal she'd had McIntosh arrange for her. She'd been over them before, during the layover in Paris and while on the plane. Maybe now that she was relaxed, something might jump out at her.

She froze when she heard a noise in the bedroom.

It wasn't repeated.

Annja stood in the bathtub. She reached for the flannel shorts and Brooklyn Dodgers jersey she liked to sleep in when she was traveling.

She pulled on the clothing as quickly and silently as she could. Surreptitious noises came from the outer room again, and this time there was no mistake.

Someone's in the room! The thought crawled across Annja's mind and sent a shiver up her spine.

16

The bathroom was a dead end. There was nowhere to go, no real room to fight even with the spacious accommodations.

Annja summoned the sword to her hand, wrapping her fingers around the hilt as she took a firm grip. She took in a deep, quiet breath, then let it out as she slowed her heart and forced herself to be calm.

The only choice was whether to stay in the room until whoever was out there came in after her or charge out to meet them. Frugal or foolhardy.

Annja decided to set her own destiny. That had always been her preferred path. Gripping the door handle, she twisted it and pulled the door open.

Four young and hard-eyed men stood inside her room, lit by the bedside lamp. All of them were dressed in American-style warm-ups and basketball jerseys, as if they'd just stepped off the court of an NBA game. Except these men were carrying suppressed pistols and machetes. Two of them stood guard near the bathroom door while the other two went through Annja's suitcases and books.

They didn't expect her to come out of the bathroom. Evidently they felt confident enough to try to search the room before any violence broke out.

Definitely not random burglars, Annja thought. They're here for the stone. She was conscious of the slight weight of it in her pocket even as she drew back the sword and launched herself at the first man.

The man lifted the pistol and fired. The bullets cut the air by Annja's head. She didn't hold back, couldn't hold back.

Months of practice with the sword had made it more a part of her than it had been when the pieces had re-formed. Annja sliced into the man's forearm. Before the shock or the pain had time to register on him, before his pistol had time to hit the floor, Annja swept the sword across his body.

She darted behind the man, taking brief refuge there. Bullets slapped into the stunned man.

Annja whirled, the world slowing down around her, and turned to face the second man by the bathroom door. He was only then registering surprise that he'd shot his compatriot instead of Annja. Or maybe he was surprised about the sword she wielded with such deadly skill.

Either way, his surprise didn't last long.

Annja lunged with the sword, bringing it up as she ducked beneath the man's outstretched arm. She heard the pistol cough twice before the sword pierced the man's chest.

The man sagged immediately. He dropped his machete and grabbed Annja's wrists. Dying, he tried to bring the pistol in line with her head.

Annja kicked her attacker backward. Still transfixed by the sword, he stumbled toward the other two men. The remaining invaders abandoned their search of the suitcases and reached for their weapons.

The suite was large, providing some room to maneuver.

Annja ran toward the only light on in the room. Jumping up, she delivered a high kick to the lamp, shattering the lightbulb in a shower of sparks.

She landed in a crouch, one hand on the floor to maintain her balance. Pistols coughed behind her, and muzzle-flashes marked the locations of the two men. They had remained close together.

The darkness inside the room was almost complete. Only a sliver of moonlight penetrated the heavy drapes and fell across the floor.

Annja gripped the sword and rose, standing straight and making for the wall, working from memory. Her bare feet made no sound as she moved.

The two men spoke in nervous voices. They spoke a dialect Annja didn't understand, but their anxiety and anger were easy to read.

Annja knew she could have headed for the door, but she couldn't be sure they hadn't locked it behind them. And fumbling with the lock in the darkness, making all that noise, would draw a hail of bullets.

The second bedside lamp winked on, unleashing a pool of dim yellow light. The man who had turned it on was squatted down behind the bed, on the other side from Annja. His partner was across the room.

Both men started firing, but Annja had already leaped forward, the sword in both hands. She brought the blade down, splitting the gunman's head and turning the sheets crimson. As she vaulted over the dead man, she kicked the light, plunging the room into darkness again.

For a moment she held her position, listening intently. The traffic noises in the street reached her ears.

"Stay back!" the man warned in heavily accented English. "Stay back or I will kill you!"

Annja tracked the man's voice, realizing he was making his way toward the door. Moonlight fell across his back for just a moment, outlining his upper body and blinking against the gun.

"Who sent you?" Annja asked, and moved to the side immediately.

Muzzle-flashes tore holes in the darkness.

"Did Tafari send you for the Spider Stone?" Annja whipped back to the other side of the room and advanced in long strides.

The man fired again, and this time the pistol blew back empty, the sound sharp and distinct. He turned and fled, his feet slapping against the floor.

Annja pursued, knowing that none of the other men were alive. She wanted at least one witness who could talk.

The door opened and the light from the hallway hurt Annja's eyes. She blinked but never broke stride, managing to grab the door before it closed.

The man broke to the right, running hard. He still carried his machete in his left hand.

Annja ran after him, driving her legs like pistons, quickly closing in on the man. Ahead, a young couple turned the corner from the bank of elevators. They saw the man with the machete and froze like deer in headlights.

The man lifted his machete, his intent clear.

Releasing the sword, Annja felt it fade away as she threw herself forward in a feet-first baseball slide. The carpet bit into her skin, promising abrasions and burns, but she collided with the back of the man's legs before he could bring down the machete.

As the man buckled under her onslaught, Annja reached up and caught his arm, controlling the machete. The young man managed to get the woman out of the way as Annja and her prey skidded into the wall.

Off balance, Annja hit the wall hard enough to drive the wind from her lungs. Dazed for a second, she held on to the man's arm, then struggled to her knees as her opponent tried to fight his way free. Annja closed her free hand into a fist and hit the man in the jaw. His eyes rolled back and he slumped over.

Breathing raggedly, her breath just coming back to her, Annja looked up at the young couple. "Do you speak English?"

"That," the young man whispered hoarsely, "was incredible! I thought he was going to kill us!"

"Yes," the young woman at his side said. "We speak English."

Annja thought she detected a German accent but wasn't certain. "Do you have a cell phone?"

"He just came out of nowhere!" the man said. "I felt like I was in one of those American slasher movies!"

Great, Annja thought, feeling the aches and pains seeping into her again and wrecking all that the bath had accomplished.

"I have a cell phone." The young woman held it up.

"Please call the hotel and ask for security." Annja started going through the unconscious man's pockets, looking for identification. "Tell them what happened."

"I saw my life flash before my eyes!" the man said. Then he held his head. "I've got to sit down. I'm going to be sick." He swayed unsteadily and sat against the opposite wall. He stared at the unconscious man. "He really was going to kill us, wasn't he?"

Annja didn't answer. The young man was going into shock. But the woman with him was clear and concise as she dealt with the hotel staff.

A shadow fell across Annja. Startled because she'd sensed no approach, she reached for the machete lying nearby. She had the wooden hilt in her hand when she saw the old woman standing before her.

The woman wore a dark red dress that almost reached the ground. A scarf of a similar color held her cotton-white hair back from her lined face. Annja guessed that the woman was seventy, with a lot of hard years behind her, but she could have been even older. She carried a gnarled wooden staff in one hand.

"You have finally come," the old woman said in accented English. "I knew that you would. My prophecies are never wrong."

Prophecies? Annja stared at the old woman.

Then hotel security arrived in force and things really got crazy.

TAFARI WALKED into the village with impunity. He carried pistols in each hand. They were the Glocks that his nephew had sent him, with extended magazines and fully automatic function. He used them to cut down two Hausa warriors who challenged him.

Neither of the men carried firearms. One had a tribal spear that was probably more heirloom than weapon, and the other had an ax used for chopping firewood. The bullets smashed into them and drove them backward.

The cries of women and children pierced the chatter of automatic weapons. Those silenced, one by one, as the raiders cut them down.

Tafari had given orders that there were to be no survivors. He kept walking, picking out targets as they appeared, changing magazines in the pistols as he needed to.

"I am Tafari!" he yelled at the villagers. "I am the death-bringer!"

He knew he looked the part. Naked except for a loincloth, his body was covered in painted tribal markings. White paint lifted his face out of the darkness and made it a skull.

His men flared around him, many of them dressed and marked as he was. Two of them carried military flamethrowers and sent streams of liquid fire rolling into the thatched huts. The wood caught instantly and burned incredibly fast.

Gray smoke poured across the sky, giving the illusion of chasing back the night.

Four jeeps circled the village deep in the savanna. Machine gunners on the rear decks executed anyone who tried to escape the slaughter at the village.

"I am Tafari!" he howled. "Beloved of the gods! I speak the words of the gods! You chose to ignore my warnings! You chose to disobey me! Now you will all die!"

In only a few minutes, the village was filled with the dead and the dying. The stink of burned flesh mixed with the acrid smoke.

His weapons recharged, Tafari led the hunt for the survivors. They killed them where they lay one by one.

When they were finished, Tafari gave orders to bring the chief and his grandson to him. Tafari stood waiting in the center of the village. He had sent men into the village to capture the two before they had begun the killing.

The chief and his grandson, a boy of nine or ten, were forced to their knees in front of Tafari. Fear strained the old man's gray-stubbled face though he tried not to show it.

"You are an abomination," the chief declared. His voice was hoarse with emotion and from the smoke. Tears leaked down his withered cheeks.

Tafari struck the old man with one of his pistols, breaking the teeth down to yellow stumps. The chief cried out in pain and collapsed to the ground. Blood pooled from his split lips.

The boy cried out and reached for his grandfather, hugging him around the waist.

Holstering his pistols, Tafari reached over his shoulder for the machete in the leather sheath and drew the weapon clear. Firelight gleamed along the blade's keen edge.

The old man looked up as Tafari swung the machete. He barely had time to get a hand up and whisper, "No!"

Then the blade sliced through the old man's hand, dropping his fingers to the ground, and cut deeply into his neck. Blood spattered Tafari's face and chest at the impact. It took Tafari two more swings to hack the head free of the skinny body.

The boy screamed in fear and backed away from the corpse. He tried to get up and run, but Zifa backhanded him to the ground.

"Don't kill him," Tafari ordered. "Someone has to carry the message."

Zifa nodded. Instead, he stepped on the boy's shin and broke the bone with a snap. The boy wept almost silently, wrapping his arms tightly around himself.

Grabbing the old man's head, Tafari squatted and held it in the terrified boy's face.

The boy closed his eyes, shivering in fear.

Tafari relished the fear. Fear was indelible. Once someone was marked by fear, that emotion left permanent scars. He reached out and slapped the boy's face. "Open your eyes," he screamed.

The boy tried to turn his head away. Zifa caught his head and forced it against the ground.

Slapping the boy again, Tafari said, "Open your eyes or I will kill you like I killed your grandfather."

The boy opened his eyes, almost convulsing in fright.

"I am Tafari. Tell everyone who did this to your grandfather. To your people. And to your village. Do you understand?"

The boy nodded.

"Say my name."

"Tafari."

"Good. Tell all that you talk to that they will not listen to Jaineba anymore. Tell them that they will not attack the refinery trucks and equipment anymore. Those things are now under my protection. Tell me that you understand."

"I understand."

"Then you may live." Tafari stood and nodded at Zifa.

Stepping back, Zifa yanked the boy to his feet. He stood awkwardly on his broken leg, lip trembling and eyes watering.

"Go," Tafari said. "Before I change my mind."

Limping, the boy made his way through the burning remnants of the village. He disappeared into the night.

"He might not live to see morning," Zifa said. "There are many creatures in the night."

Tafari caught movement from the corner of his eye. When he glanced up, he saw the pharaoh-eagle owl gliding above the treetops, skirting the flames that licked at the huts. He took heart in the omen of good fortune.

"If he does not," Tafari said, "the message will still be sent. These people will obey me."

Scanning the immediate area, Tafari found a pole about four feet long and used his machete to sharpen both ends. He thrust one end into the ground, then shoved the chief's head on top of the other end. The pole wavered for a moment, but held up under the weight.

Tafari stood back and admired his handiwork. Even if the boy died somewhere in the night, daybreak would still see his message written for all to see.

The sound of a roaring engine drew near.

Sheathing his machete, Tafari again drew the pistols. He stood waiting.

Four men rode in the jeep. They were from the communications camp and had been instructed to bring him word of the capture of the Spider Stone.

"The team failed," a slim warrior with an eye patch told Tafari.

"How?"

"They went after the woman. They thought she would be the easiest to capture. Instead, she killed three of them."

Tafari digested that. It wasn't easy. He hadn't expected the woman to be much of a problem. The way his nephew had explained what had happened in Georgia was that the police had intercepted them.

"She killed three men?" Tafari asked.

"Yes."

That put things in a different light. "What about the other archaeologist?"

"They never got to him."

Tafari waved the man away. Turning, he looked at the head mounted on the pole. It was a temporary setback. Nothing more. He wouldn't let it be anything more.

"Send more men," he told Zifa. "Tell them to kill the woman if they have to. I want the Spider Stone."

"It will be done."

Tafari gazed out across the carnage that remained of the village. The flames leaped high into the night sky, illuminating the face of the village chief. His adversaries didn't know whom they were dealing with, but he would show them.

17

"They killed *themselves?*"

Seated on a chair outside her hotel room, Annja returned the Dakar police inspector's gaze. "Yes," she replied, keeping a straight face.

The inspector's name was Oumar Mbaye. Short and stout, he wore the khaki uniform and red beret of the local police. He was in his early forties and had served on the Senegalese police department for twenty of those years. He'd expressed that to Annja in an effort to keep her calm, and maybe to intimidate her a little.

Annja was calm, but she wasn't intimidated. The only thing that had unnerved her was the old woman who stood just down the hallway.

Lurked down the hallway, Annja thought irritably. That's definitely a lurk. She glanced at the woman standing there so patiently and calmly, as if she had all night. It was beginning to look as if Mbaye's investigation was going to take all night.

"They killed each other with knives?" Mbaye's eyebrows were raised in disbelief.

"Machetes," Annja corrected. "Those were machetes that I saw. Guns and machetes. If they had knives, I didn't see them."

"But they had guns!" Mbaye almost spluttered.

"I know they had guns. They shot at me with them."

"And they *missed*."

Annja thought about that for a moment. "Perhaps that's why they brought the machetes."

"Because they were such terrible shots with the guns?"

Annja gave him a winning smile. "That sounds good, don't you think?"

Mbaye frowned at her. "No, I don't think that sounds good. Not good at all."

"Do you have another explanation?"

Pointing a finger at her, Mbaye said, "*You* killed them."

"Why would I do that?"

"Because they were in your room."

"Just for clarification, we are in agreement that the hotel room those men are lying in is mine?"

Mbaye huffed.

"And the lock was tampered with?"

"Yes, yes, yes. All of that is true. But you can't go around killing people in Dakar, Miss Creed, no matter what the provocation."

Annja agreed. "But I didn't kill anybody," she said.

Mbaye sighed.

"What's he saying?" McIntosh stood at Annja's side. He didn't speak French so he was locked out of the conversation. "He's not happy. I can tell just from looking that he's not happy."

"He's not happy," Annja agreed.

"Why isn't he happy? Are you telling him something you shouldn't be?" McIntosh had sent for a French interpreter from the embassy but no one had arrived yet.

"He has three dead men in my hotel room to explain," Annja replied. "That's a lot of explaining to do, even in Dakar."

The city was known as a crime capital and had a lot of trouble with student demonstrations. The American Embassy had issued warnings to American tourists not to gather near protesting students or in dangerous parts of the city.

"Are you cooperating?" McIntosh asked.

"He wants me to admit to killing those men."

McIntosh considered that. "Well, don't cooperate that much. I mean, if you killed those guys, don't tell him that."

"Thanks for the vote of confidence."

"It's not like this would be your first time to kill somebody. You killed those guys back in Georgia."

Mbaye smiled broadly. Then he reached inside a pocket and brought out a cigarette pack and a lighter. He lit up and smiled again.

McIntosh leaned back against the wall with a look of helpless frustration. "He understands English, doesn't he?"

"Yes," Annja said.

McIntosh cursed.

"Well, now," Mbaye said in English, "it seems we're all in agreement that Miss Creed killed the men in her room."

"He speaks English pretty well, too, don't you think?" Annja asked McIntosh.

"Why didn't you tell him you only spoke English?" McIntosh griped.

"Because the police officer who first arrived on the scene couldn't speak English. He could only speak French and an African dialect that I couldn't speak. I didn't want to get shot, so I spoke to him in French."

"It's a shame for an educated person to hide the fact that he or she has an education," Mbaye observed. "We are living in enlightened times."

"Enlightened times don't include letting hired killers go after a hotel guest," McIntosh replied.

"Americans have made a lot of enemies overseas of late." Mbaye breathed smoke out. "We can't be held accountable for the enemies your country makes."

"This doesn't look like something my country is responsible for."

"Really?" Mbaye lifted his eyebrows. "Then what does this look like?"

Annja folded her arms and waited to see if McIntosh would mention Tafari. If he did, they were going to be shuttled out of Senegal just as quickly as they'd arrived. The Senegalese government wasn't going to condone American espionage activity on their soil.

"I'll let you talk to the American Embassy," McIntosh replied.

And that would be a mistake, too, Annja thought. Once the embassy staff got involved, they'd want to be part of everything. Soon there would be a whole parade of people trekking around.

She looked at Mbaye. "How much?" she asked.

Mbaye smiled. "Ah, you've been to our country before."

"What?" McIntosh asked. "How much for what?"

Annja switched to French. "Let's speak in this language."

"Of course." Mbaye waved away a lungful of smoke.

"How much to conduct the investigation?"

"Three would-be rapists, murderers or thieves?" Mbaye shrugged. "What seems fair to you?"

"They're already caught," Annja pointed out. "It's not like you're going to have to go looking for them."

Mbaye grinned.

"What's going on?" McIntosh asked. He tried to step between them, but two of the khaki-clad policemen moved forward and blocked him from their superior.

"The fourth man says you attacked them with a sword," Mbaye said. "He claims that you killed all three of them."

"One of them was shot."

"Only after he'd been cut badly by a large blade."

"Did you find a sword?" Annja asked.

Frowning, Mbaye shook his head. "We haven't given up looking."

"Everyone needs a hobby," Annja said with a shrug.

"Perhaps you used one of their machetes."

"If I took one of their weapons away and used it to save myself, would I be found guilty of anything other than self-defense?"

"No. Of course not," the police inspector said.

"Then how much do you need to do the investigation and bring charges against the fourth man?"

Mbaye hesitated. "Two thousand dollars."

"I'll give you a thousand."

"That's robbery."

"To file a report? I don't think so," Annja said.

"I could put you in jail."

Annja remained calm. "The American Embassy would get me right out again."

"We are at an impasse," Mbaye stated.

"Not if you want a thousand dollars."

"She's being generous," a man said, also in French. "I wouldn't give you a thousand dollars to carry away the bodies of those three dead villains."

Annja turned in the direction of the voice.

A man approached from the hallway. He was blond and fair-skinned, somewhere in his fifties, Annja guessed. His blue eyes stood out like sapphires. An expensive suit draped his lean frame, and the jacket he wore could have paid for a small car.

"Mr. Ganesvoort." Mbaye inclined his head in an abbreviated bow.

The man extended a hand to Annja and took hers in his warmly. "Good evening, Ms. Creed. I'm Jozua Ganesvoort."

"Mr. Ganesvoort," Annja said.

"Please. Call me Jozua." Ganesvoort smiled.

Jozua Ganesvoort was a businessman whose family had moved from the Netherlands to Senegal 250 years ago. He was also the man Professor Hallinger had arranged to see concerning the origins of Yohance and the Spider Stone.

"This isn't any business of yours, Mr. Ganesvoort," Mbaye said.

"I disagree. Ms. Creed and Professor Hallinger are scheduled to be my guests in the morning. I would be remiss if I didn't make an effort to ensure that they made it to my home safely."

Mbaye turned to Annja. "One thousand dollars will do nicely."

Turning to McIntosh, Annja said in English, "Give him a thousand dollars."

"Why?" the Homeland Security agent asked.

"To close the case and cut us loose."

"That's bribery."

"No," Annja said quietly, before Mbaye could take offense, "that's how things are done here. The Dakar police department is undermanned and underfunded. They supplement their incomes by charging for police services."

"That's not how we do it in Atlanta."

"We're not in Atlanta," Annja reminded him.

Scowling, McIntosh shifted his attention to Mbaye. "Do you take traveler's checks?"

"Of course."

"What brought you here?" Annja asked Ganesvoort, in English so McIntosh would understand.

"A phone call, actually." Ganesvoort looked around curiously. "From a woman. She sounded rather old, but I didn't recognize the voice. She knew me, though. And she knew that you were going to be my guest tomorrow morning."

Annja searched the hallway, but there was no sign of the old woman.

I knew you'd come, she'd said.

But who was she? And how had she known?

"YOU'VE FOUND the Spider Stone, I see."

Seated beside Ganesvoort in the limousine that had pulled up in front of the hotel then swept her and Hallinger away, Annja nodded. They'd left McIntosh behind, which hadn't set well with him. McIntosh hadn't wanted Annja to leave, but he was unable to stop her. The trip to Dakar had already been paid for. She enjoyed being able to slip McIntosh's chains. It put them on more equal footing. They were in her world now, not his.

"May I see it?" the historian asked.

Annja hesitated only a second and hoped her indecision hadn't been noticed by their host. She handed him the stone.

The tiger's eye gleamed honey-gold as he turned the stone in his fingers. "Beautiful."

"What do you know about the Spider Stone?" she asked.

"Only that it could lead someone to a fabled treasure left by a ruined Hausa village. And that it was presumed lost. Most people thought the Arab raiders made off with it when they attacked the village." Ganesvoort returned the stone and looked at her with those bright blue eyes. "I presume the Spider Stone made it to the New World by way of one of the slaves?"

"Yes," Hallinger said, looking flustered. "From the accounts we've had access to, a young slave named Yohance brought the Spider Stone to the fledgling United States before there was even a United States."

"Fascinating." Ganesvoort rubbed at his chin. "I'd heard the stone had disappeared almost three hundred years ago. Before my family set up shop on Ile de Goree. Of course, I'd always believed the Spider Stone to be one more myth. Africa is a land filled with stories of vengeful gods and wondrous things. Even though we've pierced so many of her mysteries, so many yet remain." He smiled. "Of course, you already know that. That's why you do what it is you do." He spread his hands. "Now, why do you want to see my collection of ships' logs?"

"We're trying to find what ship Yohance went out on," Annja answered. "And we're hoping the captain made some notation of where he was captured."

"They didn't all make notes," Ganesvoort warned.

"I know," Hallinger said. "But several of the ships' captains were extremely detailed."

"And you had nowhere else to go." Ganesvoort grinned.

Annja returned the grin, caught up in the excitement of the hunt. "And we had nowhere else to go."

"I have a large collection of logs."

"The precise reason I called you," Hallinger said.

"With over three hundred years of slavery open to you, you're talking about a lot of searching."

"We had to figure out the time frame from how many Yohances there had been," Annja said. "We figured a median age of around twenty-five or thirty for each Yohance. Some died younger than that and some lived longer."

The car sped in silent smoothness toward the harbor. Silver-gray smog hung over the dark green water. Ships and pleasure craft lined the harbor.

"The Yohance we found went missing in 1861," Annja said.

"And what number Yohance was he?"

"The fourth."

"Then by your own criteria, the first Yohance had to have arrived in the colonies 100 to 120 years before that."

"Your family trafficked in slaves," Annja said. There's no polite way to put that, she thought.

"They did," Ganesvoort replied. "At the time, slavery was the largest commerce Ile de Goree had to offer." He gestured out the window at the city around them. "Everything else grew up around slavery. Dakar didn't really get built and come into its own until after the slave trade was outlawed. The European need for slaves as a product benefited from the fact that there were so many cultures living here. No one owed any allegiance to anyone else. Every person was fair game as someone else's prize. If the different tribes hadn't preyed on each other, not nearly as many slaves would have been captured."

"Can you imagine what it must have been like?" Annja asked. "Captured, marched in chains down to Ile de Goree and sold like a loaf of bread?" It was hard to contemplate. Slavery had always been abhorrent to her. The most horrifying thing was that some nations still practiced it, and there were hidden flesh traders who trafficked in sex slaves. Annja knew nearly forty thousand women a year went missing, most of them thought to have been taken for the sex trade.

"It had to have been horrible," Hallinger said.

"The transatlantic slave trade took root here in 1513, only eleven years after the first slave was sold, and lasted until the mid-eighteenth century," Ganesvoort went on. "Some scholars contend that fully twenty-four million people were displaced as a result in those three-hundred-plus years. Twenty percent of them died in the slave ships during the journey. They weren't fed or watered or cared for. The dead were thrown overboard to prevent the healthy from getting sick."

"Scientists who study sharks will tell you that shark migratory patterns still follow the old transatlantic slave-trade routes," Hallinger said. "They got used to feeding along those shipping lines."

The limousine arrived at the harbor and they got out. Men dressed in ship's whites and carrying pistols in shoulder holsters transferred Annja's and Hallinger's bags to a long yacht.

With the breeze in her hair and powering over the rollers in the bay, Annja relaxed a little as she stood at the bow.

"Do you like boats, Ms. Creed?" Ganesvoort asked.

"Call me 'Annja.'"

The man nodded.

"I do like boats," Annja admitted. "There's something very calm and peaceful about the ocean."

"Until you get astride her during a tropical storm. Then anything can happen." Ganesvoort studied her. "Do you know who the men were that attacked you?"

Annja shook her head.

"They belong to a man named Tafari. You've heard of him?"

Annja brushed her hair out of her face. That didn't take long. "Yes. I've heard of him."

"He's a very dangerous man, and a murderer several times over."

"There's something you should know," Annja told him.

Ganesvoort smiled. "That Tafari seeks the Spider Stone? I already know that. The man believes in myths and legends and half-buried secrets. He intends to become a legend himself. He'll kill anyone who stands in his way." He looked at Hallinger, then at Annja. "You, my old friend and my new friend, need to always keep that in mind."

18

"So this is how the rich live."

Looking up from the ship's log she was currently perusing, Annja smiled at McIntosh. The Homeland Security agent had arrived by ferry the following morning. Ganesvoort had arranged transportation, a horse-drawn carriage, to his manor house on the north end of the small island.

"Yes," Annja agreed. "It is. Some of them. Of course, Ganesvoort could have opted for the Howard Hughes lifestyle there at the end."

The manor house had been built up over the years. It had begun life as a Portuguese villa, then had been taken over by Ganesvoort's ancestors and enlarged to a sprawling fifteen-thousand-square-foot residence. Annja didn't know how many bedrooms and bathrooms the house contained, but there were many. There were a handful of dining rooms and two grand ballrooms. As a result, the rooms weren't all built on the same level, but the various architects—including the French, who'd had the last opportunity to give the structure a facelift—had managed to pull it all together with unforgettable elegance.

The manor house had a state-of-the art surveillance system and a small army of armed guards.

The room she was using was a reading room on the second floor. The north wall was nearly all glass, with a beautiful balcony that overlooked the ocean. In the distance, sailboats and fishing boats plied the waters.

"I don't like the windows," McIntosh growled.

"I love the windows," Annja replied. "It's the north light. The most even light of the day. Painters usually prefer the north light when they're working on a canvas."

"A sniper," McIntosh pointed out at the sea, "on one of those boats could cause a problem."

"Put there by Tafari, I suppose?"

"Yes." McIntosh frowned at her. "You're not taking this very seriously."

Stretching to relieve her back for a moment, Annja decided to deal with the issue head-on. "If Tafari wanted me dead, this would be a dangerous place for me to be."

"He does want you dead. Those guys last night tried to kill you."

"They would have killed me as long as they could get the Spider Stone. They planned to get the Spider Stone, then kill me. Shooting me from a ship out at sea isn't going to get Tafari the Spider Stone, is it?"

McIntosh didn't answer.

Turning her attention back to the ship's log, she said, "Think of me sitting here as being that enticing bait you wanted me to be when we got here." She smirked a little at McIntosh's frustration with her. "I sit here and he can't have me. What better bait could you possibly hope for? It's got to be driving Tafari crazy."

"That's not what I meant."

"It *is* what you meant. Your best hope is that Tafari gets as tired of waiting as you do and makes a move against us so you can nab him."

McIntosh appeared to give that some thought. "What do you think the chances are of him doing that?"

"*I* wouldn't do it," Annja said. "I'd wait until I left the house and probably this island."

"That's you. You're probably smarter than Tafari."

"Thank you. I am definitely smarter than Tafari. On any day of the week that ends in *Y*."

"Don't get cocky."

"I'm not. You see, I know I have a weakness," Annja said.

McIntosh looked at her, not understanding.

"When I figure out where Yohance came from and I know where the map shows, I'm going to go there. I'll bet Tafari knows that. That's when he'll get his opportunity to get the treasure and kill me, too."

That possibility turned McIntosh's frown even deeper.

Annja sat at a French provincial desk that had probably seen service in one of Louis XIV's courts. The chair, of course, was modern although built in a style that accented the desk. Comfort, when working for hours leaning over old documents and maps, was paramount.

"I still don't think you're taking this seriously enough," McIntosh said.

"On the contrary. I'm taking this very seriously. That's why I'm working as hard as I am."

"You don't normally risk your life doing your job."

Annja lifted an arched brow. "Really? You don't call exploring almost forgotten ruins—where cave-ins can occur and diseases run rampant—risky? Going to remote dig sites where a hospital is two days or more away? Falling from a cliff or through a trap some ancient dead man set to keep thieves from his remains? And that doesn't take into account bandits, robbers, slavers, mercenaries or drug traffickers that you can run into who think you have something they want or that they can use you in some fashion to get past the next checkpoint."

McIntosh tried to interrupt.

Annja didn't let him. "Do you know that most countries still distrust archaeologists? Well, they do. Want to know why? Because archaeologists have a long history of being spies for the United States and British governments. A lot of governments see us as a necessary evil. We bring in money to help them extract a past they might never see without outside funding." She paused. "Archaeology isn't as bland as you seem to make it out to be."

"Not the way you do it," McIntosh grumbled.

"What does that mean?"

"It means that you seem to attract trouble."

Annja couldn't argue with that, so she didn't. Instead, she turned back to her work. Almost five minutes passed in silence.

"How long is this going to take?" McIntosh asked.

Only slightly irritated because she'd been expecting the question from the moment McIntosh had arrived and started pacing, Annja said, "As long as it takes."

"You're reading books." McIntosh approached her and took the top book off the stack.

"That's what archaeologists do."

"I thought you broke into graves, found cities that had

been buried in lava, looked for dinosaur bones and located shipwrecks."

"We do that, too."

McIntosh hefted the book. "If you were getting paid by the pound, you'd make a fortune."

Annja looked at McIntosh pointedly.

"What?" he asked.

"You're talking. It's hard to read when you're talking. I mean, I can do it, but then I'd be ignoring you. So I'm giving you warning, I'm going to work until lunch. If you talk to me before the lunch bell rings, I'm going to ignore you." Annja turned back to the book.

And she ignored him.

HOURS LATER, seated at the beautiful table in one of the dining rooms, Annja piled her plate high with food. Plates of suckling pig and pheasant, fresh fruit, a half-dozen salads and several desserts, including three different sorbets, covered the table.

"This is wonderful," she said.

"I see you're ambitious," Ganesvoort observed.

Annja felt only a little self-conscious. She'd always been a healthy eater, and the past few days she hadn't exactly been meal conscious. "I haven't eaten this well in a long time. Thank you very much. I'll be embarrassed later."

Ganesvoort smiled. "Don't be embarrassed. It's my pleasure. My cook thanks you, too. It's not often that she gets to go all out. My tastes are simple and don't challenge her. I throw the occasional party simply to keep her from turning in her resignation out of boredom. But she tells me that party preparations are not as personal as cooking for overnight guests."

"I'm glad she likes cooking for guests. We may be here for a few days." Annja sipped her wine.

McIntosh looked up from his plate. "Days?"

"Or weeks." Hallinger used his knife and fork industriously, throwing himself into the meal, as well. Annja had noted the color in his face, as well as his energy.

"Why weeks?" McIntosh asked. "I thought this was a simple research job."

"Because there are a lot of logs to go through," Annja replied.

"We don't even know if the information we're looking for is here," Hallinger added.

"Aren't those logs alphabetized?" McIntosh asked.

"Some of them are, Agent McIntosh," Ganesvoort said. "However, I must apologize. My collection has merely been a hobby, a sweet passion, not something I felt I had to pursue every day. I've only cataloged about two-thirds of the journals and logs that I've bought over the years. I've read and am familiar with far less of them."

"Isn't someone in charge of cataloging things like that?" McIntosh asked.

"Like what?" Annja asked.

McIntosh shrugged. "*Historical* things."

"Who's to say what a historical thing is?" Hallinger asked.

McIntosh thought about that for a moment. "I don't know."

"Nor does anyone else."

"But there are historical preservation societies. I worked a murder case that involved a group like that in Atlanta."

"Those societies," Ganesvoort said, "are just as self-serving as my own interests. They choose houses or other landmarks for preservation because they want something to champion. I enjoyed reading ships' logs and imagining what a maritime life might have been like back in those days. When I sit down with one of those old books, it's like I'm taking that voyage myself. The story, the men, the problems, they all come alive around me. Even in the unskilled writings of the captains, first mates and officers of the watch."

"I'm that way about open and unsolved cases," McIntosh said.

Ganesvoort nodded. "I see. In its own way, an open case is very much a historical document, dealing with murders that happened years ago."

Annja hadn't thought about a police investigation like that.

"Right," McIntosh said. "When you start looking through an unsolved case, you have to put your mind back in the time that the murder took place. Figure out what the people were doing, what they were thinking."

"And what their world was like on a day-to-day basis," Annja said.

"Yeah."

"That's what an archaeologist does," Annja said. "We take artifacts—things left behind by others—"

"Clues and evidence, as well as hunches based on case data that lead to profiling, to use your terminology," Hallinger said.

"—and we attempt to reconstruct the world those people lived in. What they struggled for and what they dreamed of," Annja finished. "In the end, though, we know we've only been able to deliver our best guess. Eventually, someone will come along to challenge or refute what you said. Like when Michael Crichton postulated in *Jurassic Park* that dinosaurs were fleet and warm-blooded like fowl rather than ponderous and slow-moving like lizards. That turned the science community on its collective ear, even though the conjecture had been out there for a long time. Crichton made the theory popular and put it into the public eye. Laymen started asking questions, and scientists—wanting funding and attention—acted on it."

"History," Hallinger said, "in the end is subjective. People never know what to throw away or what to keep. These days, we try to keep most everything. But even recent things, things that touch our daily lives, get recycled as junk. Did you ever read comic books or collect baseball cards when you were a kid?"

"I did," McIntosh admitted. "I still have the baseball cards, but I sold the comics when I started getting into girls. Comics and girls don't mix."

"Depends on the girl," Annja said. "I still read comics these days and graphic novels, too. Picture storytelling has been around since the first cave painting."

McIntosh smiled. "I would never have guessed that you read comics."

"There's a lot," Annja said, "that you don't know about me."

For a moment, McIntosh held her gaze, then he nodded and dropped his eyes.

Annja forced her attention back to her own plate.

FOUR DAYS LATER, they got a break.

Hallinger sprinted into the room where Annja was working. McIntosh had taken to looking through the English ships' logs for the name Yohance. He was a quick reader, but bored easily. Still, it kept him quiet most of the time.

"I found him!" the professor exclaimed as he burst into the room carrying a large ship's log.

After days of looking at them, Annja knew that ships' logs came in different sizes and degrees of craftsmanship. Some of them had been made by abbeys or by printing shops. But just as many had been handmade.

The people who had kept them were just as varied as the logs. Educated and uneducated men assembled their thoughts on the pages as best as they were able. Ships' captains, first mates, quartermasters, officers of the watch, common sailors and even cabin boys—those who had become somewhat literate—had all left their marks.

Despite the pressure to solve the riddle of the Spider Stone, Annja had found herself entranced on more than one occasion. Understanding Ganesvoort's hobby of choice was easy. Whole worlds opened up in those pages.

"You found Yohance?" Annja whispered the name, afraid to say it too loudly.

"Yes." Hallinger marched into the room like a commanding general. "The time frame is right. It says here that the slaves were brought aboard in July of 1755." He plopped the log down in front of Annja.

"'Yohance' is a common name," she said, striving to keep her hopes in check and to play the devil's advocate.

"I know, but it appears that our Yohance's arrival on the ship garnered attention from the captain and ship's crew. Actually caused a bit of a furor."

"What kind of furor?" Annja asked.

"Several of the ship's crew thought the boy was cursed. Or marked by the gods. Most of the sailors at that time were very superstitious. There was even some discussion of heaving the boy overboard at one point."

Annja turned the log so she could better see it. The writing was French, put there in a fine, strong hand by Captain Henri LaForge of *Cornucopia.*

"Where's Yohance's name?" McIntosh leaned over Annja's shoulder, squinting at the cursive writing.

Annja was conscious of him there, of the heat from his body and the scent of his cologne. But the possibility of discovery took precedence over whatever feelings his proximity stirred up.

"Here." Annja placed her finger on the first mention of Yohance's name.

"I see the name," McIntosh growled, "but I can't read the rest of it."

"That's because it's in French."

McIntosh shot her a look of impatience. "Maybe you could translate."

Before Annja could begin reading, Ganesvoort entered the room. Lights danced in his eyes. "You found him?" their host asked.

Smiling, Hallinger looked up at him. "I did."

Ganesvoort clapped the professor on the back. "So it is true?"

"At least this much of the story. It remains to be seen if the treasure is real."

"My little hobby has turned out to be worth something after all."

"It has," Hallinger said.

Ganesvoort flopped in one of the nearby comfortable chairs. "Thank God. I was beginning to feel that this one had slipped by us."

"Well," McIntosh said, "it didn't."

"The chances of such a thing being mentioned are so

small," Ganesvoort stated. "Twenty-four million slaves passed through this island. God knows how many ships and ships' captains. With this kind of luck, we could go to Monaco and become fabulously wealthy."

"I thought you already were," McIntosh said.

"I am. But you know what I mean." Ganesvoort turned his attention to Annja. "Does the listing show where Yohance was from? Usually you don't get much information."

"This is more than a listing." Annja held the book up for him to see. "There appear to be a number of entries."

Ganesvoort leaned forward like an enthusiastic child awaiting a favorite bedtime story. "Come on, then. Let's have the story."

Annja sipped from her bottle of water and began to read aloud, translating the French to English effortlessly.

19

July 14, 1755
Henri LaForge, Captain of Cornucopia
Afternoon
Prevailing Winds, Easterly
Weather, Good

Our arrival in Ile de Goree was met with relief by my crew. After the tropical storm that very nearly laid waste to us in the Atlantic, we were all very happy to be alive.

We've spent the last six days partaking of the island's delights. I myself spent some time with my good friend Andrew Wiley, captain of *Bess,* which he named after his beautiful bride. We talked and ate, told of our troubles and our travels. Then we went to the auction block and both bought slaves to fill our holds.

Everything proceeded without incident until we arrived back at the ship with our goods.

"Goods?" McIntosh interrupted. "He's referring to the slaves?"

"Yes," Annja answered.

"They were considered nothing more than cargo," Gansevoort added. "I don't think anyone truly realizes how inhumanly these people were treated, despite everything that's been written."

Annja continued reading.

I feel very confident of the lot I bargained for. They were newly arrived to Ile de Goree. I learned that they were taken by fellow tribesmen, which is all to the good, I think. Although I've been involved in a number of engagements with pirates and am accustomed to living my life through quick wits, a musket and a good length of steel, I don't think I'd like to tempt the fates by leading expeditions into the interior to gather slaves.

Most of the men are in good shape. They should give several years of labor wherever they end up, once they are gentled. A few of them are belligerent and think they are cunning. I'll have that beaten or starved out of them by voyage's end.

The women are young and healthy, and no few of them are comely enough for what they are. They will make good domestics and breeding stock.

A few of them are already with child. If they survive the voyage, they will fetch an extra penny on the auction block. Wiley said he's heard of some captains who keep the more comely looking women aboard ship and let the men have at them, ensuring a pregnancy and more money when they sell them by adding calving and proving they're fertile.

There was a strange incident which has got my crew talking, though. There is a young boy, perhaps ten or twelve, about the same age as my Georges, who has caused consternation. His name is Yohance, I have discovered, and he is rumored to be a medicine man or something like that. Since my crew tends to be more superstitious than God-fearing, they put great stock in stories of curses and the other black arts that seem so prevalent among this species.

This situation will bear closer scrutiny because several of the other slaves we have on board treat this boy with a deference that I can't for the life of me understand. He's not even attained a man's growth.

"Obviously several of Yohance's fellow tribesmen were bought at the same time," Ganesvoort said.

"Yes," Hallinger said. "That fits with what we were able to find out from Franklin Dickerson's journal back in Georgia."

Annja took another sip of water and continued with the next entry.

July 17, 1755

We are at present three days' journey out of Ile de Goree. Thus far, the wind has proved capricious at best. We've not been able to hold a strong heading and have had to shift constantly.

Several of the crew have reported rumors that we

have been cursed for taking the boy Yohance from his homeland.

I have not yet ascertained who started this rumor, but I intend to have none of it. Rumors fester like boils aboard ship, without a proper way of dealing with them. Once I find out who is behind it, I will have the skin off that man's back.

"With that in the log," Hallinger said, "Captain LaForge was evidently putting his crew on notice. But it didn't do any good."

July 19, 1755

The situation has worsened. Today Colbert, a gunnery mate, fell upon Yohance and demanded that he lift whatever curse is suspected of being placed on the ship. We've been two more days with the fickle wind, and a storm is brewing in the west, showing signs of giving chase to us. The men are mortally afraid of going through such a blow again.

In response to the attack on Yohance, two of the slaves rose up and pulled Colbert down, beating him unmercifully. Jacques de Mornay, my first mate, had to shoot one of the slaves before order was returned to the hold.

The slave died. There was no saving him. I ordered the body thrown overboard to the ever-present sharks. I also informed Colbert that I was taking the price of the slave out of his wages. However, I fear dissension is rapidly spreading through my crew.

Annja studied the next entry and was surprised. "This is written in Latin." She looked up at Hallinger.

The professor agreed. "I looked back through the ship's log. Whenever Captain LaForge wished to remain circumspect in his musings, he used Latin."

"He was a highly educated man," Ganesvoort said. "How did he end up doing something as dangerous and hard as being a ship's captain?"

"From the earlier entries I read," Hallinger said, "LaForge was born to a wealthy family. His father was a highly successful merchant, and his mother was linked to nobility. But Henri LaForge chose not to be the merchant his father wanted him to be. He went to sea instead, taking over one of his father's ships so that he could see more of the world that he'd read about."

Annja understood that choice. She'd felt the same way while growing up in the orphanage. Her one touchstone throughout her youth had been her martial-arts classes. Sister Mary Annabelle, eighty years old and irrepressible, had taken part in the *tai chi* classes where Annja had started out.

Before and after classes, Annja had talked to the instructors whenever she could. Many of them had been from Japan or Korea. Those conversations had whet the appetite to travel that staying cooped up in the orphanage under the supervision of nuns and reading histories had already inspired.

"Do you read Latin?" McIntosh asked.

"Yes," Annja replied, and she continued with the narrative.

July 22, 1755

My first mate has had some experience with slaves in the wild, and he understands some of their language. He learned from some of the other slaves that Yohance is a medicine man among his people, and that he is believed to have great power.

What concerns me is that I think Jacques, who normally has a good head about him, might believe some of these stories that we might be under some curse from an African god. I reminded him that we are both men of strong faith, and that none of the magic practiced in those dark lands will ever be proof against God.

I worry that he might be succumbing to the same fears that plague the other crew members. We met in my cabin and shared a bottle of good port that I normally keep for the end of a successful voyage, but I don't think either of us felt entirely satisfied when we parted.

July 24, 1755

The storm overran us last night. We caught only the outer fringes of it, but it was enough to thoroughly unnerve my crew.

Cariou and I were hard-pressed to keep control of the situation. The storm hit just after dusk, during the dark hours of early evening while we were sitting down to dine.

The ship reacted violently in the blow. Several yardarms snapped off, which are being replaced today, though the storm conditions persist and I fear we're mired within the storm, always bumping into the violence of it. It feels as though we are caught in some grand trap and are doomed.

To make matters worse, the slaves began wailing and calling on their deities to save them. Their moans and fearful cries further took the strength from my men. Cariou and I had to arm ourselves and threaten to shoot any man that abandoned his post.

Even then I feared that someone would.

In the worst of the gale, the boy, Yohance, somehow quieted the slaves. I think that he knew we would kill one of them to make an example for the others if they did not quiet. Instead, he sang some song, something that I never discovered the nature of. After a time, the storm eased and we were once more in control of our course instead of being tossed about like a child's toy.

However, the crew now treat Yohance differently. We've still got a long voyage ahead of us, so I have to take steps to end this. He is not some magical being as the slaves would have us believe. I refuse to entertain that notion even for a moment.

"That sounds as if he's having his doubts," McIntosh commented dryly.

"If a man gets out on the sea long enough," Ganesvoort stated quietly, "he can convince himself of nearly anything."

"The stuff you've read about the Spider Stone," McIntosh said, "doesn't mention anything about this, does it?"

"It does mention a curse." Annja sipped her water again.

"A curse?" Uncertainty darted in McIntosh's eyes. "Neither of you mentioned anything about a curse."

"I thought you wouldn't believe in something like a curse," Hallinger said.

Maybe you're beginning to have a few doubts yourself, Annja thought. "Still believe archaeologists lead laidback lives?" She wasn't able to resist taunting. Just a little.

"Curses don't exist," McIntosh replied.

But Annja knew the mood had altered as she read the entries. There are still any number of things out in the world that we can't explain, she thought.

"Do you carry a lucky charm, Special Agent McIntosh?" Hallinger asked.

McIntosh looked self-conscious. "A pocket angel. A lot of the guys I know carry one. Or something like it."

"Because you believe it will help protect you?"

"As a precaution. When my dad was on the job, he carried one, too. It's like crossing your fingers. Doesn't really mean anything."

"Actually," Annja said, "crossing your fingers is a throwback to England's belief in witches. Crossing your fingers would ward off witches. Basically making the sign of the cross with your fingers. If you encountered a witch, making the sign of the cross would send her on her way."

"Belief in magic is an ingrained trait," Hallinger said. "You won't find a culture anywhere that didn't or doesn't believe in some sort of sorcery or magic."

Annja returned to the ship's log, still on the Latin entry.

> I had Yohance brought to me tonight. I wanted to put an end to all this foolishness. Since I didn't speak his dialect and the boy had no English, I had de Mornay in attendance because he could speak the boy's savage tongue. I swore the man to secrecy, made him give me his gravest oath that he would not let slip anything that we discussed in my quarters.

The boy, Yohance, was afraid. I could see it in him. That vulnerability again reminded me of my own son, Georges, and how he might fare under these harsh conditions. But Yohance kept himself composed despite being outnumbered and outgunned.

I had my first mate ask the boy his story, how he came to be in Ile de Goree.

The boy told us of his village near the confluence of the Semefé and Bafing Rivers.

Annja stopped reading and looked at Hallinger. "Did you read this?"

The professor nodded. "I wanted to wait until you were up to speed before we began searching. There's still a lot of area to cover. And that's if Captain LaForge and his first mate actually got everything right."

"Doesn't that map on the Spider Stone show two rivers joining?" McIntosh asked. "That seems like it would be hard to miss."

"No," Annja said. "The problem we've had so far is that there aren't large numbers of Hausa living in Senegal. If they're not here now—"

"Then chances are good that they weren't here then," Hallinger finished. "The Hausa people date back to 500 A.D., and their ancestral lands in Nigeria have been occupied by civilized peoples since prehistoric times. Between 500 and 700 A.D., the Hausa began consolidating, developing seven city-states that were believed to have been founded by Bayajidda, a hero of their people who supposedly had a magic knife fashioned for him. He used the knife to fight his enemies and rescued the queen of Daura and her people from a giant snake."

"The queen married Bayajidda," Annja said, taking up the tale, "and they had seven sons. By the thirteenth century, the Hausa controlled most of the trade in those areas. They also mixed with the Fulani people, whose roots are Muslim. After a series of jihads in the early nineteenth century, the Fulani took over, forming the Sokoto Caliphate, which became the Fulani Empire."

"Wars generally ruin records and documents," Ganesvoort put in. "They also tend to scatter people. For Yohance's people to be where they were—"

"Somewhere near Kidira from the sound of it," Annja said, looking at a map she had on the desk.

"—they had to have gone far from their homelands," Ganesvoort said.

"Not necessarily," Hallinger said. "Yohance's people may have already been scattered."

"There are pockets of Hausa scattered all across West Africa," Annja added. "According to the words on the Spider Stone, Yohance's people had already fled from invaders."

"Probably the Yoruba." Hallinger stroked his chin. "They'd been an aggressive people until the Fulani Empire put them out of business."

"So what happened to Yohance?" McIntosh asked.

Annja smiled. That's the thing about history, she thought. Everybody thinks it's a boring subject until they learn it's really about people.

Annja returned to translating the captain's writing.

> The boy was reluctant to say anything more, but I knew I had to get to the bottom of the medicine-man myth. When I asked him about it, he refused to answer.
>
> I've dealt with reluctant men before, and I'm not

leery of employing tactics that some would deem harsh or cruel. A man has to know what a man has to know.

After growing frustrated with questioning the boy, I took out a knife and cut off his left ear. After all, a slave doesn't use an ear to work, and the amputation didn't make him deaf.

Yohance cried and became very afraid.

I told him I would cut the throat of one of the other boys if he didn't tell me what I wished to know. Looking at his own ear lying there before him, he believed me. And that was good because I don't make idle threats.

He told an incredible tale. I believe it was a complete fabrication, but I knew he hadn't created the tale. It had been handed down through his people.

His people hold to the savage belief that their gods are some kind of animal. Or gods can be found in animals. Heresy, all of it, and spread by the Devil himself to undermine the faith of good Christians.

According to Yohance, the spider god of his people, gave them a vast treasure after he allowed their village to be destroyed. He also gave them a weapon, a curse that they could visit on any enemy.

I didn't believe any of it, but I could tell that de Mornay did. I remonstrated the boy, told him the error of his ways regarding how he was causing the other slaves to act, and I told him that I would hold him responsible for their actions. If anything further happened, I swore to him that I would tie a bag of cannonballs around his neck and hurl him into the Atlantic. Then I sent him back to the hold.

I have every confidence that I have seen the end of this matter.

When she finished reading the entry, Annja felt slightly sick. She had a strong stomach and she'd read about and even seen much worse in her own work, but the thought of the boy being so harshly treated at the hands of uncaring men touched her.

"That's it?" McIntosh asked.

"There's one other important entry," Hallinger said. "Just a few days later. It's written by Captain LaForge's lieutenant."

Annja read the entry.

August 2, 1755
Maurice Cariou, Lieutenant of Cornucopia
Evening
Prevailing Winds, Northerly
Weather, Poor

It is with a heavy heart that I take up the pen to finish the work begun by my captain, the good Henri LaForge. I pray that he is with Our Lord, and that his name will always be remembered with favor.

The storm that has constantly dogged our tracks on this voyage caught up with us once again last night. I've never seen such a determined effort on part of something that is without purpose, human or divine, that acted so cold-heartedly.

While we were lashed about, Captain LaForge took the deck and gave his courage and strength to our crew. During the worst of the storm, a sail came loose and whipped across our rear deck, malevolently wrapping the captain in the ropes and dragging him overboard. He was gone, vanished into the sea before we could do a thing about it.

I shall be glad when this voyage is over. Ever since we have taken on the boy Yohance, luck and fortune have been against us. I struggle not to be a superstitious man because I don't want to affront God, but in these circumstances I find myself hard-pressed not to at least wonder.

"Interestingly enough," Hallinger said, "if you read the entries before that one, you'll see that the storm never once let up. It stayed on the ship's tail. Many of the ship's crew grew increasingly agitated. Captain LaForge had to take more and more aggressive means to keep the situation under control. After he cut off Yohance's ear, the crew turned against him, believing that he was responsible for the storm's continued fury."

"What you're saying is that you don't think LaForge's death went exactly the way his second-in-command said it did," McIntosh said.

"You're the expert in our midst when it comes to murder," Hallinger said. "What do you think?"

"I think it's awfully convenient that a whole ship's sail could come loose in a major storm and only take out one guy."

Annja agreed. Then she turned her thoughts to the puzzle of the Spider Stone again. They had a direction. They almost had a location. All they had to do was get there.

Looking at Ganesvoort, Annja asked, "What's the quickest way to Kidira?"

20

Looking up from the train seat, Annja saw the smiling face of one of the two young boys in front of her. As it turned out, the fastest way to Kidira was on the Dakar-Niger Railway. Going hundreds of miles overland by car would have taken nearly twice as long, even factoring in the five-hour delay in leaving Dakar. Punctuality wasn't one of the railway's strong suits.

Nor was comfort. The train generally concerned itself with cargo first and passengers second. Or third or fourth or fifth, Annja was quick to realize. Cargo was the big ticket for the railway, moving goods in from the coast to the interior.

She was jammed into a narrow seat with little room. There was no dining car, so meals had to be packed on. Fortunately, Ganesvoort's chef put together an excellent picnic basket.

McIntosh slept only a few seats over, lulled by the slow sway of the train. The CIA agents accompanying them occupied other seats. Three rows up, Hallinger and Ganesvoort conferred, going over topographical maps on Hallinger's computer just as Annja was doing, comparing the pictures they'd taken from the Spider Stone to the physical features of the land.

The two boys and their mother had sat in the seats in front of Annja. The mother had looked tired and frazzled. She'd stayed on her cell phone nearly the whole trip, evidently stressing over the conversation. Something somewhere wasn't going right.

"Hi," Annja said to the small boy.

The boy leaned over the back of his seat and peered at Annja's notebook computer. "Playing video games?" His English accent was unmistakable.

"Not exactly." Annja grinned at the boy's curiosity. She guessed that he was five or six, dressed in a red T-shirt, denim shorts and high-top basketball shoes.

"My brother plays games on his computer."

"He does?"

The little boy nodded. "Yeah. All the time. He gets in trouble with my mom because he doesn't know when to quit."

"I see." Glancing over the top of the seat, Annja saw the little boy's older brother by maybe three or four years was sound asleep. The mother had walked to the other end of the train car, evidently seeking a better connection for the phone.

"My name's Bashir." The boy stuck out his hand.

Annja took the hand and shook it. "Nice to meet you, Bashir. I'm Annja."

"You have a pretty name."

Chuckling, Annja said, "Thank you."

The boy waited maybe a heartbeat, then looked at her in

exaggerated annoyance, as if she'd missed something she should have automatically known. "Don't I have a pretty name?" he asked.

With the prompting, Annja immediately understood what she'd done wrong. "Yes, you do. I was trying to think if I've ever heard that name before, and I don't think I have. You have an unusual name, too."

Bashir smiled then. "My mom says my name means 'bringer of good news.' What does your name mean?"

"I don't know."

Bashir looked puzzled for just a moment. "Didn't your mom tell you what your name means?"

"No," Annja said truthfully, feeling just the smallest twinge of pain stab at her for a moment. "She didn't."

"Oh. My brother's name is Kamil. It means 'perfect.'" Bashir leaned in and cupped his hands around his mouth. His whisper was still loud. "Only he's not perfect—he's a slob."

Annja laughed. "I see."

Bashir looked at her curiously. "Are you an African?"

"No."

"I had to ask 'cause I found out there's white Africans, too. I didn't know that till I came here with my mom."

"I'm an American," Annja said.

"Our ancestors were Americans, too. But we're English now. Before we came here, we lived in London. My mom says our ancestors went to England after President Lincoln freed the slaves." Bashir thought some more. "Can I see your marble?"

"My marble?"

"Yeah." He pressed his hands together and smiled, revealing a gap where his two front teeth had been. "The pretty yellow one."

He meant the Spider Stone. Annja had had it out earlier, looking at it again and trying to get a deeper feel for it.

"Do you promise to take good care of it?" she asked.

"Sure."

Annja took the Spider Stone from her pocket and gave it to the boy.

He turned it around and around in his hands, studying it with complete fascination.

Bashir handed the Spider Stone back to Annja. "Why does it have a spider on it?"

"That spider represents Anansi. Do you know who Anansi is?" Annja asked.

Bashir's forehead wrinkled. "Some kind of hero?"

That's close enough, Annja thought. "Right. He's a hero. Anansi is a spider who lives here in West Africa."

"A spider?"

"Well, sometimes he can turn into a human."

Bashir grinned. "Brilliant. Do you know any stories about him?"

"I do." Annja put the computer aside and gave Bashir her full attention. "Anansi is one of those guys who seems to always get into trouble. Because he's always doing something or because he's after something he wants. And he wants a lot."

Outside the train windows, the countryside whipped by. Most of it was savanna, dry and covered with scrub brush and stunted trees.

"One day Anansi decided he wanted to be the king of all stories," Annja began. "So he went to his father, Nyame, who was the sky god."

"Anansi's dad is a god?"

"It's just a story."

Bashir looked at Annja as if she were a simpleton. "I know that. I'm not a baby."

"Sorry," Annja said.

At that moment, the mother arrived. She looked embarrassed. "I really must apologize," she said. "I asked him not to bother anyone."

"It wasn't a bother," Annja said. "It was kind of nice to take a break. And you have a terrific kid."

Bashir beamed. "She was telling me about Anansi. He's a spider god who can be a spider or a human, and he's supposed to live right here in West Africa, only he's really just make-believe."

"I hope you don't mind," Annja said.

The woman sat down, turned so that she could face Annja and smiled. "No, but I should warn you that you're dealing with an overactive imagination that requires constant feeding and attention." She offered her hand. "I'm Tanisha Diouf."

"Annja Creed. Nice to meet you." Annja shook her hand.

"How far are you going?"

"Kidira," Annja said.

"We are, too."

"With the kids along, it looks like vacation, but with all the phone time involved, it looks more like work," Annja said.

"Work. Definitely. I'm an engineer for Childress Construction."

"Is that part of Childress Corporation?"

Tanisha grimaced. "I see you've heard of us."

"Only this morning while waiting in the train station. I scanned the newspaper and saw Childress mentioned."

"Not a lot of people here like us," Tanisha said.

"Because of the oil refinery that's being built?"

"Exactly. Childress Corporation is the parent. The construction arm is one of the subsidiaries. I happen to be the engineer in charge of the project."

"Sounds like a big job."

"It is. Some days, like today, I think it's too big. Being a single mom is hard enough without being a single mom out of the country. But the opportunity and the pay is great. When I finish this, I can put both my boys through college on the bonus money I'll earn." Tanisha glanced at the topographical maps Annja had been studying. "What do you do?"

"I'm an archaeologist."

"Now, *that* sounds interesting."

"Some days are more interesting than others," Annja replied.

"May I?" Tanisha gestured toward one of the maps.

"Be my guest."

The woman picked up the map, then another one. "I don't think this is far from where we're putting the refinery in, actually."

That got Annja's attention immediately. "Really?"

"Really. What are you out here looking for?"

"A Hausa village that was destroyed in 1755."

"The sad thing is, you'll probably find lots of those. There's a lot of unrest in the savanna even now. Our work sites keep getting attacked by tribes that don't want us there. At least, they have been getting attacked. The last few days have been pretty quiet. You'll want to be careful out there."

"I will," Annja said.

Tanisha handed the maps back. "You're not traveling alone, are you?"

"I'm with a small expedition."

"Let me make a phone call. If it looks like we're heading in the same direction, maybe I can get you in with us when you have to go overland. If that's all right."

"I'd appreciate that." There is safety in numbers, Annja thought. But she feared it might also mean that she might endanger Tanisha Diouf and her children.

ALMOST TWO HOURS LATER, Annja stood on the small platform outside the passenger car. The train's wheels rumbled over the tracks in steady monotony. Darkness filled the savanna on either side of the railroad line, but the silver moon lit the sky.

She sipped from a bottle of water and ate pineapple chunks from a small plastic container Ganesvoort's cook had supplied. Fatigue ate at her, but she knew it was from spending the past few days doing nothing physical. She'd been active all her life. Inactivity seemed to take more out of her than physical exertion did.

Standing, breathing rhythmically, feeling warm despite the chill of the wind pulling at her clothing, Annja stared into the darkness around the train. She felt at peace, and a sense of belonging. There was a power in the land around her, and she sensed it in a way that she never had before. She soaked up the sensation, reveling in it, and her heart lifted.

Then she realized she wasn't alone. Someone was watching her.

"Here."

Annja spun, facing into the train car.

The African woman from the hotel stood before her, leaning on her staff. She wore a black grand *bubu,* and the extra material belled around her.

"You feel it, don't you?" the old woman asked. "You feel

the pull of this land on you." She waved at the savanna. "This is where the world began, where humanity took root and spread across the world. We all belong to Africa. So many have forgotten that."

Annja was silent.

The old woman smiled. "It's just me, daughter. You have nothing to fear from me."

"What do you want?" Annja asked.

"Nothing that you can't give."

"Don't talk to me in riddles."

"I'm not. I'm telling you the truth," the woman said.

"Why are you following me?"

"I'm not following you. At this time, we happen to be traveling in the same direction. You pursue the answer to the Spider Stone. But you're not the one to solve that."

"I've already solved it," Annja said. "All I have to do is find the cave where Anansi put the treasure."

"You're not here for the treasure."

No, Annja admitted to herself. I want to see what's there. I want to read the books that were left. I want to know what those people knew. I want to look back through that window in time to another world. Even if only for a little while.

The old woman shook her head. "That is not your path. You are here only to go so far, Annja Creed."

"How do you know who I am?" Trepidation jangled inside Annja. She knows you from the hotel, she reasoned. All she had to do was talk to the police or the hotel staff. What was more mystifying was how the woman knew Annja was at the hotel to begin with.

"You have finally come." Annja remembered the woman's first words to her.

"I know who you are because I've been trained and

blessed by the gods to know these things," the woman said. "And I know you by that sword you carry."

Annja wondered how much of the fight in the hotel the woman had seen. Only Annja, Roux and Garin knew about Joan's sword. *My sword.*

"You're a warrior," the woman said. "You have been blessed—or cursed, depending on how you wish to view it—to affect changes in the lives of people who hang in the balance."

Annja shook her head in disbelief. So much of what the old woman was saying reminded her of the talk she'd had with Roux in her loft all those months ago. If she didn't sound so much like Roux right now, I'd swear she was crazy. Then again, maybe both of them are crazy.

She might have believed that if she hadn't seen the sword become whole again, if she couldn't pluck it out of thin air whenever she wished.

"I came here tonight to warn you," the old woman said.

"Warn me about what?"

"Your enemies are close."

"By design," Annja said. "I meant to draw Tafari out. I can take care of myself."

The old woman nodded. "I know. But you must take care of others, too."

Annja resisted the impulse to ask whom she was supposed to protect.

"Tanisha Diouf has a part to play in this," the old woman said. "She and her two children must be protected. They are going to be in the eye of the storm." She pointed toward the front of the train. "Now look. Your enemies have gathered."

Unwilling to look, thinking that it was some kind of trick,

Annja hesitated. Then the train's brakes locked up and the metal wheels shrilled across the steel tracks.

Off balance, distracted, Annja fell, tumbling toward the edge of the platform.

21

Annja flailed for the railing around the platform. Her left hand caught, but the right hand missed. Around her, sparks shot out for yards, showering the ground and the brush. Small fires had already started in the wake of the train. The squeal of metal on metal as the wheels skidded along the tracks sounded like the howl of a gigantic beast.

She regained her balance as her right hand took hold.

An explosion of light struck the locomotive. The sound of the detonation followed.

The train whipsawed like a snake. Train cars flipped from the tracks onto their sides. Bedlam filled the night.

Annja looked for the old woman. She was nowhere in sight.

The train car shuddered as it slammed to a full stop. Then it reared up like some rebellious beast. A roar of incredible clanging and shredding metal filled Annja's ears. At the front of the train, the lights of several vehicles suddenly flared to life.

Trap! Annja thought. Either the attackers had used an anti-tank weapon of some kind or they'd mined the tracks.

She leaped from the train, landing in a crouch. Covering her mouth to keep from choking on the huge cloud of dust the wreck had created, Annja scanned the landscape. The vehicles—jeeps and motorcycles—closed in rapidly.

She darted behind a tree as a motorcycle rider spotted her and lifted a pistol in his left hand. The rider was African, dressed in Kevlar armor, his face painted like a skeleton. Bullets smashed into the tree, tearing bark free in chunks.

The rider leathered the pistol and gunned his machine after Annja. Other shots echoed over the broken terrain as she ran.

Abruptly, knowing the man was on the verge of running her down, Annja stepped aside and wheeled to face her attacker. She timed her move, trusted her strength and resiliency, and swung her left arm out, clotheslining the man and knocking him from the motorcycle.

The man landed at Annja's feet. The impact had knocked the air from his lungs. She kicked him in the face, rendering him unconscious.

Kneeling, she stripped an assault rifle from the man, took the bandolier of extra magazines, and the pistol and holster, as well. She buckled the belt around her waist, reloaded the pistol with one of the extra magazines on the belt and stood with the assault rifle in hand.

She wasn't sure what kind of rifle she was holding—she guessed a Russian or Chinese weapon—but she knew how to use it. At the moment, that was enough.

Armed, she ran back toward the train. Whoever the attackers were, and she was pretty sure whom they belonged to, she didn't think they were going to take any unnecessary prisoners.

TANISHA DIOUF MADE herself stand. Dazed, she looked around for Bashir and Kamil. Her children were the center of her life. They were all that she had left of the dreams she and Kevin had had when they married.

"Mom! Mom!" Bashir yelled, tears streaming down his face. "The train wrecked!"

Kneeling, Tanisha helped her youngest up from the clutter of baggage that had tumbled from the overhead compartments. "Easy, Bashir. I've got you." She put her arms around him, felt him shaking and shivering in his fear.

He held on to her tightly.

Gently, Tanisha disengaged from him and took one of his hands in hers. Panic welled up inside her, threatening to spill out of control. *Where's Kamil? Please! Please don't let anything have happened to my baby!* She looked around, but the car had plunged into total darkness.

A light flared to her left. Someone had a flashlight.

In the glow of the beam, Tanisha saw that it was Jaineba. The old woman stepped through the wreckage of the train car as calmly as though she were out for a Sunday walk.

"Jaineba," Tanisha called.

"I hear you, daughter," the old woman said. "You're going to be all right. You've just got to keep your wits about you."

"My son," Tanisha said. "Kamil is missing."

Pausing, Jaineba braced her staff against her shoulder and reached down into the debris. She grabbed Kamil's hand and pulled him free. Kamil stood, but he had a cut above his left eye that bled terribly.

"Kamil!" Tanisha let go of Bashir's hand and grabbed Kamil's head in her hands. She turned his face toward the light to better see the cut. It was deep and would require stitches, but it wasn't life-threatening.

"I'm all right," Kamil protested. "What happened?"

"I don't know." Tanisha gazed around.

The men who had been with Annja Creed had weapons in their fists. Some of them were taking still more weapons from luggage cases.

Seeing the men with guns didn't surprise Tanisha. They'd seemed to her to be the type of men who would carry weapons. They moved calmly and efficiently.

"Where's Annja?" one of the men asked.

"She was just here, Agent McIntosh," one of the other men said.

Agent? Tanisha was surprised about that. She'd guessed that the men were bodyguards for the archaeologist, hired to protect the expedition she was directing.

"She went outside," Tanisha said.

McIntosh directed his flashlight on her. "Who are you?"

"Tanisha Diouf. Annja and I were talking earlier. I saw her go out the back of the car."

The American agent cursed and started for the back door.

"What happened?" someone else asked.

"The train's under attack," the agent said.

Tanisha realized why the train had been attacked. A large part of the cargo was equipment—bulldozers and other earth-moving equipment—to replace the machines that had been destroyed by the tribesmen fighting against encroachment onto what they claimed were their lands. She was sure the Childress Corporation was their target.

"Come on," Jaineba said, waving to her. "We must get the children out of this place. It's very dangerous."

Tanisha nodded and started to follow the old woman to

the back of the car. She was disoriented because the car lay on its side.

A shadow fell over her. Looking up instinctively, Tanisha saw a man—not a man, she corrected herself, a skeleton—squatting next to the shattered window. He had a rifle in his hands.

All of the memories of the voodoo ceremonies she'd seen in and around Dakar came back to Tanisha in a flood. She'd never believed in any of it, not the zombies, not the *loas* riding willing hosts who gyrated to the savage beat of drums and bit the heads off chickens for tourists.

None of that is real, she told herself.

But she was certain she was staring into the face of death. She tried to open her mouth in warning, but she knew she would never get the words out in time.

ANNJA RAN to the overturned train car she'd been riding in. From thirty feet away, she saw one of the attackers clambering along the side. The skeleton-faced man stopped and took aim with his rifle.

Raising the assault rifle to her shoulder, Annja squeezed off a burst. The man jerked as the bullets struck him, but she hadn't hit any mortal areas. Spinning, the attacker lifted his weapon and took aim.

Before he could fire, before Annja could move, the window at his feet exploded in a hail of shattered glass. Gunshots rolled from inside the train car, and the skeleton-faced man jerked like a marionette in the hands of an unskilled puppet master. Then the dead man collapsed.

A moment later, McIntosh came through the door at the back of the train car. He held his pistol in both hands and moved well enough that Annja knew he wasn't hurt.

A jeep roared along beside the train. A man in skeleton makeup hung on to a light machine gun mounted on the rear deck.

"McIntosh," Annja yelled in warning. "Look out!"

McIntosh went to ground at once, taking cover behind the platform beside him just as the jeep's searchlight swept over him and the machine gun chattered.

Using the tree beside her to steady the assault rifle, Annja opened fire. Her bullets raked the side of the jeep, missing the driver, as well as the gunner. Okay, so you're not Annie Oakley, Annja thought, adrenaline surging.

McIntosh fired from cover, a carefully measured 2-round punch that caught the driver in the face. The jeep swerved out of control and slammed into a tree. The gunner flew out of the vehicle and landed in a heap. Before he could get up, McIntosh shot him, as well.

"Who are they?" McIntosh asked.

"They didn't exactly introduce themselves," Annja replied.

McIntosh jogged over to the jeep and helped himself to the dead men's weapons. Other agents did the same. McIntosh also helped himself to one of the bloody Kevlar vests and tossed the other one to Annja.

"Put that on," he growled.

Two other motorcyclists closed on their position. McIntosh and three of the agents took aim and cleared the seats.

"What do you suppose the chances are that the brakeman had a chance to call in the attack?" one of the agents asked.

"Even if they had a radio and were in contact with someone at the railroad," another agent said, "it's going to be hours before anyone comes looking for us."

"The jeep might still be drivable," one of the men said.

"See if you can get it started," McIntosh said. "We need to get the women and children out of here."

Annja started to respond to that, thinking McIntosh was being sarcastic and referring to her. Then she saw Tanisha Diouf and her two sons. The old woman, Jaineba, was right behind them.

Tanisha was hunkered down beside the train, holding Bashir in one arm while she held Kamil's hand with her free hand. She looked frightened.

The jeep roared to life. The agents quickly hustled Tanisha, her sons and Jaineba into the vehicle. One of the agents manned the deck-mounted light machine gun.

"Clear the battle zone, then take cover," McIntosh ordered. "Keep the civilians safe and healthy. We're going to see if we can keep the opposition distracted and whittle the odds down."

The agent wished them luck and pulled out, keeping his lights out so he wouldn't be noticeable immediately.

McIntosh pulled the team together, organizing them into two groups. "We go forward," he told his troops. "Slowly. Take out anybody who isn't us and isn't a civilian."

"With those skull faces they're wearing, there won't be much worry about who's who," one of the agents said.

They went forward slowly, and they killed everyone who was wearing a skull face. They also added to their armament and ammunition with every encounter. Annja immediately saw that McIntosh's agents were far more skilled at this kind of warfare than their attackers.

"When we left Dakar earlier today," Annja said to McIntosh while they regrouped, "you were upset because you thought we might lose Tafari."

McIntosh grunted sourly and looked down at the dead man at his feet.

"I think maybe we have his attention," Annja said.

TAFARI CURSED the ineptitude of his men as they lost battle after battle. He watched through night-vision binoculars, only catching glimpses of the woman and the men who protected her.

"They're too skilled," Zifa said. "Our people haven't ever been up against men like this. Our warriors have had an easy time of it killing ill-equipped tribesmen."

Gazing through the binoculars, Tafari watched as one of his jeeps suddenly swerved and overturned. A jeep with a flamethrower mounted in the back suddenly burst into flames and became a ground comet as bullets tore through the fuel tanks. Burning quickly, the jeep slammed into one of the train cars, came to an abrupt stop and sagged as the tires melted and blew.

"All we're going to do tonight is lose more men," Zifa reasoned.

Tafari knew Zifa was right. There were still plenty of warriors he could use, but the ones who survived the night would tell the others if he used them so coldly.

Besides, he had access to other men, trained mercenaries, who could track and kill Annja Creed and the Americans. He hadn't expected the resistance they'd had tonight. There'd been no way of knowing what those men were like.

He had expected the train wreck to have caused more damage than it had. No one else had recovered as quickly as Annja Creed and her bodyguards had.

"All right," Tafari grated. "Call them off." But he promised himself there would be another opportunity. Soon.

And when that opportunity came and the American archaeologist was within his grasp, she would die a very slow, painful death that people would remember for years.

More than that, the treasure that Anansi had given the Hausa people would be his.

"THEY'RE PULLING UP stakes and leaving," McIntosh said.

Beside him, hunkered down behind one of the train cars, Annja watched as the skull-faced warriors withdrew from the battle.

"Do you think it's a trick?" she asked.

"No," McIntosh said. "I think they've had all they could stand. But we're going to stay put until we know for certain." He glanced at his watch. "It'll be dawn in a couple more hours. We'll see how things look then."

"We need supplies," Annja said. "If they return in the morning, with more men, we don't want to get caught out here without water." She nodded at the overturned train. "We also need to find out if anyone in there needs medical attention."

"You're not a doctor," McIntosh said.

"I'm trained in first aid," Annja said. "I've stitched myself up when I had to."

McIntosh stared at her. "You've stitched yourself up?"

"And a few other people when we were too far from civilization or didn't have access to medical care."

"The lady's right, McIntosh," one of the agents said. "If there's people in that train who've been hurt and there's something we can do for them, I think we need to get it done."

McIntosh nodded. "All right. But we operate in two-man teams and stay in constant radio communication." He and the other agents wore walkie-talkies with earbuds and pencil mikes that lay along their jaws. "Annja, you're with me."

22

Annja jogged to the nearest passenger car and heaved herself inside. There were only three passenger cars. The rest were all cargo cars. They'd go through them, too, looking for railway personnel and supplies—water, food and first-aid kits, but there was less chance of anyone being inside those cars.

McIntosh wasn't happy about her decision to be on one of the search teams. He'd wanted her to stay put. But as she'd informed him, she was highly capable when it came to field medicine.

The car was dark inside.

Annja wanted to use her flashlight, but McIntosh had forbidden their use and she understood the reasoning. A flashlight would attract sniper fire if their attackers had only drawn back to a safe range instead of leaving the area completely.

Nine people were inside the car. All of them were frightened. Thankfully, all of them spoke French so Annja was able to calm them down and allay their fears that they were the attackers.

One of the men had a compound fracture of his left leg. With the slight glow of the moon in the car, Annja could see where the white bone had pushed through the dark flesh of his thigh. The femur was jagged and uneven. He'd bled heavily at first, but most of that appeared to have stopped.

McIntosh cursed.

The man's eyes widened and he clutched at the hand of the woman cradling his head in her lap.

"Stop," Annja told McIntosh, kneeling beside the wounded man.

He was in his early sixties, white-haired and clearly frightened. His eyes rolled and his breath came in short gasps. The woman who cradled his head in her lap looked as though she was his wife. Three small children, probably grandchildren, sat nearby.

"This man is scared enough," Annja went on in a calm voice. She smiled reassuringly at the man. "If you get upset, he's going to panic."

"If that wound doesn't get closed up, it's going to get infected. This train isn't the most hygienic environment."

"I know."

"If infection sets in, he could lose that leg."

Annja forced herself to draw a deep breath. She knew that, too.

"Have you ever dealt with an open fracture before?" McIntosh asked.

"No," Annja admitted. "But I know how to handle it. I need a med kit and some kind of anesthetic."

McIntosh talked briefly over the radio. Within a few

minutes, one of the agents showed up with a medical kit they'd salvaged from the locomotive.

"The engineer and the brakeman are both dead," the agent said. "Took a direct hit up there. They probably died instantly."

Annja didn't let the news touch her. It was too depressing. So far they knew of seven people who had died in the attack. One of them had been a child.

You'll grieve later, she told herself. Do what you can for the others now.

She opened the med kit and found ampoules of morphine. In a calm voice, she told the man that she was going to give him something to take some of the pain away, and she told him there would be pain involved in her fixing his leg.

Grimly, face ashen in the darkness, the man nodded. "Thank you for everything you're doing, miss."

"You're welcome. Now just lie back and try to take it easy." Annja used an alcohol swab on the inside of his right elbow. She gave him the morphine and waited.

Gradually, the old man's eyes glazed and his breathing slowed and deepened.

Annja turned to McIntosh. "I can't do this in the dark."

McIntosh sighed. "I know. Give me a hand and we'll cover the windows as best as we can."

Together, they scrounged for something to use to cover the windows and found bolts of cloth in one of the cargo cars. They cut the material into squares with pocketknives and used strapping tape they'd found there to hold the cloth in place.

By that time, the old man was deeply under the influence of the morphine.

"I'm going to need you to help me do this," Annja said.

"If I knew he'd get medical attention within the next two hours, I'd just immobilize the leg. I'm going to have to assume that it's going to be longer than that. We've got to align the break."

"Tell me what to do." McIntosh put his rifle down nearby. Following Annja's directions, he gripped the man's upper thigh.

The man groaned a little.

"I'm hurting him," McIntosh said.

"It's going to hurt," Annja replied. "If I could put him out, I would."

"You've got more morphine there."

"I could give him too much. I've given him all I think I safely can. Just hold on to his thigh. When I start realigning the bone, I'm going to pull it back into the flesh. If that jagged end slips around too much, it could cut the femoral artery and he'll bleed out in minutes and there's not a thing we can do about it." Annja looked at McIntosh. "Are you ready?"

He gave a tight nod.

Working carefully, Annja stripped the man's shoe off and gripped his foot by the heel and by the top. She pulled steadily, ignoring the man's cries of pain and his wife's plaintive cries to stop what they were doing.

Finally, after a lot of hard work, the broken femur oozed back through the hole in the flesh with a slight sucking noise and disappeared. Annja kept on working, feeling the ends of the bone grate together until she judged she had the best fit possible.

Annja then fashioned a splint for the man's leg using materials she salvaged from the train.

After she'd finished, the man quietly went to sleep.

"Watch him," she told the woman. "Keep him still. If there's any problem, come get me."

"Of course," the woman said. "Bless you for all that you have done."

Annja smiled at the woman. "He's going to be fine. You'll just have to take care of him for a little while after the doctors finish with him."

"Always," the woman said proudly. "I always take care of him."

A FEW MINUTES LATER, Annja stood outside again. The wind felt cool after being inside the train car. McIntosh put a bottle of water in her hand. She opened it and drank gratefully.

McIntosh nodded toward the train car. "What you did back there, most archaeologists don't do that, do they?"

"Not unless they have to take care of someone who's been hurt. Most of us have taken first aid."

"How many times have you done this?"

"Counting this time?"

McIntosh nodded.

"Once."

DAWN STREAKED the eastern sky purple and gold. As night swiftly disappeared, so did some of the fear that had hung over them since the attack.

If it hadn't been for the skull-faced corpses littering the ground, and the fact that another passenger had succumbed to his injuries, the morning might almost have seemed normal.

Annja sat on the ground with her back to a tree and felt the world warm up around her. She wanted a long bath and a comfortable bed, but her mind kept buzzing with thoughts of the Spider Stone. They were close to the area where Yohance had come from. She felt certain about that.

She took the stone from her pocket and studied it again. Her backpack lay nearby. One of McIntosh's agents had recovered it and brought it to her. A brief examination of the computer revealed that it was still in working order.

Footsteps drew close to her. She looked up and saw McIntosh approaching.

Professor Hallinger and Jozua Ganesvoort slept on sleeping bags that had been taken from the cargo cars. Both had spent the night tending to the injured passengers.

She waited for McIntosh to speak.

"We still haven't made contact with Kidira," he said. McIntosh definitely looked worse for wear after being up all night. His clothing was bloody and dirty. He carried the assault rifle in his hand, as if it were a growth that had sprung up overnight.

"They'll send someone," she said.

"We've got enough jeeps to get everyone out of here."

"That would mean crossing a lot of open space, though," Annja said without disguising her concern.

McIntosh sighed. "I know. I've been thinking about that, too." His radio squawked for attention. "McIntosh."

"We have a problem," a man said. "One of the two sons of the lady engineer has a laceration above his eye. We haven't been able to get the bleeding stopped. She wants to know if Ms. Creed could take a look at it."

McIntosh looked at Annja.

Annja nodded.

"Sure," McIntosh said. "We'll be right up." He offered his hand and helped Annja to her feet.

She hoisted the backpack over one shoulder and bent down

to retrieve the med kit. Most of the supplies had been exhausted.

"Last night," McIntosh said as they walked toward one of the jeeps they'd commandeered, "that woman said you'd gone outside the car."

"I did," Annja said.

"Why?"

"I needed some air."

McIntosh snorted as he started the engine. "You're lucky you weren't killed."

Looking at the wrecked train, Annja said, "We all are."

"CAN YOU CLOSE the wound?"

Annja pushed the two edges of the laceration above Kamil's eye together. The edges met perfectly, offering mute testimony that it had been a slice and not a tear. Blood wept slowly down the side of the boy's face.

"I can," Annja said, "but I'm not a doctor."

Tanisha stood behind Annja, looking over her shoulder. "I know," Tanisha said. "But the wound needs to be closed. Kamil says he's feeling light-headed. I'm afraid he's lost too much blood."

"Light-headedness could be from lack of sleep or a concussion," Annja said.

"The size of his pupils match. If it was a bad concussion, the pupils wouldn't match and he'd have a horrendous headache."

Tanisha was anxious about her son's condition. Annja felt the tension coming off the other woman in waves. *It's not just the wound. It's about being out here, as well. Not knowing what's going to happen or if her kids are going to be safe,* she thought.

"I don't have a headache," Kamil said.

Tanisha and her boys sat away from the train with the other civilians. The precaution was in case Tafari's men returned, hoping to catch them unawares. They had food and water and shade, but Annja could tell they were all worried.

Maybe McIntosh is right, she thought. Maybe we should take our chances about going cross-country.

But they were more than an hour away from Kidira by train. Traveling by jeep over the rough terrain would certainly add to that time.

"I need to sit down," Kamil said. "I feel sick."

"Okay," Annja said. "Have a seat." She held on to the boy's arm and helped him sit. Then she looked at Tanisha. "I can close the wound, but I'm not a professional. If the hospital has a plastic surgeon on call, Kamil won't have much of a scar. If I close the wound, I don't know what it'll look like."

"If the cut stays open and gets infected," Tanisha said, "it won't matter if a plastic surgeon is on call at the hospital. The hospital is hours away, and there's no telling how long the wait will be once we get there. I don't want to risk an infection."

"Do you want to do this, Kamil?" Annja asked. During childhood in the orphanage, she hadn't had much control over her life. She'd gone to doctors and dentists when and where she'd been told. She'd resented the impersonal actions. She didn't want to treat Kamil that way.

"Not really," the boy answered.

"We're going to do this," his mother replied, her voice firm. Then it softened. "I don't want you to get worse, Kamil. If this wasn't necessary, I promise you I wouldn't have it done like this."

"Okay." Kamil didn't sound very happy, but he reached out to take his mother's hand.

Annja prepped the wound, cleaning it out with antiseptic and applying topical antibiotics. "Close your eyes, please."

Kamil did, and sat tense as a board.

"Ooh, Kamil," Bashir whispered, eyes wide. "Annja's got a needle. A *big* needle."

Kamil groaned unhappily.

"Hey, Bashir," Annja chided. "I thought your name meant you brought *good* news."

The younger boy clapped his hands over his mouth. "Sorry," he said quietly.

Working quickly, Annja injected local anesthetic around and into the wound to numb it. She used the smallest curved needle in the med kit and put six close-set stitches above Kamil's wound. The smaller and closer the stitches, the smaller the scar.

When she was finished, Annja washed the blood away, put more topical antibiotic on the closure and bandaged the wound.

Once done, Annja had a moment to relax. She suddenly realized she hadn't been alone when the train was attacked. She looked for the old woman, Jaineba.

"Looking for someone?" Tanisha asked.

"I saw an old woman last night," Annja said. "You were with her when you came out of the passenger car."

"Jaineba?"

Annja remembered the name and nodded.

Looking around, Tanisha shook her head. "She was here earlier, but I don't see her now. In fact, I don't know how long it's been since I saw her."

"Is she a friend?" Annja asked.

"Maybe," Tanisha answered. "I think she believes she is. She's a Hausa wisewoman. She lives up in the hills around here."

"Here?" Annja asked. "Not around Dakar?" Excitement flared in her as she thought about the few Hausa villages that were in the area. Most of the Hausa in West Africa lived in Nigeria, not Senegal.

"I don't know if she's ever been to Dakar."

"She's been to Dakar. She was there last night," Annja said.

Tanisha looked at Annja doubtfully. "I don't mean to sound as though I doubt your word, but are you certain it was Jaineba you saw? Some old people tend to look alike."

Annja nodded. "It was Jaineba. She knew me."

"Had you met before?"

"Never."

"Then how did she know you."

"I have no idea."

"That's strange," Tanisha said.

Taking a bottle of water from the box of supplies they'd gathered from the train, Annja silently agreed. Then again, strange things had started happening to her the day she'd found that piece of the sword in France. Strange things had continued happening ever since.

THE SAVANNA FILLED with people an hour later. Tribesmen in loincloths or T-shirts and shorts came with their wives and children from all directions and descended upon the train like carrion feeders.

McIntosh stood, his rifle at the ready.

"Don't shoot," Annja said. "They don't mean us any

harm. They're just here for the cargo." She didn't know how she knew that, only that she sensed no menace.

"Hold your fire," McIntosh called over the radio.

All around them, his men held their weapons up.

The tribesmen smiled and waved and yelled out greetings in English and French. Most of them were empty-handed.

They didn't leave empty-handed, though. Crawling through the cargo, the men, women and children made their selections—as much as they could possibly carry—and returned to the trees and grasslands, disappearing almost at once. Within the hour, there was no sign that they'd ever been there.

"Shopping day," McIntosh commented. Then he sat down in the shade.

Annja joined him. "Someone let them know the train had been derailed," she said. "If they know, other people have to know, too."

"I'm going to give the railway another hour," McIntosh said, "then we're going to caravan out of here. If we'd left this morning, we'd already be in Kidira. I don't want to be out here when it gets dark again."

Me neither, Annja thought. The idea of being trapped in the open by Tafari's men again wasn't a happy one.

FORTY-THREE MINUTES LATER, a train from Kidira chugged into view. The people who'd been stranded by the attack gave voice to a small cheer.

Gendarmes, the military law-enforcement body outside the metropolitan areas of Senegal, occupied the train in force. Dressed in green fatigues and blue berets, they stepped off the train armed to the teeth and took control of the area without hesitation.

The passengers and their luggage were loaded onto the new train. Work crews and security guards wearing black uniforms with Childress Security Division stamped on them stayed behind to begin salvaging what they could.

ANNJA, HALLINGER, Ganesvoort and McIntosh took one of the private salons in the new train and sat down to figure out how they were going to proceed with their treasure hunt.

"I think we should turn back," McIntosh said.

"Turn back?" Annja asked in disbelief. "It was your idea to come."

"It was," McIntosh admitted. "But I was thinking that Tafari would be easier to handle than he is. I thought we could get him off to himself long enough to lock him down. According to our intelligence, his troops were scattered. After last night, we know that's not true." He leaned back in his seat. "Much as I hate to admit it, we're outgunned."

"Just because you're giving up on the possibility of getting Tafari doesn't mean we should back off finding the treasure that Anansi left the Hausa," Hallinger said.

McIntosh shook his head. "Listen to yourself, Professor. You're talking about chasing after an unknown treasure left by an African spider god. It's a story. Make-believe. Nothing more."

Hallinger held up his thumb and forefinger a fraction of an inch apart. "We're this close to finding Anansi's treasure trove."

"You don't know that," McIntosh said.

Anger mixed with Hallinger's words. "We didn't come this far just to give up."

"If you keep this up," McIntosh said, "you're going to get killed. It could have happened last night. I knew it was a mistake to leave Dakar. I should have put my foot down then. We're not set up to deal with something like this. We should have been able to grab Tafari somewhere along the way. That was the plan."

"That was *your* plan," Hallinger replied brusquely. "Annja and I came to find out the truth about the Spider Stone. Just because your plan isn't going to work out doesn't mean ours won't."

"I'll pull the funding on this operation," McIntosh said.

"And I'll underwrite it," Ganesvoort stated quietly. He looked at Hallinger. "If you'll permit me. I've never been part of something like this, and I have to admit that it holds a certain allure."

"You're on Tafari's turf out here." McIntosh sounded exasperated. "Are you people not listening?"

Annja ignored the conversation, concentrating on the topographical maps she'd taken from her backpack. You're not going to see anything you haven't seen before, she told herself. It was hopeless. The map on the Spider Stone didn't match up with anything she could see on paper.

McIntosh was right. They'd come to the end of the chase. The puzzle couldn't be solved. She didn't have enough pieces to make it work.

Worn and tired, not knowing her next move, Annja looked out the window. High in the sky, she saw a lone falcon riding the wind currents. The bird dropped like a stone, plummeting to earth and scooping up a small hare.

She felt as powerless as the hare, and she didn't like it.

23

Seated in a jeep with the canvas canopy up, Tafari waited outside Kidira at an abandoned warehouse and watched the train roll toward the railway station. The building was just outside the city's border so none of the guards would bother him. Outside the city limits, the country turned immediately hostile and dangerous.

Tafari knew the woman archaeologist would be on the train and that vexed him. The night's events had not happened the way he'd imagined them.

Furthermore, the destruction of the train had caused an unplanned rift with his partner. That partnership was a lucrative one, and it promised to be even more so in the future.

"Here he comes," Zifa said.

Zifa's comment was unnecessary. Parked out by one of the truck loading docks, there was no traffic. The luxury Mercedes couldn't have been missed.

Tafari stepped from the jeep. For the meeting, he'd put on one of his camouflage khaki uniforms. It was what all of his men wore when he wanted people to recognize them and know he had sent them there.

The Mercedes pulled up and sat idling. The rear window rolled down.

"Ah, General Tafari," a suave voice called from the back seat. "Join me."

"I'm fine out here," Tafari replied. "I prefer the night air to the air-conditioning inside the car." He wore body armor under his jacket. In addition to the pistols on his hip and under his left arm, he also wore one snugged against his back. With his hands clasped behind him, it was within easy reach.

Tafari viewed the partnership as one of convenience and not trust.

"Then I'll join you." The man got out of the car. Tall and elegant, with black hair and blue eyes, and wearing a tuxedo, Victor Childress was CEO and chief stockholder of Childress Corporation. If he had a pistol under his jacket, it didn't show.

"The train was a mistake," Tafari said. That was as close as he would come to an apology.

"A very costly one," Childress agreed. "Some of that equipment is going to take weeks to replace. And I'd already spent weeks getting those units."

Tafari said nothing. What had been destroyed had been destroyed. His pride and his purpose would remain resolute.

"Why did you do it?" Childress took out a gold cigarette case, selected two cigarettes and offered one to Tafari.

Tafari took the cigarette and leaned in for a quick light. The cigarettes were a personal blend, far superior to anything he could ever get his hands on. He blew out the smoke and let the wind carry it away.

"The woman archaeologist was on the train," Tafari said. "She eluded me in Dakar. She's traveling with a group of killers that I think belong to the CIA or an American military detachment. I also believe they were sent here after me."

"Not for the purpose of protecting the woman?"

"The woman is a lure to get me out of hiding. When my nephew was arrested in the United States, his connection to me would have become known to the American government."

"Then blowing up the train was a good idea," Childress said.

"Last night it was."

"It's just unfortunate that I had so much equipment on that train. And that they're still alive. It's going to be weeks before the Canadians put up the money to fix the train."

That didn't concern Tafari. He never used the train. Even after the Canadians had bought the railway and improved the traveling conditions and timeliness, the train offered too many opportunities for his enemies to get to him.

Childress looked at the city in the distance. Lights lit Kidira, but it was dwarfed by Diboli, the city just across the Senegal River that made up the border between Senegal and Mali.

"Do you really believe this treasure exists?" Childress asked finally.

"Yes."

"What do you think is there?"

Tafari shrugged, not wanting to make his partner greedy. He'd seen greed dissolve a great number of partnerships, especially those that were made out of convenience rather than passion or a shared belief.

"Gold. Ivory. Gems. Perhaps some art pieces museums or collectors might pay handsomely for. Senegal has a long history of trade empires. Even before the slave trade took root here, the Hausa and my people, the Yoruba, pushed vast fortunes throughout the trans-Saharan trade routes."

"Someone could have found this treasure and stolen it away a long time ago," Childress said.

"If that had been the case," Tafari said, "someone would have heard of it. The legend would not have persisted."

"It could be a myth, nothing more."

Tafari dropped his cigarette to the ground and crushed it underfoot. "The Spider Stone is real. My people have seen it. If one is real, then I will believe the other is real, as well. Until I find out differently."

"You need a partner in this endeavor."

"No," Tafari said, "I don't." He had already partnered with Childress in the oil-refinery business. Jaineba encouraged the tribesmen to attack the equipment when they could, but Childress had cut Tafari in to make object lessons of those tribesmen who interfered. Once the Kenyan oil was being refined in the Childress refinery, Tafari would become a rich man.

Childress turned to the warlord and smiled. "Yes, you do. Especially one who can deliver the woman to you."

"You can do that?"

"I can. One of my employees, Tanisha Diouf, called me to ask if we could accompany the archaeologist group into the savanna. Evidently the location of the treasure is somewhere near where we're building the refinery." Childress shrugged, his hair blowing in the wind. "She'd asked me that *before* you blew up the train. All I have to do is say yes."

"A partner like that," Tafari said, "would be good to have."

"I'm glad you see it that way," Childress said. "I thought you would."

Tafari also thought that if Childress became too much of a problem, it would be just as easy to bury him with the rest of them.

AT THE POLICE CHECKPOINT in Kidira, Annja had to show her ID and allow officers to go through her luggage and computer. She'd traveled enough and gone through the process enough that having her panties and bras put on public display was no longer embarrassing.

When the security check was finished, she shoved everything back into her suitcases, shouldered her backpack and walked out with Hallinger.

"This isn't turning out the way we'd planned, is it?" Hallinger asked.

"No."

"Jozua meant what he said about underwriting whatever we want to do."

Annja glanced at Ganesvoort. The man was already arranging taxis for the group to take them to their hotel. She wasn't even sure if they had a hotel, but watching Ganesvoort in action, she was willing to bet he'd arranged one.

"I know," she said. "But at this point, until we can refine our search area or beef up our protection, I don't think wandering around the savanna is such a smart thing to do."

Hallinger looked disappointed. "Let's at least sleep on it before we make a decision."

Annja agreed. She didn't like giving up on anything.

There's a way around this. I'm just too tired to think of it at the moment, she told herself. She remained hopeful, to a degree, but the effort was hard.

THE HOTEL WAS a dump. Even with all the money he had, it was the best Ganesvoort could do.

Annja sat on the bed in her underwear and a T-shirt, sweltering in the heat. There was no air-conditioning, and hardly any wind blew through the solitary window that opened up onto an alley. A tall building next door blocked whatever wind might have been out there.

Loneliness and disappointment filled her. She couldn't talk to McIntosh because he was still upset that they hadn't agreed with him about leaving. Hallinger and Ganesvoort had been down in the lobby poring over maps and pictures when she'd left them.

She wanted to talk to someone. She'd tried Bart McGilley's number but all she got was his answering machine. It was the same with the three numbers she had for Roux. Wherever he was, he was choosing to be unavailable. She'd drawn the line at calling Doug Morrell because she'd been avoiding his phone calls for days and really didn't want to deal with a backlog of guilt.

Feeling dejected and slightly overwhelmed, she sat on the bed with her back against the wall and her computer on her thighs. Slowly, carefully she scrolled through everything she had, glancing frequently at the Spider Stone until, finally, she couldn't keep her eyes open anymore.

A CELL PHONE CHIRPED for attention and a man answered. Waking with a jolt, Annja realized someone was in her room and that she was sleeping on top of the bedclothes. Her back was to the door and to whoever was watching her.

She focused on the sword. All she had to do was close her hand around the hilt and it was in bed with her.

"You're awake," a familiar gruff voice said. "Don't pretend that you aren't. I saw the change in your breathing. And don't come up swinging because I didn't come here to—"

Angry, Annja twisted and threw herself from the bed. She brought the sword up between her and her uninvited visitor.

Garin Braden sat in a straight-backed chair that looked entirely too small for his stature. His magnetic black eyes glinted with amusement as he held empty hands up at his sides. Long black hair framed his ruggedly handsome face. A goatee covered his chin but not the sardonic smile. His suit was elegant, carefully tailored.

"What are you doing in my room?" Annja demanded.

Garin held the cell phone close to his ear just long enough to say "I'll get back to you," then he closed the device and dropped it into his pocket. "I came to see you, of course."

"How did you find me?"

"Magic," Garin answered. "I looked in my crystal ball and—*poof!*—there you were." He paused. "Why don't you put the sword down?"

"Because I like the sword," Annja replied. She also liked the fact that Garin was afraid of the sword. After he'd lived fearlessly for the past five hundred years, it calmed Annja a little to know that he was afraid of her. "And the last time you and I were alone together, you tried to kill me."

That had been in her loft in Brooklyn. She'd surprised him and ended up with the sword at his throat, ready to kill him in a split second if he hadn't backed off. Roux had arrived about then and kept her from doing it.

"If I wanted to kill you," Garin said, "I could have done it while you were sleeping."

Annja didn't know if that was true or not. When it came to Garin, she had no idea what to believe. She might choose to get along with him, but she'd never trust him if she didn't have to.

"Look," Garin said in a calm voice, "I came here to help."

"Me?"

He made a show of looking around. "I don't see anyone else here. Which is a sad thing, because I was told Special Agent McIntosh is a rather good-looking man."

"Let's get back to how you found me," Annja said.

"Boring," Garin told her.

"Tell me and I won't split your nose with my sword and let you bleed all over that expensive suit."

"Fine. Credit cards."

"Credit cards? I haven't used any credit cards."

"No, but Special Agent McIntosh has. They're all on Homeland Security accounts. Hacking into their system and finding that out caused some consternation, I tell you. I tracked the credit-card usage from Georgia to Dakar to here."

"McIntosh didn't pay for my room."

"No, but Ganesvoort did, and I knew he was traveling with you."

Annja thought about that, searching for Garin's angle. He had one, she was certain. The man always had one.

"Trust me," Garin said.

"No." Her answer was flat and immediate.

"You should."

"Why?"

"Because I know something about Anansi's treasure that you don't. In fact, I think I know where it is."

"Then why aren't you claiming it yourself?" Annja asked.

Garin sighed. "I'm rich several times over. Even if I were to live forever, which I hope to, I could maintain my lifestyle of extravagance on just the interest my investments and companies make." He smiled. "I wanted to do the treasure hunting with you. To vicariously enjoy your success."

That's not the whole truth, Annja told herself, but it's close. She still didn't lower the sword.

"Annja," Garin said softly, "you're a beautiful woman. I have to tell you, I could probably spend the day staring at you in that T-shirt and panties." He ran his eyes over her.

Annja suddenly felt exposed. She held her aplomb with difficulty.

"But they're not going to let you eat breakfast downstairs in the restaurant like that," Garin went on. He smiled again, flashing white teeth. "Of course, we could order room service and stay in."

"You are a filthy, disgusting pig," Annja said, irritated because she didn't know what to do. Curiosity wouldn't permit her to throw Garin out of the room without hearing everything he had to say, and she wasn't quite ready to kill him.

Yet.

She willed the sword away and it vanished. Then she took a pair of jeans, clean underwear and bra and a cotton top from her suitcase. She strode toward the bathroom, away from Garin.

"Hey, Annja," he called.

She stopped at the door. "What?"

Smiling, he said, "Could you come back here and walk there one more time? I've never really noticed how your—"

Annja stepped into the bathroom and slammed the door, cutting him off. She was frustrated by Garin's crude nature, but part of her was glad to see him and she didn't understand that at all.

"WE REALLY SHOULD have gone somewhere else." Garin stared at the menu with no enthusiasm. The plastic protecting the typed sheets was stained. "Surely they've got a better restaurant than this."

"This isn't a date," Annja pointed out.

The restaurant was small, more like an afterthought to the hotel than anything else. The menu was extremely limited, but the food smelled good enough to make Annja's stomach rumble in anticipation.

"Maybe I'll just have a coffee," Garin said.

"Eat something," Annja urged.

He peered at her over the menu with interest. "Why? Are you worried that I'm going to starve?"

"I'm hoping you'll choke." Actually, she didn't want to eat alone. She could, and often did, but not when there was an alternative. Maybe Garin was a cold-blooded killer, a thief and a cheat, but he could also be breakfast company.

"Now, there's a cheery thought. And after I've flown so far to see you," he said.

"It's not that far from Germany to Senegal," Annja replied. "And it's not like you actually came to see me. You've got an ulterior motive."

"You've got such a bad impression of me."

"People who try to kill me generally leave a bad impression."

"I'm surprised you came to breakfast with me at all, in that case."

Annja glared at him. "Me. You. Small talk." She shook her head. "It's not going to happen. Get around to whatever brought you here and let's deal with it."

A server came to the table. She was short and plump, in her middle sixties and missing her front teeth. She smiled at them and said good-morning.

Garin ordered for them both, in the native dialect, and in a manner that got a bigger smile out of the tired server.

"You ordered for me," Annja said when he turned back to her.

"I'm sorry," Garin said. "It's a habit I sometimes forget about. When I was a young man, ordering for a woman was both an expectation of the woman and an art for the man. I didn't mean to offend you."

Surprisingly, Annja believed him. "No. Actually, I thought it was kind of charming."

He smiled and looked pleased with himself, erasing some of the charm.

"Seriously, though," Annja said, "we need to talk about why you're here." She glanced at her watch. "You've got fifteen seconds."

"A challenge then."

"Thirteen."

"I think that if you're not careful when you enter Anansi's treasure vault, you're going to unleash a plague that could destroy most of western and northern Africa."

Annja stared at him.

"How am I doing so far?" Garin asked.

24

After the unexpected announcement, it took Annja a moment to find her voice. "You're lying."

Garin laughed at her. "I'm lying? That's the best you can come up with after I tell you that a plague is waiting to be released?" He sipped his coffee. "Why would I lie?"

"To get my attention."

Garin gestured expansively. "I already have your attention. Despite my slight indiscretion—"

"Trying to kill me isn't a slight indiscretion."

"A momentary lapse in judgment."

Annja started to protest again.

Garin held up a hand and looked irritated. "*Whatever* you wish to call it." He took a breath. "Despite that, you talk to me whenever I wish because you're willing to do whatever it takes to get knowledge out of me that you wouldn't otherwise have."

Folding her arms across her breasts, Annja said, "You're not the only man I know who's lived more than five hundred years. In fact, I'm not at all sure how long Roux has been around."

"Nor am I," Garin admitted. "But I am sure of one thing. You won't be able to make casual conversation with Roux and have him trot out his past to be picked over like a buffet line. The only time he tells you anything is when he has his own motivations for doing so. Believe me. I've tried."

"He's trained you well."

Garin grimaced. "I'm not at all like that old fool."

"Maybe you are, more than you like to admit." In fact, upon observing the two of them together, Annja had the distinct opinion that the two acted very much like father and son.

Five hundred years of failed expectation and rebelliousness. Man, that'll leave a mark, she thought.

Garin cursed and shook his head. "We've never seen eye to eye. Roux continues to insist that good will triumph over evil."

"I guess you can't afford to think that way."

"Because you think I'm evil?" Garin asked, sneering.

"Yes."

"I'm not evil. I'm merely a man after my own pursuits."

"You've killed and stolen to get them," Annja said.

"So have you."

Annja gasped. She *had* killed. No more than thirty-six hours ago.

"You killed people to save your life, or to save the lives of others," Garin said. "So you excuse yourself for it. I don't have a problem with that. I excuse myself for the same reasons."

"*You* tried to kill me."

"Will you get over that already?" Garin breathed impatiently. "You threatened me."

"How?"

"The sword. Everything that I am, everything that I have gone through, is because of that sword. Now it is in your hands. When that happened, when I first realized that you had it, can you imagine how I felt?"

Annja couldn't.

"After five hundred years, I'd begun believing that it would never return. Then you came along. And it did. After it had been shattered into pieces. I was afraid. When I attacked you, I wasn't in my right mind. You can't just label people so conveniently," Garin said. "Do you honestly believe Roux is a pure force of good?"

Annja didn't know. She wanted to believe the best of Roux, but he had bailed on her when she had so many questions about the sword and what she was supposed to do. He'd just given her some pop-psychology answers and left her to deal with it. He'd made it clear he didn't see any need to be further involved.

But he'd also told her that she could affect the balance between good and evil. Did she believe that?

Garin scowled. "Roux has filled your head with that crap about the destiny of the sword, hasn't he? And you've really bought into it."

Annja didn't care for the demeaning tone of Garin's words.

"He told me the same thing, once upon a time," Garin said. "Do you know what we did?"

Annja shook her head.

"Roux chased women and gambled across Europe and Asia," Garin said. "Then Roux became intoxicated with the idea of Joan."

"Why? What drew him to her?" Annja asked.

"Probably the same things that draw him to you. She was young—younger than you—and independent. A woman who wouldn't give herself easily to any man."

Annja knew that Roux liked young women. He was rarely without their company at home and abroad from what she had seen.

Frustrated with the conversation, and not liking how it was making her feel, Annja said, "We're not here to talk about Roux."

"I only wanted to put him in perspective so you could better see me," Garin said. "You paint me as a villain, yet I'm the one who showed up here to help you."

Annja restrained from asking him why. "Why do you think the treasure of Anansi has a plague in it?" she asked instead.

AS GARIN SPOKE, he studied Annja. He knew that she didn't trust him. He didn't care. She didn't have to trust him, but only had to let him into the expedition. That was all that he wanted.

But he couldn't get the image of her sleeping atop the bedcovers out of his mind. She was a tall woman, and full-bodied, equipped with warm curves over muscle. Strength sheathed in beauty. That was what she was.

Before he was able to truly launch into the story, the server arrived with their breakfast. Despite his complaining about the probable condition of the food, it looked and smelled good.

They ate while he talked, moving through the mango, bananas and *uji,* sorghum bread and beef strips. He'd ordered as much for her as he had for himself. He'd seen Annja eat before and had been impressed.

The hunger to know what he knew showed in her eyes. She wanted to ask him about what he'd seen, what he'd done, and he knew that, as well.

"I was here in West Africa during the slave trade," Garin went on. "In fact, I knew Jozua Ganesvoort's ancestors. For a time I did business in Ile de Goree."

"Selling slaves?" she asked. The accusation was soft in her words, but it was still there.

"No," he lied. "I sold goods and managed a banking operation." That was the truth. He'd dabbled in many things.

Annja continued eating and listening.

"There's more to the legend of the Spider Stone," Garin told her. "In the Old Testament, God smote the pharaoh and his people with plagues."

"Ten in all," Annja said. "I'm familiar with the story. There's been some conjecture that the plagues may have been the result of activity in the Thera volcano 650 miles away. The Nile could have been polluted by the volcano stirring up the silt and rendering the water undrinkable. That would have accounted for the dead fish, as well. It might even have been red algae, a blood tide. With the water gone bad, the frogs would have abandoned the river and allowed the insect population to grow. Disease-carrying insects could have infected livestock and given the people boils. Plagues of locusts happen even without any of these other events, and enough of them can even make the sky dark. With the volcano involved, perhaps it was ash floating in the air. As for the firstborn dying, if the food was ruined they may have died from the diseases it carried."

"And what does the field of archaeology say?" Garin asked.

"When it comes to the Bible, archaeologists are divided," Annja admitted. "Some treat it as a historical document, and others believe it's a work of fiction."

"Designed to keep the believers in line."

"Perhaps."

Garin smiled. "What if I told you that those Biblical citizens weren't that far removed from people today? That there existed within their ranks men who would use whatever means necessary to achieve their ends."

"That's mankind in action," Annja said. "No surprise there."

"True. However, research I've done indicates that some of the people scattered after the pharaoh figured out that the disease that ran through his city wasn't all due to the Hebrew god. The pharaoh's men discovered that some of the diseases had been deliberately started by men."

"Where did you get this information?" Annja asked.

Garin reached into his pocket and took out a USB flash drive. "I have copies of the document."

Annja pushed her empty plates away and put her computer on the table.

Watching her become absorbed in the task, Garin felt a glow of success.

WORKING QUICKLY, Annja opened the flash drive. There was only one file on the device. She copied it to her computer—she couldn't risk Garin snatching it away whenever he wanted—and opened the file. There were several folders tucked inside the main file. Most of them were jpegs.

"They're photographs of tablets recovered from a Hausa village about a hundred years or so after they were written," Garin said. "Evidently the author couldn't live his life in anonymity. That's probably how the pharaoh found out about his culpability in the plagues."

Annja studied the first photograph of a clay tablet. It

appeared to be similar in nature to those used in Egypt at the same time period.

"I can't read them. Can you?" Garin asked.

"No," Annja replied.

"Select the next jpeg and you'll see a translation."

The next file had a picture of the same tablet with a translation overlaid on it in white letters. Annja read the story.

> While I lived among the dark men and feared Pharaoh's revenge, I had cause to once more use the potion I had concocted to ravage Pharaoh's army. My adopted village was approached by a young man, no more than a boy, who said that his own village was beset by enemies.
>
> I was touched by the boy's story of how Anansi, the spider god of his people, directed him to me in a dream. I knew that he probably came to me because I have solved many problems for this village where I have chosen to stay.
>
> He appealed to my vanity, praising me as one who has been chosen to be spoken through by his gods. Since his people do trade as much as they do and carry news of many countries, I thought it would be best if I maintained their friendship.
>
> I gave him a pot of the potion and told him to spread it in the water of his enemies. I told him that only a small amount would be necessary, for it was very powerful and water in these lands is a precious commodity, just as it is in Egypt.

Annja launched into the second set of tablets. Excitement stirred within her, along with fear.

I saw the boy again today. He told me that the men who attacked his village are now dead. The potion has always performed well.

When I asked him what he did with the rest of the potion, he told me that Anansi directed him to put it in the place of treasures so that it might be used again if needed.

He gave me a small bag of emeralds and rubies. Before he left, he also showed me a small stone he's inscribing that will tell the history of Anansi's promise to protect his people. On one side, the stone bears the image of an atrocious spider. The other holds the language of his people.

Finished with the translations, Annja stared at Garin. "Is this true?" she asked.

He nodded. "You're hunting something that could kill you and a lot of other people."

"And you're here because you care about people?"

"No," Garin said. "I'm here because I care about you."

Annja didn't believe him. There was more. She waited.

Garin cocked an eyebrow and grinned. "But there's more, Annja. For five hundred years, only Roux and I have shared the mystery of the sword. I'd given up on it. But you came along and made that mystery new again. Made it attainable once more. Or at least clothed it in that illusion. And you've turned our two-sided war into a three-way battle. I've never gotten the best of Roux. With you at my side, I think that balance of power could change."

"Why would I ever help you?" Annja asked.

"Because one day, you may not have a choice. Roux is

not your benefactor. If you get in his way—and you might—he'll step on you."

A chill threaded down through Annja's spine as she faced the possibility that Garin might be speaking honestly.

"Well," Garin asked, "do we have a deal? Or did we just have breakfast?"

25

Annja made the introductions, giving Garin's name as Gar Lambert, a professional treasure hunter she'd bumped into while in town.

Hallinger and Ganesvoort seemed pleased by the possibility that someone familiar with the area—and someone who had armed men at his disposal—could join the expedition.

McIntosh and his entourage weren't so easy to convince. They sat together at the back of the room Garin had reserved for the meeting.

"It's amazing how you just happened to come along," McIntosh said.

"Not so amazing," Garin replied. He'd changed clothes, dropping the suit and slipping into jeans and a khaki shirt. He also affected an American accent. The skill of weaving different accents and behaviors was something Annja had noticed in both Roux and Garin. Both men were as skilled as trained actors. "I've been watching the news. I knew Annja was in West Africa. We've already been here for weeks."

The dozen men who followed Garin were hard-eyed and silent. Most of them looked as if they'd fit right in with the Kidira citizens. Except that most of the Senegalese didn't look like killers.

"When we ran into each other earlier," Annja said, "I explained what we were doing." She looked at McIntosh. "I also told him we were short on manpower."

Garin smiled. "Naturally, I couldn't let Annja go trekking around the wilds of the savanna unprotected. Especially not with Tafari gunning for her."

"Naturally," McIntosh said sarcastically.

Annja didn't say anything, although the expression on McIntosh's face made it tempting. She kept quiet, and after a few minutes, everyone began discussing how they were going to get the expedition under way.

"HOW WELL do you know this guy?"

Annja glanced at McIntosh as they walked along the sidewalk.

Garin and his crew of mercenary cutthroats had set out to finalize the vehicles and armament they were taking.

"I trust him," Annja said.

"With your life?"

"Yes."

"What about the lives of the rest of us?"

Annja stopped and wheeled on McIntosh so fiercely that he backed up a step. "I trust him with the lives of other people as much as I trust you with them, Agent McIntosh."

Passersby started going around them, giving them a wide berth.

"Furthermore," Annja said, "you and your men don't have to take this trip if you don't want to."

McIntosh got his feet under him and leaned into her. "I came this far with you. I'm not going to turn tail now."

"We're not on your turf anymore," Annja said, feeling a little concerned for him. "This isn't Atlanta. That wilderness out there isn't like anything you've ever dealt with. This is my game now."

"Except for your buddy. Looks like it's his game, too."

"He's been around this kind of thing longer than I have," she said.

"Tafari is still out there somewhere, Annja."

"I know," she said. "That'll give you the chance to capture him like you wanted. You should be glad."

"Well, I'm not." McIntosh was breathing hard.

Annja got the impression he was about to do something stupid, like try to kiss her. That's the last thing I need right now, she told herself.

McIntosh cursed and walked away.

"SOMEBODY'S COMING."

Annja looked up from her computer and stared down the trail that cut through the savanna. Kidira was hours behind them, and the western sky was starting to turn purple with the dimming of the day. They were making their way toward a distant hill to the west. Locals, Annja had discovered when she'd asked, had called the place Brothers of Water. Given that the Spider Stone showed a suggestion of waterways in the map—at least, she *hoped* it was a suggestion of waterways—Anansi's treasure was likely to be hidden somewhere near there.

Garin rode in the lead Land Rover. His driver halted. The other drivers behind him fanned out, all of them parking in a formation that allowed for defensive moves.

"I need you to stay put, Ms. Creed," Annja's driver said. He rolled the vehicle to a stop, then closed a big hand around the assault rifle between the seats.

Annja put her computer away. She wore a .45-caliber semiautomatic on her hip. Her T-shirt and cargo pants were soaked through from the heat. She wore a New York Yankees baseball cap and wraparound sunglasses.

All of Garin's crew had drawn their weapons. McIntosh and his people had, too. The possibility of an outside threat seemed to unify the two forces.

The approaching Land Rover halted a few feet in front of Garin's vehicle. Tanisha Diouf slid out of the passenger side. She was dressed in khakis, a green T-shirt tucked into her pants. Stopping, she called out, "Annja Creed."

Annja stepped out of the vehicle and onto the trail. "Tanisha."

The woman's face split into a wide, generous smile. "You've been invited to join us."

"Us?" Annja echoed.

Tanisha pointed to the side of her Land Rover. Childress Corporation was emblazoned on the side. "I talked to Mr. Childress. He agreed to help you get as far into the savanna as safely as you can. If you're interested."

"I am," Annja said.

Tanisha walked over to her. "I was hoping you would say that. My boys have been worried about you. They thought maybe something had happened to you after you left us."

Annja grinned. "I'm glad nothing's happened to you."

"Mr. Childress believes the train was attacked by bandits hoping to steal some of the cargo," Tanisha said. "The next time he has a shipment coming in, it'll be protected."

Annja nodded.

"Mind if I ride with you?" Tanisha asked. "We can talk along the way."

"Sure."

Garin's men repositioned themselves, making room for Tanisha.

"Follow that vehicle," Tanisha instructed the driver. "We've got a base camp not far from here."

Tanisha looked at Annja. "Do you have those maps you had on the train? Let me have a peek and maybe I can get you closer to where you need to go."

"ARE YOU an investor, then?" Victor Childress peered at Garin.

"Yes," Garin replied. "Well, not really investing so much. That's a little rich for my blood. But I do speculate. If something catches my eye."

Annja sat at the folding table their host had provided. Everyone was relaxing after a generous meal.

Bashir sat on her lap and kept distracting Annja with whispered comments despite his mother's admonitions. Kamil had allowed Annja to take a look at his cut, even though it interfered with his manly acting. She'd been pleased to find the wound was healing well.

"Oil is where the money is," Childress said. "If you have it, you make money. But do you know who else makes money?"

Annja knew Childress had consumed a fair bit of wine with the meal.

"Who?" Garin asked as if he was intensely interested. For all Annja knew, maybe he was.

"The people who transport it and sell it at the pump, of course," Childress said. "And the corporations that refine oil."

"I guess that's true enough," Garin said.

McIntosh was ignoring the conversation for the most part. His attention was directed at the dark savanna outside the ring of lights that lit the camp.

"Did you know that Nigeria, not that far from here, actually," Childress said, "is the largest African producer of oil?"

"No," Garin replied.

"Well, they are. Unfortunately, that country is being torn apart by American oil interests and a corrupt government. Hobbled as they are, battered between gangsters and native militias, they can't enter a competitive market. Also nearby, Mauritania's army ousted their president and are looking to do business. In the past, they've had to go through American companies. Childress Corporation is here to change that."

From the short time she'd been around the man, Annja could see that Childress had a high opinion of himself. With McIntosh and Garin already butting heads over who was the alpha male of the expedition, there was too much testosterone in the air.

"I contracted with the Senegalese government to set up a refinery out here," Childress said. "We're in the process of building it now. At the same time, another facet of Childress Corporation is also laying pipe from Mauritania to Senegal. When everything's finished, we'll pump the oil across from Mauritania and refine it here. We hope we'll pick up some business from Nigeria, as well."

ANNJA WORKED in the small dome tent she'd set up for the night.

A shadow darkened the door and Garin's deep voice said, "Knock, knock."

"Come in." Annja sat cross-legged on the floor of the tent. The computer was plugged into an electrical outlet maintained by one of the camp's generator trucks.

Garin entered the tent, having to hunker low. He scowled, then spoke in Latin. "Speak this language. I don't want to be understood by the guards posted nearby, or by the bugs."

"What bugs?" Annja asked in Latin.

"Our host is spying on us."

"Why?"

Garin grinned. "Because he's not a good guy. All that talk he had of setting up a refinery to do fair business with Mauritania and Nigeria? Do you know what he's really banking on?"

"No."

"Bandits. Oil thieves. They've got them all over those countries. As Mauritania was getting ready to enter the oil market, the army pushed out the president, broke off relations with the Americans and went into business with an Australian firm. Nigeria has been conducting sporadic warfare over oil for years. Tanker trucks are stolen from those fields all the time."

"That's going on in the Middle East, too," Annja said.

"Everyone's watching the Middle East," Garin said. He shook his head. "Childress is setting himself up well. He can deal with the bandits in all those countries to subsidize his legitimate business, and have an oil refinery that can sell gasoline right back to the locals, as well as ship it out to the rest of Africa and even Europe. It's a sweet setup. But do you know what he needs?"

Annja didn't like where her mind automatically went because it left Tanisha and her children exposed. "A local warlord to handle all the strong-arm work," she said.

"You know," Garin said, "you don't think like an archaeologist."

"To the contrary," Annja said, "if you study history, you'll see that every culture, nation or people that existed or exists was influenced by what they had or what they wanted or needed. If they had something, they lived a life of other people trying to take it away from them. If they wanted or needed something, they lived a life struggling to get it." She sighed.

She looked at Garin. "So we can't trust Childress."

"No." Garin grinned. "But we let him think we do."

"You think he's going to sell us out to Tafari?"

"I think he already has. Once you find Anansi's treasure, the jaws of the trap will close."

"Then it makes no sense to try to find it," Annja said.

"Now you disappoint me. If we try to leave, deviate from our mission of trying to find the treasure, the jaws of the trap will close anyway. We'll have to fight and maybe lose a lot of people. But if we find the treasure, Tafari and Childress should at least be distracted. Then we'll act to do what we can."

"We could try to slip away. Choose the path of least resistance." Annja didn't want to chance getting McIntosh, Hallinger or Ganesvoort hurt. It was her fault that they'd come this far.

"What about the woman? The engineer and her kids? The other innocent people who are part of this operation? Do you want to just leave them out here?" Garin asked.

Annja knew she was tired because she hadn't thought far enough. She'd been using all her energy to try to find a match on the maps. She shook her head.

"I'd be willing to bet that Tafari or Childress will use your connection to them against you," Garin continued. "After you had the little boy on your knee for most of the night, you've left yourself—and them—open to that." He paused. "If it was me, I would use them against you."

Annja knew he told her that honestly, even though it would remind her of the reasons not to like or trust him. But he knows I don't have a choice now, she thought. I have to trust him. And maybe, if he wants to find Anansi's treasure, he has to trust me.

She took a deep breath and let it out. "What do we do?"

In the darkness of the tent, Garin's lips curled back in a wolfish smile. "When the time is right, we'll act."

Annja nodded.

"I'm going to have to come see you more often, little angel," Garin said in a light tone. "You do lead an interesting life." He turned and crawled back through the tent flaps. "I just hope the cursed luck of that sword doesn't get you killed." He tossed her a smile over his shoulder as he disappeared into the night lying in wait outside.

THE CARAVAN STARTED out early the next morning. In spite of all he'd drunk and the lateness of his evening, Victor Childress was one of the first to be ready. He wore safari clothes and carried a big-game hunting rifle slung over his shoulder.

"Since I seem to be having trouble with the local toughs," he said, "what with the equipment sabotage and the train wreck, I thought I'd get better equipped."

Annja looked at him, wondering if what Garin had told her the previous night was really true. Childress seemed amiable and harmless, actually enthusiastic about helping. But she couldn't shake the feeling that Garin was right.

It takes a villain to know a villain, she told herself. She wondered again about Garin's own motivations, and whether he was the villain she'd thought him to be. Here he was, laying his life on the line. But for what?

"You don't have to come," Annja told Childress. "I think we've got enough people to handle everything."

"Nonsense." Childress sipped gourmet coffee from a stainless-steel mug. "If you and your group hadn't run off those sods that ambushed the train, they might well have made off with all of my equipment. I'm certain that's what they were after."

Annja wondered if he was attempting to allay any suspicions about Tafari.

"While we're waiting on replacement equipment," Childress said, "I can spare Tanisha and a few of my men to help you out for a few days. Once the new equipment gets here, we'll have to tend to our own kettle of fish."

Annja made herself smile and thank him.

The group set out across the savanna, following the course she'd developed from the map on the Spider Stone.

BY MIDDAY, everyone was hot and tired. They followed trails made by wagons and carts when they could, picked up fragments of footpaths and game trails when they couldn't and blazed new paths when they couldn't do anything else. One of the Land Rovers went down with a flat tire, bringing the caravan to a halt.

Annja stood in the shade of the vehicle she rode in and compared the terrain to what she understood from the Spider Stone. *Either it's starting to look familiar because I've been looking at it too long, or we're getting close.*

As she opened a bottle of water, McIntosh joined her. His

shirt was dark with sweat and a film of dust that stuck to the moisture. She tossed him a bottle of water from the cooler in the back of the Land Rover. His men and Garin's had set up a defensive perimeter around the vehicles.

"I keep getting this feeling we're being followed," McIntosh said as he opened the water and drank.

"We are." Annja nodded upward at the large birds that floated gracefully in the still sky. They were two feet long with a wingspan nearly three times that. Brown feathers covered their plump, ungainly bodies, and their heads were a pinkish bald knob.

McIntosh shaded his eyes and looked up. "What are those?"

"Hooded vultures. You'll find them in the wild, as well as around towns."

"I thought I saw some like them in Kidira."

Annja nodded. "They feed near slaughterhouses more often than they feed out in the wilderness. They're the smallest of the African vultures, but the swiftest. Generally they're the first to find a carcass, but they're so much weaker that everything else drives them away."

"They've spotted us and think we're going to croak, huh?" McIntosh said.

Despite her misgivings, Annja smiled. "I hope not."

McIntosh spoke without looking at her. "I think you're right about Childress."

She'd gone to McIntosh's tent after Garin had left hers, and told him what Garin suspected. McIntosh had said he doubted that Garin knew what he was talking about.

"Why the change of heart?" Annja asked.

"Do you know many millionaires who figure they have time in their day to intentionally go out and try to get themselves killed?"

"What are you talking about?"

McIntosh looked at her. "I don't think Childress would be out here beating the bush with us unless he thought he had a lock on things." He nodded toward the man, who was conferring with some of his own men. "Whatever's going on in his mind, he thinks he has a free pass."

Annja agreed.

"I think we need to drop this," McIntosh went on. "Just tell Childress that you were wrong, that Anansi's treasure is a big hoax—"

"He's not going to believe that if Tafari doesn't believe that."

"Tell him the treasure isn't located anywhere around here."

Annja was quiet for a moment. The men had finished replacing the tire on the Land Rover, and everyone was preparing to continue.

"It is, though," Annja said. "And I'll bet Tafari knows it is, too." She took out the Spider Stone and looked at the map etched on its surface. She knew every line of it by now. "Leaving isn't the answer. We're too deep into it now. The only way out is to go through with this."

26

"You haven't asked me why."

Looking up from the maps they were studying as they ate, Annja studied Tanisha Diouf. "Asked you why what?"

"Why I'm out here."

Annja didn't understand.

"In the savanna," Tanisha said. "When I could be home in London with my kids." She glanced at Kamil and Bashir. The boys played in the nearby scrub, going deeper and deeper into the wilderness as they got braver. "To hear my mother tell it, where I should be with my kids." She sighed. "There's nothing worse than a mom call."

Annja had seen Tanisha talking on the satellite phone earlier.

"Does your mom call to give you grief over what you do?" Tanisha asked.

"I kind of missed out on that," Annja said.

"You lost your mom?" Tanisha looked stricken. "I'm sorry. I didn't mean to bring up anything that would—"

"Actually, I was raised in an orphanage."

"I've seen you on that show—"

"Chasing History's Monsters," Annja said.

"—and no one ever mentioned it."

"Not exactly something you want advertised on a television show like that," Annja said. She waited a beat. "So why are you?"

"Why am I what?" Tanisha asked.

"Out here. In the wilds of West Africa. With your boys."

"I was working for Childress in London. Operating some of the drilling platforms he's working in the North Sea. I had a deal set up with him where I was two weeks on-site and two weeks home with my kids. Still available for calls, though." Tanisha ate another peach slice. "Then he approached me about this." She waved her fork around to take in the savanna.

"Was the offer too good to turn down?"

"It was good. Don't get me wrong there. But it was something else that made me come here."

Annja waited.

"I grew up in London," Tanisha said. "But my grandparents grew up in the United States. In Georgia. Near Atlanta. Before that, according to my father and grandfather, my people were here."

"West Africa?"

Tanisha nodded. "They were from the Hausa." She looked at Annja. "The same people who made that Spider Stone." She shrugged. "So, in a way, taking this job meant that I could see my homeland. I didn't know if it would make a difference."

"Does it?"

Tanisha hesitated. "I don't know. The job and the boys

have been keeping me frantic. The sabotage and destruction of the equipment has been the worst. That always causes a drain on time and energy." She took a deep breath and let it out. "But sometimes, when I'm alone or it's really late at night, or when I'm talking to Jaineba, this place just feels like home." Shaking her head, she looked at Annja. "Isn't that weird?"

Annja thought about the sword she carried, the one Joan had carried into battle. I've seen stuff a lot weirder than that, she thought.

AN HOUR LATER, they came to a rise and Annja looked down into the slight valley below. A small stream, nothing like the Senegal River or any of the other three that fed the country, wound through the valley and—for a time, just as the Spider Stone map showed—became two streams.

There was something about the land that drew Annja's attention. Pieces of the Spider Stone's map and the topography files she'd been studying fit together inside her head.

She had the driver stop and she got out at the top of the hill.

Garin, noticing that she had stopped, ordered his vehicle to a halt also. He clambered out with his assault rifle in hand.

"What is it?" he asked.

"We're here," Annja said, controlling the excitement that filled her. "This is the Brothers of Water."

Garin looked around at the area. "You're sure?"

Annja nodded. She saw the landmarks she'd been searching for—the hills that formed a bowl-shaped depression and the two streams that made a wishbone only a little to the right of her position. There, like the Senegal River was formed by the mixing of the Semefé and Bafing Rivers, the two streams came from one, then pooled into a depression at the bottom of the valley.

"It's here," she said. "Or it doesn't exist at all."

THEY BEGAN in the center of the valley. Annja marked off sections by natural landforms. The hunt kicked off in earnest.

"What are we looking for exactly?" McIntosh asked.

"A door," Annja said. "At least, that's what I think it is. On the map on the Spider Stone, it shows a rectangle that I think is a door."

"But you might be wrong," he said.

"Archaeology isn't as exact a science as mathematics or physics," Annja said. "There's a lot of guesswork involved, conclusions that you draw that may never be proved."

"The rectangle could just as easily be an unmarked grave," he said.

Annja replied grudgingly, "Yes. But that's not what the stone says."

TAFARI WATCHED the woman search the valley. Hours passed and the sun settled over the western horizon. Still, she didn't give up.

Nor did he.

He lay on his chest on another hill and held a pair of binoculars to his eyes as the woman continued her quest. Eventually, some of those hunting in the area were pulled off the search to set up camp.

Zifa crawled up to him and handed him a satellite phone. "Childress," Zifa said.

Taking the phone, Tafari cradled it to his face and said, "Yes?"

"I think this is a waste of time," Childress complained. "Whatever she thinks she has, whatever you think she has, she doesn't have it."

Tafari said nothing. He kept watch through the binoculars. Below, the searchers were starting to use flashlights, not even giving up to the night.

"Did you hear me?" Childress demanded.

"I did," Tafari replied.

"What are you going to do?"

"Be patient."

"It's just a superstition," Childress argued. "If there was anything to find here, it would have been found by now."

"Sometimes," Tafari said, "secrets don't come out so easily. What you're talking about in this place, the gods have hidden."

"In the morning," Childress said, "I'm leaving. This has ceased to be amusing."

"You would never make a good hunter," Tafari told the man. "And if you leave now, you can consider our partnership in the matter of this treasure at an end."

"Why?"

"If you're not here to labor for the fruits, you won't be allowed to partake in the banquet."

Childress sounded upset. "I did my part. I delivered the woman."

"But now you've become a part of it. If you leave this expedition early, that could warn her. She already senses that she's being followed."

"If she does, I haven't seen any sign of it," Childress said.

"You're a civilized predator," Tafari said. "You don't know what to look for out here. The woman does. If you leave tomorrow, you will end our agreement because your departure will jeopardize my effectiveness in trailing her."

"All right," Childress grumbled. "I'll be here for a few more days. No more than that." He broke the connection.

Tafari handed the phone back to Zifa.

"There is a problem if the woman continues in the direction she's headed," Zifa said.

"What?"

"The village we destroyed a few days ago lies less than two miles farther in the direction she's going."

Tafari had almost forgotten about the Hausa village they'd eliminated. "Maybe it would be good if she and her friends see that place," he told Zifa. "That way she'll know what I'm capable of."

FRUSTRATION CHAFED at Annja as she stared through the darkness. But the feeling that she was at the edge of discovery wouldn't go away.

Moving slowly through the brush, her eyes burning, she searched for anything that might suggest a hidden place. Graves could often be found by earth that sank in after them. So could collapsed buildings and remnants of cities. Refuse built up over time, and she had no way of knowing how long ago Anansi's treasure had been hidden.

"Annja."

She ignored McIntosh's call, knowing he would only want to try to talk her into giving up the search for the night.

"Hey." McIntosh caught up to her, flashlight bobbing through the scrub brush. He took her by the elbow.

"Let go," she said.

He took his hand back. "I'm not asking you to give up," he said. "Just to wait. It's dark out here. Somebody's going to get hurt. Come eat. Get some rest. Then start again in the morning when it's light. Everything will look different then."

He's right, she thought. She forced herself to take a deep breath. One of the most important things she'd learned while on digs was that the expectations of the leader tempered those of the people working the site. Pour on the expectation too early, keep them working too long and too hard, and there would be less to work with.

"You're right," she said.

"ANNJA," Tanisha called.

Groggy from being sound asleep, her dreams filled with spiders, maps and murderous men, Annja blinked her eyes and focused on Tanisha Diouf as the woman unzipped the tent and climbed in.

"What's wrong?" Annja asked.

"Bashir's missing," Tanisha replied. "I looked for him, but I can't find him anywhere."

Fear tightened Annja's stomach, and she felt a chill against the back of her neck. Rain slapped against the tent, and from the sound of it she knew the ground outside was soaked.

"How long has he been missing?" Annja dressed quickly.

"Five, maybe ten minutes. I went looking for him, but I couldn't find him." Panic ate at the edges of Tanisha's words.

Annja pulled on her hiking boots and laced them up. A glance at her watch showed her it was just after 6:00 a.m. It didn't sound as though anyone else was up. "We'll find him. Are Garin and his men up?"

"The sentries are."

"None of them saw Bashir?"

"They saw him walk into the brush. They didn't see him walk back out."

Annja grabbed the pistol and slung the assault rifle. Reaching down, she grabbed her backpack. It contained medical supplies, rope and extra gear.

"Why did Bashir go into the brush?" Annja asked.

"To use the bathroom. He's shy about that. Kamil knows he's supposed to go with him, but he said he couldn't wake up." Tanisha shook her head. "I didn't even know he was gone until I woke up a few minutes ago and he wasn't there."

Garin was up when Annja left her tent. So was McIntosh.

"What's going on?" Garin asked.

"Bashir is missing," Tanisha cried.

Garin looked over to one of the hard-eyed sentries.

The man shook his head, then spoke German. Annja listened.

"Did you see the boy?" Garin asked.

"The boy went into the brush," the man said. "He does that. Likes to be by himself. Shy kidneys. I didn't think anything of it."

"Has anyone been around?"

"No."

Garin held the assault rifle, barked orders to his men and looked at Annja. He spoke in English. "Let's find the boy."

FOLLOWING Bashir's trail across the muddy ground was easy at first. The rain had softened the surface enough that his footprints sank into the ground. However, that same rain also threatened to wash them away.

Annja moved quickly. Mud clung to her hiking boots and made her feet heavy. Sucking noises sounded every time she lifted the boots clear of the muck.

Bashir had managed a circuitous route through the brush. From the way he stopped and his feet turned around, it was evident he was tracking something. A short distance on, Annja found the tracks of a hare.

"A rabbit," McIntosh said, dropping to one knee to examine the tracks.

"Bashir saw them all day yesterday," Tanisha said. "He wanted to make a pet out of one of them."

A short distance ahead, Annja saw where a sinkhole had opened up in the earth, leaving a gaping maw almost four feet across. Her heart trip-hammered in her chest. She'd suspected that Anansi's chamber was underground, but there was no way of knowing how large it was.

"Oh, my god," Tanisha gasped. She jerked into a run.

27

Annja caught Tanisha around the waist and held her back from the sinkhole.

"Let me go!" Tanisha struggled, but Annja was able to hold her.

Garin moved in to help.

"Bashir may have fallen into that hole!" Tanisha said. Her tears mixed with the rain.

"I know," Annja said as calmly as she could. "If he's in there, we'll get him. But we won't be able to help him by losing our heads." She stared into Tanisha's eyes. "Do you hear me? Don't waste time."

Tanisha nodded.

Annja passed the woman off to McIntosh, then shrugged out of her backpack and took out a coil of rope. She tied the rope around a tree in a quick, practiced flip.

"I've got you," Garin told Annja, taking hold of the rope.

Annja nodded at him, then knotted the rope around her waist and went as quickly as she dared to the edge of the sinkhole. She focused on saving Bashir, not finding the little boy drowned in a huge pool of mud.

She eased over the edge of the hole, taking heart in the fact that the sinkhole hadn't crumbled any farther and that the mud pile at the bottom of the hole wasn't large enough to cover even a small child.

Annja spotted muddy footprints on the stone floor of the tunnel. Crouched down at the bottom of the drop, some ten or twelve feet below the ground, she realized that she was standing in a passageway.

"Annja," Garin called.

"I'm all right. Bashir's not in the mud." Annja knelt and examined the stone flooring. Flat stones made up the bottom of the passageway. More stones supported the sides. A quick check over her head, dragging her fingers along the tunnel's ceiling, told her that stones had been used there, as well.

Thin streaks made from small fingers stained the walls. As Annja studied them, the mud began to run.

"Bashir was here, though," she called up. "The sinkhole leads to a tunnel." A puddle of water came halfway up her boots. He got scared he was going to drown, she thought. Or that no one was going to find him.

"Where is he now?" Tanisha asked.

Annja peered into the darkness. "I don't know. Get some flashlights and get down here."

TAFARI ROUSED the instant Zifa touched him. "What?" he asked.

"Childress called," Zifa said. "It appears that Annja Creed has found a tunnel to an underground structure."

"Get the others," Tafari ordered. "Let's go see what the woman found." He strapped on his guns over his loincloth, then opened the tin containing the paint he used to mark himself as a warrior of his people. He started putting on the skull face by touch.

"BASHIR." Annja called the boy's name as she went forward through the passageway. The floor tilted, heading deeper into the earth. Her voice echoed ahead of her, letting her know that she'd barely seen any of the underground space that existed. *"Bashir."*

"Annja?" The boy's voice came out of the darkness. In the next moment he was stepping into her flashlight beam. He was covered in mud. "Annja!"

She knelt, holding on to the boy as he desperately wrapped his arms around her. Then he was sobbing, shaking against her, knotting his fists in her shirt.

Annja didn't say a word, just held him and let him know she was there. She rubbed his back.

"I was lost," he said.

"I know," Annja replied.

"I was chasing after a rabbit. I didn't know it was leading me into a trap."

Annja smiled. "I really don't think the rabbit built this, do you?"

Bashir pulled his head off her shoulder and sniffled. "No. Bugs Bunny would never live in a place like this." He looked around.

"That's probably true," Annja agreed. "Are you all right?"

He nodded.

Annja made him step back so she could survey him from head to toe. Muddy and teary-eyed, Bashir didn't seem to be any worse for the wear.

Holding on to his hand, Annja walked him back to the

sinkhole. McIntosh, Garin, Tanisha and Childress had gathered around the opening. They lowered a rope and pulled Bashir up. Mother and son had a tearful reunion.

"Is it down there?" Childress asked, more animated than ever. "Anansi's treasure?"

"I don't know," Annja said. "I didn't reach the end of the passageway. It goes on for a while."

Lightning flickered against the cottony-gray sky of early morning. Thunder pealed like a cannon, drowning out the constant hiss of the falling rain for a time.

"With the sinkhole opened up like that," McIntosh said, "the rain could flood the passageway."

"We could try to close it up," Childress said.

"No," a woman said.

They all turned and found Jaineba standing at the edge of the savanna. She wore a brown grand *bubu* and leaned on her staff.

"This is the time to seek out Anansi's treasure," Jaineba said. She strode from the tree line and stopped in front of Tanisha. "This is why you were brought back to our people, daughter. Blood of your blood was sworn to protect this place and these secrets."

Blood of your blood? Annja thought.

"Me?" Tanisha asked.

"I have seen you in my dreams," Jaineba said. "And this one, too." She nodded at Annja. "Your coming was foretold to me months ago. It was time for this place to be found." The old woman put her hand on Bashir's head, then on Kamil's. "These two are of the warrior blood of the Hausa who once lived in these lands. Those people were friends to my people. Their medicine man was charged with preserving the secrets of Anansi that were given to his people. But he was taken from these lands by slavers after his people were destroyed."

Annja listened, not knowing how much of the old woman's story to believe.

"You are Yohance's descendant, daughter," Jaineba declared. "I see his blood in you."

Tanisha shook her head.

"It is true," the old woman said. "Just as Yohance was charged with caring for the Spider Stone and the secrets it contained, so are you now charged with bringing forth the secrets Anansi left in this place."

"But that can't be true." Tanisha's voice was hollow.

"Search yourself, daughter," Jaineba encouraged. "You have told me before that you feel tied to this place in ways that you don't understand. Now it is time to see that your spirit longs to be here so that it can join the spirits of your people."

"My mother and father have never wanted to come to Africa."

"Not everyone who is gone from this place will feel the pull." Jaineba stared into Tanisha's eyes. "But you feel it strongly."

Tanisha said nothing.

Thunder boomed.

Kamil and Bashir pulled in closer to their mother.

"Which is it to be, daughter?" Jaineba asked. "Do you turn your back on your true past? Or do you seize your destiny?"

Destiny. The word hit Annja with a jolt. When she'd picked up the sword fragment, she'd set her foot upon her own destiny. And it had led her here.

"I'm going down there," Garin stated gruffly. "Even if it's only to get out of this rain." He looked at Annja.

Annja knew it was Tanisha's decision to make. She looked at the woman.

"This is your passion, your love, isn't it?" Tanisha asked. "To see old things. Relics and artifacts. It's not about the gold or silver for you."

"No," Annja answered honestly. "It's about touching the past." She made herself smile. "For all we know, that passageway goes nowhere. Or to a flooded room. Anything that might have been in there could have been taken long ago." She couldn't help thinking about the plague that Garin had insisted still remained within the chamber below.

Tanisha was quiet for a moment. "All right," she said in a soft voice. "Let's go see what there is."

THEY CAME to the end of the passageway. A large wall of stone blocked the path.

"A dead end?" Childress said, playing his light over the craggy stone surface. "That's what we came down here to see? A dead end?"

Annja handed her flashlight to McIntosh, then went forward to examine the wall. Tanisha joined her.

"Do you think we're dealing with a counterbalanced wall?" Tanisha asked.

Turning to McIntosh, Annja said, "Play the flashlight beam along the bottom of the wall."

McIntosh did.

"Watch the silt in the rainwater," Annja said.

As they watched, the murky sand and mud slid quietly under the edge of the rock. The two surfaces had been fit together so smoothly that the delineation between them wasn't readily apparent.

"The Egyptians did a lot with counterbalanced walls," Annja said. "Since we're not so far away from that culture, and the Hausa who built this wanted to remain secretive, maybe they mimicked some of the engineering feats the Egyptians used."

"Found it," Tanisha said, her hand resting at a point midway down the wall to the right side. "Everybody step back. I don't know which way this is going to turn."

After everyone was clear, Tanisha triggered the release mechanism. A four-foot section of the wall swiveled. Rock chips and pebbles ground audibly under the massive weight of the hidden door.

Taking her flashlight back from McIntosh, Annja stepped through the door on one side while Tanisha slid through on the other. Their flashlight beams hit the treasure waiting on the other side at the same time.

Childress cursed in stunned surprise.

The room was huge, at least 150 feet across. Several fortunes in gold and silver, ivory and gems, occupied stone shelves made of carefully placed rock. The riches immediately pulled the attention of Garin and his men. Likewise, McIntosh and his group of CIA agents were drawn in.

Hallinger and Ganesvoort seized on the same thing that caught Annja's attention. Clay tablets sat in neat piles.

Mesmerized, everyone moved forward.

"Can you read it?" Hallinger whispered to Annja as she carefully lifted a tablet.

She looked at the row of characters. "I can pick out some words here and there, but this is even older writing than what's on the Spider Stone."

"Do you know what we have here?" Hallinger asked. Then he answered his own question before she could make the attempt. "This is the history of a people. Probably a history that isn't even known today."

Annja knew. This was the kind of find all archaeologists dreamed about. This was the kind of event that made careers.

It was also the kind of thing that allowed them to be caught off guard.

Assault rifles on full-auto opened fire. A hail of bullets struck Garin's mercenaries, chopping many of them down where they stood with their hands filled with gold coins or jewels. Some of them managed to pull their own weapons and start firing back.

It was enough to break the line of skeleton-faced men into confusion as several of their number pitched over dead. Annja could tell by the surprise on their faces that they hadn't expected to get routed—even if only momentarily. She was certain the attackers were Tafari's men.

"This way!" Tanisha yelled, throwing herself toward the back wall.

Garin and McIntosh had their assault rifles up, opening fire and spraying bullets at the warriors in the other doorway. Half of their men were down and probably dead.

Return fire from Tafari's men hammered piles of treasure. The room plunged into relative darkness as many of the flashlights winked out and the ones that survived were extinguished so they wouldn't draw fire.

Tanisha kept her light on. She ran toward the back wall without hesitation, seeking something on the wall. Annja was surprised when that section of the wall spun out to reveal another tunnel.

The survivors raced through the second door, hurling themselves from the death room as Tafari's men launched a new fusillade of bullets.

On the other side of the door, Tanisha reached up and adjusted the hidden mechanism. The massive door shut again. The gunfire became muffled.

Garin leaned against a wall and changed magazines in his assault rifle. "How did you know about the other door?" he asked.

"That end of the room was the same size as the other one," Tanisha answered. "And I couldn't imagine anyone only building one way into that room, knowing they could be trapped by a collapsed passageway."

"If you'd guessed wrong," Hallinger gasped, holding a hand to a bloody wound in his side, "we'd all be dead."

"We were almost dead anyway," Garin said. "That was a stupid mistake." He grimaced in displeasure. Blood wept from cuts on his cheek and forehead. Either he'd been grazed by bullets or splinters of flying rock.

"That means this tunnel has to lead to the surface somewhere," McIntosh said. He took a flashlight from his pocket and shone it around.

"Unfortunately, we don't know how far away that might be," Garin said. "And the whole time we're looking for another way out of here, Tafari is loading up as much of the treasure as he can. Including, possibly, the plague."

"My boys," Tanisha said. "My boys are still out there."

Her words, the desperation and the fear, filled the passageway with silence.

Annja took stock of them. Other than Garin, McIntosh, Hallinger and Ganesvoort, who had a wound in his thigh that needed tending, only three other men had survived the attack. Sporadic gunfire from the treasure room let them know no one else would live.

Without a word, Tanisha took off, running toward the end of the new passageway.

Annja ran after her. She knew if Tafari found the boys, he would kill them.

They ran through the darkness, sometimes stumbling and falling, but getting up again and going on.

Behind them, Annja heard the massive door open, followed by a brief volley of gunfire, and knew that they were being pursued.

TAFARI POINTED his assault rifle at the open door of the treasure room. "Hold your fire," he ordered his men.

They'd already fired into the darkness. It had taken them a while to figure out the mechanism of the door. Too much time, he now saw.

"They got away," Childress said.

"I see that," Tafari said angrily. He quickly divided his men and sent a group of them down the throat of the passageway after those who had escaped.

"They can't get away to tell someone," Childress protested. He gestured at all the gold and silver. "It'll take days, maybe weeks, to get all of this transported out of here. The rain will make that even harder. Carrying this much weight, trucks will get stuck." He reached out and picked up a small fired-clay pot that caught his eye.

The pot was white, covered in gold filigree and sealed with wax. It was an oddity against the other treasures.

Tafari glanced around the room. It was more than he'd ever thought might be there. He reloaded his weapon. "They won't get away," he said. Lifting the assault rifle, he pointed it at Childress. "And I don't need a partner anymore." He pulled the trigger and unleashed a 3-round burst.

Childress dropped like a rock, a look of surprise frozen on his face.

Tafari plucked the pot from the dead man's hand and ran down the passageway. He had the engineer's children. That gave him an advantage no one yet knew about.

28

The tunnel came to an abrupt end.

Annja swung her flashlight up and examined the ceiling. There was no hint of a door. Whatever had been there all those years ago had filled in with silt and debris.

"Move," Garin ordered, slinging his assault rifle and reaching into the combat vest he wore. He extracted a grayish lump of what looked like modeling clay. "Plastic explosive. There's going to be a lot of noise. Cover your ears and get back."

Annja grabbed Tanisha's arm and pulled her back. Hallinger had one of Ganesvoort's arms slung over his shoulders and was supporting the man's weight. Both of them were breathing hard, almost to the point of exhaustion. She knew they couldn't go on much farther.

Garin prepared the charge.

When the plastic explosive detonated, a thousand pounds or more of mud was blown outward. A lot of the mud came down, splattering all of them.

Even with her ears covered and her mouth open to equalize pressure, Annja was temporarily deafened by the blast. The concussive force had knocked everyone to the ground.

But when the chaos ended, the hole was open and passable.

Annja recovered quickest. She pushed herself to her feet and climbed up the pile of muddy earth, emerging into the rain on a slope overlooking the valley. Getting her bearings, she looked around and spotted the camp. She could see a group of men guarding Kamil and Bashir.

The two boys sat on the rear deck of a jeep, looking wet and frightened. Their hands were bound.

The explosion had alerted the guards. One of them manned the .50-caliber machine gun mounted on the rear deck and he opened fire immediately.

Garin was just climbing out of the hole.

"Down!" Annja shouted. She couldn't really hear herself so she wasn't sure if he heard her. She ran toward Garin, leaping up and hitting him squarely in the chest with both feet.

Caught by surprise and hit hard, Garin tumbled back into the hole.

Annja hit the ground and rolled down the incline. The machine gun rattled, the rounds tearing chunks out of the ground as the gunner closed the range. She realized that somewhere in the chaos she'd lost the assault rifle and the pistol. All she had now was her sword.

That's all I need, she told herself grimly. She leaped, throwing herself forward in a swan dive down a particularly steep section of the hill. Hitting hard, she rolled and slid behind a copse of baobob trees. The extraordinarily thick trunks of the trees provided good cover.

Annja stayed in motion, though, circling the trees to the left. Bullets hammered the trees, shearing through some of the smaller branches and dropping them to the ground.

Once in the tree line near the camp, there was plenty of cover. She used it, closing in on the guards.

Almost on top of them, Annja spotted Jaineba stretched out on the ground. The old woman's chest was soaked with blood.

Horror and anger shot through Annja, forming a powerful concoction of emotions. She summoned the sword to her right hand and ran.

The men were busily engaged exchanging shots with someone on the hill. She thought it might be Garin or McIntosh, or perhaps both. They were having a hard time because Kamil and Bashir were too close.

The three guards suddenly turned to face her, bringing their weapons to bear.

Annja willed herself to go dead inside. There was no option to be merciful. Whatever chance the boys had depended on her.

She ran straight at the men, plunging the sword through the heart of the first man, then stopping her forward momentum and pivoting on her right foot, yanking the sword free as she came around. Still holding on to the sword with both hands, she whirled, cutting the second man as she sliced through his ribs under his right arm and through his heart.

Lifting a foot, she kicked the dying man free of the sword and turned to engage the third man, who was aiming the machine gun toward her. The heavy-caliber rounds tore through the ground and the brush and poked holes in some of the tents and one of the Land Rovers.

Annja threw the sword, stepping into the effort with all

the grace of a baseball pitcher delivering a fastball. The sword sailed straight and true, piercing the man through the solar plexus and knocking him back from the machine gun.

Vaulting up onto the jeep, Annja grabbed the sword and willed it away. She tore at the ropes that bound the boys, then tucked them into the back seats of the jeep.

She ran to Jaineba and saw that her chest rose and fell in a shallow rhythm. Annja carried the woman and belted her into the passenger seat. Jaineba groaned in pain and Annja chose to view that as a good sign.

Bullets were cutting leaves from the trees, coming from the group of men boiling from the sinkhole. Tafari led them.

Luck was with her. The jeep didn't require keys. All it had was a starter button. Annja hit the button and got the engine turning over.

"Hang on!" she shouted to the boys, then let out the clutch. All four tires screamed for traction on the wet ground. After they'd chewed through the top layer of mud, they grabbed hold and sent the jeep screaming forward.

Driving wildly, in skips and jumps, Annja brought the jeep to a stop in front of Hallinger and Ganesvoort. She got out while McIntosh, Garin and three other men provided covering fire.

After helping Hallinger put Ganesvoort into the back of the jeep, Annja turned to Tanisha and said, "Get them out of here."

Tanisha didn't hesitate to slide quickly behind the wheel. She took off and bullets chased the jeep up the hillside.

Garin tossed Annja one of the assault rifles he was carrying. "I picked that up where you dropped it. You'll need to reload."

Annja did, taking a magazine from the bandolier across her chest.

From a prone position, Garin fired spaced shots that took down targets among Tafari's skull-faced warriors.

"According to the map," Annja said, "there's a rope suspension bridge over a hundred-foot chasm only a few miles to the west. If we can get another vehicle, and if we can beat Tafari there, we might be able to stage a strategic retreat."

"I hate retreats," Garin said. "Just means you have to fight someone again. I'd rather finish this."

"We're severely outnumbered here," Annja pointed out.

"Yeah," McIntosh said, firing deliberately, "but the numbers are getting less and less all the time."

A growling-engine noise arrived about two seconds before the jeep did. It screamed up the hill on the blind side, airborne and almost coming down on top of them.

Annja threw herself to one side, waited till the jeep landed, then sped in pursuit. If it had kept going, she would never have caught it, but the driver cut the wheels to come around in a tight turn. Still running, Annja ripped bursts through the driver and his two passengers before they recognized her as a threat.

The jeep stalled out.

Annja grabbed the dead men's clothes and hauled them out. She crawled behind the wheel. She pulled the vehicle around and headed back to the others.

"Let's go!" she shouted over the gunfire.

Tafari and his men were loading into vehicles. It wouldn't be long before their position on the hillside was overrun.

As soon as the last man was aboard the jeep, Annja released the clutch and sped off in the direction Tanisha had driven. She hoped Tanisha had remembered the bridge. As Annja topped the rise, she saw that the bridge was closer than she'd thought, just at the bottom of the hill. Tanisha was already headed across it.

Annja drove as fast as she dared, closing in on Tanisha. The jeep slewed wildly as she overdrove the control. She had to downshift to recover, and lost speed doing so.

But they were closing on the suspension bridge. Tanisha was already halfway across.

"Get ready," McIntosh called from the back. "They're coming. Start evasive maneuvers."

Annja rolled the steering wheel back and forth, feeling the soft earth peeling away under the tires. Worse than that, the gearbox was picking up mud. She feared it might fail at any moment.

"Incoming!" McIntosh yelled. "Bear right! Bear right!"

Annja pulled hard right, almost flipping the jeep. Beside her, Garin cursed.

The grenade landed just ahead of them to the left. Mud rained down on them and a yawning crater opened up. It was close enough that Annja's left tires both dipped sickeningly into the hole and threw her out of control again.

McIntosh brought up his rifle and fired steadily.

Glancing at the cracked rearview mirror, Annja saw one of the men fall from the lead pursuit jeep then get run over by one of the others.

At least three vehicles followed them. Annja knew even if they made it across the bridge, they'd never be able to escape. And they were being followed too closely to stop and somehow destroy the bridge.

If we stop, Tafari will put one of those grenades right into us, she thought. The best Annja could hope was that the blast would destroy the bridge and Tanisha and her sons would go free.

She turned to Garin. "Take the wheel."

He stared at her. "What?"

"Take the wheel!" When Garin did, Annja squeezed out onto the running board and let him take her seat.

"What are you doing?" McIntosh yelled.

"A true act of desperation," Annja replied. She knew she'd be pushing her strength and speed to the limits—if she pulled off what she was thinking of. And there was a good chance that she wouldn't.

But it was all that she had left.

"Incoming!" McIntosh yelled again.

"Hold on!" Garin warned, then he yanked the wheel.

This time they almost drove straight through the explosion. The concussion nearly tore Annja from the jeep. Smoke and mud filled the air and nearly overcame her.

When she looked forward, she saw they were at the bridge. The tires rumbled over the wooden planks, and the vehicle swung and swayed enough that Annja felt certain they'd never make it across.

A rocket from another jeep shot past them, then impacted on the opposite chasm wall. The sound of the explosion echoed in the hundred-foot drop.

Garin cursed.

Tafari abandoned his rocket launcher and took up his assault rifle. Standing in his seat, he shot at Annja.

Annja held tight. Tafari's jeep had gained the bridge. She waited for the right moment, then released her hold on the jeep and leaped. She grabbed hold of the bridge's rope support and somehow managed not to be torn free. She spun around and touched down on her feet. Reaching over her shoulder, she took a deep breath and summoned the sword.

Realizing what the madwoman intended to do, Tafari shouted at the driver, "Run her down! Run her down *now* or we are dead men!"

The jeep wobbled dangerously.

"Keep it on the bridge!" Tafari howled. "Keep it on the bridge or I'll kill you!" He pointed the assault rifle at the driver's head.

Annja raised the sword and prepared to cut the ropes.

It's too soon! Tafari realized, watching the jeeps on the other side. The first vehicle was clear of the bridge, but the second vehicle would be lost if she cut the ropes too soon.

Everything slowed down in Annja's mind. She saw Tafari's jeep bearing down on her. She cut one rope and swung out over the gorge. The maneuver took her out of the path of the bullets and bought a little time. It had to be enough.

Annja swept the sword through the bridge supports on the left side. Garin had made it safely across the gorge. Ahead of her, Tafari stood up in the jeep and tried to swing his rifle around.

Too late, Annja thought, feeling the bridge tilt sickeningly.

The bridge twisted. Tafari kept his finger on the trigger, firing the whole way through. Bullets cut the air beside Annja, coming within inches.

Swinging wildly, she saw a white clay pot spill from a pack in the rear of Tafari's jeep.

The plague!

She made a grab but the jar slid over the edge of the failing bridge. The remaining ropes gave way, and Tafari's jeep flew out over the gorge. When it hit the ground, it exploded into an orange fireball.

Breathing hard, hardly believing she was still alive, Annja clung to the shredded ropes as Tafari's surviving warriors lined up at the gorge's edge and brought their weapons to bear.

Twisting, Annja swung through the air away from her enemies. She turned to meet the gorge wall with bended legs.

For a moment, sporadic fire hammered the gorge face around her. Then she heard rifles from above and knew that Garin and McIntosh were returning fire. Tafari's remaining men quickly lost interest in being a private shooting gallery and backed away from the gorge.

Annja held on to the rope, caught her breath and made the long climb to the top.

Epilogue

"When are you coming back home?" Doug Morrell asked.

Annja held the satellite phone to her ear and grinned as she watched Kamil and Bashir playing with the baby elephant in the middle of the Hausa village.

"Soon," she told him.

"The reason I'm asking," Doug said, "is because I'm getting some heat from the network. You've been in the news a lot lately, but you haven't done a piece for the show."

"Haven't found any monsters the show would be interested in," Annja said.

Tafari was dead. She, Garin and McIntosh had climbed down to the bottom of the gorge and made certain of that.

"Well, I may have one for you," Doug offered.

"Some place cool, I hope," Annja said. She'd had enough of the sun and the heat for a while. In Brooklyn, people were already starting to feel the first bite of winter. She was ready to see snow.

"Ever heard of the *wendigo?*" Doug asked.

"There's no such thing as a *wendigo,*" Annja said. "That's just a myth created by Native Americans who turned cannibal either by circumstance or by choice."

"My people think the show's fans want to see a *wendigo.* There's one in Canada," Doug insisted.

"Send Kristie."

"Nope. The last time we sent Kristie, she got frostbite. She wasn't happy. Her fans don't like it when she has to cover up in a parka. Her ratings took a definite dip. I got called on the carpet over the whole thing."

"Look, I'll give you a call in a couple days," Annja said. "When I've got a better handle on things here." She broke the connection before he could argue.

Annja walked through the village. Even though she didn't know the language she felt comfortable there. Not as if it was home, but it was a good place to stay.

The baby elephant was frustrated with all the children around it. Dipping its trunk into the gallon water bucket, it drained the bucket nearly dry. Kamil, Bashir and nearly every other child in the village held their breath expectantly.

The elephant unleashed a deluge of protest. The kids ran squealing, laughing and spluttering.

Stepping into the hut where Jaineba was being cared for, Annja saw the old woman was awake.

"You are still here?" Jaineba asked.

Annja frowned. "Why does everybody keep asking me that? It's like I'm not welcome."

The old woman smiled. "Come. Sit." She patted the ground beside her. Despite her age, she was recovering well from the gunshot wound to her shoulder.

Annja sat.

"Don't you worry. You're welcome. You'll always be

welcome in this place. Everyone keeps asking you because everyone else has already gone," Jaineba said.

It was true. Garin had left almost immediately, taking a share of Anansi's treasure with him, of course. The plague pot hadn't been recovered, but an environmental team found no evidence of any contamination of any kind. Annja didn't know if the plague threat was ever real. She also didn't know what Garin was up to but she decided to let that thought go for now.

McIntosh had returned to Atlanta, riding high on commendations from the Department of Homeland Security. He'd invited her to visit his ranch some time. Annja thought she might really enjoy that. However, she didn't know if she would ever take him up on it.

Professor Hallinger had to report back to the university, and Jozua Ganesvoort had returned to Ile de Goree to see if he could plunder any more legends from his collections of captains' logs.

"I've got a lot to do with the Hausa tablets," Annja said. Most of them had been destroyed during Tafari's attack in the treasure room, but enough remained to add to some of the knowledge of trade in the area.

"Do you like that kind of work?" Jaineba asked. "Working all day in a room by yourself?"

"It's what I trained to do," Annja said.

"But it's not what you want to do now. Not entirely. You're a champion. You're going to meet people and help them with their problems. Help them have clearer eyes. Like you did with Tanisha."

"I didn't do anything with Tanisha," Annja protested. "She decided to stay here all on her own." Her part of the treasure would allow her to do that.

"That's not true," the old woman said. "If you hadn't come here seeking answers to your own puzzle, she'd have never found her true way."

Annja didn't argue. It didn't do any good to argue with Jaineba. She would either win or insist at a later date that she had.

The old woman dropped her hand to cover Annja's. "You're changing, child. Growing new eyes and seeing new things. You'll be more than you ever thought you could be, but you can't go back to being what you once were. That isn't what being a champion is about."

"How do you know all this?"

Jaineba smiled. "Because I've known champions before, and I know how they live." Her face saddened. "I know how they die, too. So you be careful out there, Annja Creed, while you're finding your way through your new life. Given the chance, I'd like to meet you again when you get back this way."

The sound of children's laughter invaded the hut and brought a smile to the old woman's face. Then she turned back to Annja.

"Your life is going to be hard at times," the old woman said. "Filled with some hard choices to make and hard things to see."

"I kind of get that, but I don't know what I'm supposed to do about it," Annja said.

"Well, child, what you should do is take time to wash the elephants."

Puzzled, Annja smiled and shook her head. "Take time to wash the elephants?"

"That's right."

Bashir parted the cloth covering the door and stuck his head into the room. "Hey, Annja."

"Hey, Bashir," Annja replied.

"Want to help wash the baby elephant?"

Annja looked at the old woman in surprise.

Jaineba nodded solemnly and shooed her away with one hand.

"Sure," Annja said.

"Great!" Bashir trotted over and extended his hand.

Annja let the boy help her up. Then she held Bashir's hand, enjoying the boy's excitement, and went out into the bright sunlight to wash the elephant.